Strike Zone

GINGER WALLS

First paperback edition August 2024

Book Cover design by Books & Mood

978-1-962755-04-7 (paperback)

www.GingerAlana.com

Contents

This book is dedicated to the people who send text messages like rapid fire and the best friend who secretly loves them for it.

WYATT

EARLY OCTOBER

I have been bamboozled.

Hart did me dirty.

I take a swig of my beer, staring down the man who invited me to the *party*. He's sitting in the living room with his girl-friend, Lauren, on his lap—whispering in her ear and making her blush.

"Party at the girls' dorm," Hart said. "You in?"

It's like he doesn't even know me. Of course I was in.

"Hmpf. Party, my ass," I mutter to myself. I should have known better. Hart thinks having three people in a room at any given time constitutes a party. There are five of us here. It's me, two of my roommates, Koa and Hart, and their girlfriends, Sydney and Lauren.

Sydney ain't really Koa's girlfriend but he sure is looking at her right now like he wishes she was.

Let the record state, this ain't no party. This is a double date and I'm the fifth fucking wheel.

1

"Wyatt?" Sydney asks, getting my attention. I lift my eyes from my beer bottle and wait for her to finish pulling a hot pan out of the oven. "Can you go get Charlie and Wren for me? They were supposed to be here twenty minutes ago with wine."

"I reckon," I say with a sigh. Standing up from my seat at the table, I drain the rest of my beer.

I could slip out of here. Find something or *someone* more interesting to occupy my attention for the night. There has to be someone roaming the halls looking for a good time. Someone else who also needs to escape and forget life and responsibilities for an hour or so.

"Thanks. Charlie's more likely to stop messing around and come over if you ask her," Syd says with a sly grin. This girl is always trying to play matchmaker. Now that Lauren and Hart are together, she's moved on to me or maybe this Charlie girl. She should worry about her own love life. I'm doing fine on my own.

"Which dorm is theirs?" I ask with my hand on the door-knob.

"Right across the hall. You'll see their names on the door." *How convenient.* "And wine. Don't forget the wine," she says. I salute her and open the door.

The empty hallway is not looking very promising. A few girls walk by, but they have their arms full of books and are likely heading out for a study group. No thank you. Hard pass.

Not the distraction I'm looking for tonight. I need something a little stronger to take my mind off what really holds me hostage, and preferably an activity where clothes are optional.

I glance at the sign beside their door. '*Charlie and Wren*' is written in perfectly formed letters. It's so neat, you might think it's been typed up on a computer and printed.

I'm seconds from knocking on the door when the most heavenly voice starts floating through the air. Stepping into the middle of the hall, I swivel my head left and right, trying to locate the source. Then I realize it is coming from the dorm room in front of me.

The words filter through the wood door and splinter something deep inside of me. There's this strange feeling slippin' under my skin, slitherin' around like a rattlesnake waiting to strike.

I know once I knock on their door I'll be greeted with silence again. I don't want her to stop, but I have to know who that voice belongs to.

Resting my hand against the door frame, I tap the door a few times. As I suspected, the singing stops almost immediately.

After a few moments, the door opens to reveal a pretty redhead with sparkling emerald eyes. I don't shy away from checking her out. My eyes roam over her body taking in the lush curves of her hips and chest.

"Can I help you?" she asks with a curl to her lips that tells me she knows *exactly* how she can help me.

"Yes, darlin', I think you can. Your presence has been requested across the hall." I gesture toward Sydney and Lauren's place. "Along with your roommate and a bottle of wine."

"Right, game night." She turns on her heel and walks toward the kitchen. "Wren isn't here. She's uh…at the library." This must be Charlie then.

"You're here alone?" My question makes her pause.

"Mmhmm."

Charlie is my mystery voice.

I follow her, even though she didn't invite me in. Their living room is neat and orderly. If it weren't for a few pictures on the wall and side table, you wouldn't think anyone even lived here. I've never seen a dorm room this neat before. And I've been in quite a few dorm rooms.

She stands in front of the open fridge searching for something. When she bends over to reach the back, I have to swallow a groan. Her ass looks incredible in the black, skin-hugging dress she's wearing.

"I guess it will just be the two of us then," I say, taking a step closer.

Her hand freezes on whatever she's been looking for and pulls it out of the fridge. *The wine.* The night is looking up. I can be persuaded to stick around and play a few games of charades if it means time with this girl, and a bottle of wine.

"Tempting." Her eyes roam from the tip of my boots to the backward hat on the top of my head, clearly checking me out. "But I have a date." She shoves the wine into my chest. "Here take this. Tell Sydney and Lauren I'm sorry."

She shoos me towards the door. This is the first time I've been kicked out of a girl's dorm room. Usually I'm the one rushing to exit the room before my jeans are even zipped up all the way.

"I'll see you around," I tell her while showcasing my best panty-dropping smile. The one that makes my dimples pop. The one that's going to have her thinking about me tonight instead of whoever she's on a date with.

Her cheeks blush as her tongue flicks over her lip. "Maybe." She wraps her hand around the doorknob and gracefully pulls it open, ushering me further out the door.

I stop short, causing her to bump into me before she can close the door in my face. "No maybes about it," I say, my voice huskier than usual. I briefly enjoy the blanket of pink that covers her chest before walking back across the hall.

Always leave them wanting more. That's what my oldest brother Ford told me when I started taking an interest in girls.

My mind doesn't stop thinking about Charlie's voice for the rest of the night. I attempt to distract myself by messing with Sydney during a game of trivia. It's fun to rile her up by answering questions wrong on purpose. She's as competitive as her brother Nash. I know I'm doing a good job at making her mad when Koa tells me to lay off, officially ending my good time.

When Hart reaches his limit of socializing and kicks us out so he can have Lauren to himself, I don't complain.

Back at home, laying on my bed, my eyes drift closed. The song Charlie was singing plays over and over in my mind.

It's like she was singing that song for me because the words hit me hard—whatever makes me happy? Whatever I want? Those things can't be found here at Newhouse.

I scrub my hand down my face. I know I won't be able to shake it loose until I have her. I only need her one time to get her voice out of my head. I can't have her reminding me everyday that I'm miserable and not where I want to be.

Get ready Charlie, I'm coming for you.

1
WREN

Dry Cleaning.
Bank.
Clean out my purse.
Car detailing.
No. I did that last week. This week is my closet. Deep cleaning on a four-to-six-week rotation is the best way to keep everything orderly and immaculate. It isn't a foolproof system but it has been working well for me the past few years.

My closet has been the hardest to keep up with while in college. It's taken me years to get the proper system setup correctly. You would be surprised how easy it is for a cream blouse to get mixed in with the ivory.

Especially if you have a roommate like mine. I love Charlie, but she is chaos incarnate.

Organize closet.

Office supply run.

I continue to write my to-do list in my planner. I'll add it to my electronic planner after my tutoring session. I flick my wrist to check the time on my gold watch. They should be at the library any minute.

W. Rivers

I glance down at the blank student profile I've prepared.

The student center didn't give me any additional information. I didn't ask either. I never do. I don't get paid for my tutoring sessions. I do it to flex my skills. It's an opportunity for me to put my problem-solving abilities to the test.

If I want to secure a job at the top of my father's firm, without using nepotism as a step stool, I need to be the best business analyst he has on the team.

Tutoring is not the same as saving a company from going belly up, but the concept is similar in nature. I evaluate their study habits, determine where the disconnect is with class material, and come up with a plan to help them succeed.

It's all very simple.

Ten past five. They're late.

I begin to pack up my highlighters when a large form casts a shadow over the table.

"Hi, darlin'," he croons, as he takes the seat across from me. I visibly cringe. I know that voice. I hate that voice. It's attached to *him*.

Wyatt Rivers.

One of the pitchers for the Newhouse Knights baseball team. He's also the most annoying student that attends Newhouse University, at least according to me. If I issued an official survey, I doubt he would make the top ten list considering three-fourths of the student body wants to sleep with him or probably already has.

I haven't been tortured by his southern twang for months. Thankfully with finals and winter break it's been easy to make myself scarce. I haven't seen him since the night our little friend group attended the Halloween party at The Armory.

Well, they called it a party. I considered it more along the lines of my worst nightmare.

Not that I have any reason to be in his vicinity. I don't do sporting events, parties, or social gatherings of any kind for that matter. I typically enjoy the company of one person at a time versus larger crowds.

Wyatt Rivers is the last person I would ever want to spend one-on-one time with.

"Those are cute." He points to my sticky notes with hedgehogs on them.

"I know. That's why I bought them." I move the square pad of paper closer to me even though it completely destroys the order in which I like to keep my supplies. *Sticky notes, pens, pencils, highlighters.* I begin to line them up again to keep my eye from twitching.

Wyatt smirks as I attempt to find some semblance of structure. I'm glad I can amuse him. However, we aren't here for comedy hour. We're here because he needs a tutor.

"Here." I slide the student profile paper toward him. "You need to fill this out if I'm going to assist you. What class do you need help with?"

The new semester started a week ago. I was surprised to already have a student assigned to me for tutoring. One could assume he is simply being proactive since he's an athlete, but that doesn't line up with my observations of this man in our brief interactions.

The only thing he's proactive about is using protection. Even that assumption could be a stretch.

Wyatt scans the paper, making grunting noises so often I begin to wonder if he has something caught in his throat.

Then I notice the dimple in his smile peeking out from under the bill of his cap. Which by the way, is absolutely disgusting. It's soiled in what looks like years of sweat and dirt.

His long hair flips and curls haphazardly covering his neck and ears adding to his lackadaisical attitude towards personal grooming.

"I don't need your help with any classes," he says, sliding the paper back toward me. "But this is, ah, very detailed." His lip curls, mocking me.

My eyes trail from his middle finger, up his forearm, over the green T-shirt stretched tight over his bicep. Pushing my glasses back up on my nose, I stare at him through slanted eyes. I don't appreciate him wasting my time. "Why did you sign up for a tutoring session then?"

"I wanted to see you."

I scoff. I can't imagine a world in which Wyatt Rivers would have a reason or need to seek me out. I think I made myself clear the last time I spent more than five minutes with this man that he is not high ranking on the list of people I like.

"This should be good. Why did you want to see me exactly?" I fold my arms over my chest.

"Do I need a reason to see a friend? Maybe I wanted to catch up. How was your holiday break?"

"It was fine," I reply. I don't want to be rude. "We both know that we're not friends."

"Don't be like that now. We had a great time at The Armory together." He flashes a smile that doesn't feel genuine, but it's one he's practiced often. It appears on his face so effortlessly. I wear a similar one when I'm forced to spend time with my father's business associates.

I shudder thinking back to the night at The Armory. Too many drunk people wearing ridiculous outfits packed in a small space like sardines. As soon as we got inside, I high-tailed it straight to the bar. My friend tequila was calling my name.

For whatever reason Wyatt trailed behind me in his Scottish kilt and sporran. If he called me lass one more time, I would have strangled him. He already insulted me once by assuming I was wearing a costume. Like that is something I would do.

I don't know what part of my tailored blazer, slacks, and sensible blouse screamed Halloween costume to him. It's a classic look—my go to choice for most social outings.

"We must have different definitions of the phrase *great time.*"

He shrugs dismissing me. "I didn't see you running away."

"I was barricaded in by your mob of fans. There was nowhere for me to go." Thanks to his little fan club I spent my time that night choking on floral perfume and listening to women jockeying for his attention.

If I took a shot every time someone—male or female—offered to take care of him in the bathroom, I would have been at the hospital getting my stomach pumped within the first ten minutes. Hmm...that might have been a better alternative now that I think about it.

I was counting down the seconds until I could be back in a quiet, controlled environment. I promised Charlie I would stay for thirty minutes, and I did. Once the timer went off on my phone, I paid my tab and left.

"You should consider yourself lucky. Your seat was prime real estate."

"And to think, I didn't even have to flash my boobs to get it either," I snark.

His eyes widen in shock before dipping to my chest. "I didn't miss much."

My nostrils flare and my hands clench without warning in my lap. *Didn't miss much. Smug little...*

Standing from the chair, I place my palms flat on the table. I lean forward allowing my blouse to dip low enough for him to peer down my shirt.

He holds my stare with curiosity. *That's right. You never know what I'll do next.* It's easy to assume with my large frame glasses and blazers that I am a quiet wallflower. While I do enjoy a peaceful afternoon, I am not afraid of speaking my mind.

Years spent in the beauty pageant circuit when I was younger has made me confident in my own skin. There is no room to be shy or uncomfortable when you have a limited amount of time to change into your next gown or costume.

I jerk my eyes away from him and pretend to be intrigued with the wood graining on the table. I even fiddle with one of my pens to keep up the ruse.

He takes my bait and allows his eyes to wander down to the hollow of my throat, the top of my cleavage, and the lace cups covering my breasts. They look amazing, by the way.

I tilt my head in his direction in time to catch him absent-mindedly licking his lips.

"You can't miss something that was never yours," I say, a breath away from his face before retreating.

He shakes his head loose, and his mane of hair swishes from side to side. I smile to myself as I begin to pack up all my belongings. The fact that I've entertained his company for this long is galling.

"What are you doin'?" His calloused palm lands on top of my hand halting my movements.

"Packing up. Do you mind?" I give his dry, cracked knuckles a pointed look silently asking him to move. What does he do all day with his hands? Hasn't he ever heard of moisturizer?

"Not really." His lip twitches on one side.

I blow out a frustrated breath. My hair whips around and lands over my glasses. He watches as my hair swings back and forth like a pendulum until I finally push it off my face.

I attempt to free my hand but his grip only tightens. I stare at him. *Really.*

"Sit. *Please.*" He gestures toward my chair.

"Let go of my hand first," I counter.

"Sit and I'll let go of your hand."

My stubborn side wants to keep fighting with him, but I'm starting to lose blood flow in my fingers from his punishing grip.

"You are such a child," I quip as I sit down.

He bristles. I've touched a nerve. It wasn't my intention. Pulling off a verbal slap in the face is yet another skill in my arsenal. My father has warned me more than once about my sharp tongue.

My mouth opens to say something reassuring, maybe apologize, but before I can speak he is smiling and back to his jovial self. *Or is Mr. Happy Go Lucky a front he puts on?*

"Yeah, that's me." His tone straddles a line between sadness and sarcasm.

"I didn't realize that was a sore spot."

"It's not."

"Fine." I raise a questionable eyebrow.

"Good."

"Great." I force a smile. "I'm sitting. What do you want?"

He glances at me for a moment, as his pointer finger lingers over my neat row of pencils before pushing every other one, making them uneven. I scratch at my chest that's now warm to the touch.

Directing my focus back to his face, I wait for him to speak even though my fingers itch to fix everything he just destroyed. Two can play this game. I am equal parts stubborn and perfectionist. I guarantee I will outlast him in this match.

"Charlie," he finally answers.

"Excuse me?" Charlie? As in my roommate. I must have heard him wrong. What does he want with her?

"I need your help getting a date with your roommate." I would laugh if we weren't in a library surrounded by several groups of people trying to study. Ever since an anonymous article was printed about the top hook-up spots inside the library last semester, it has become more popular than a dating app.

"You date?" I question. I blink hard attempting to register this information.

"Well, no. I need you to get me in a room with her. *Alone.*" He leans back in his chair until it's on two legs. What I wouldn't give for it to slip out from underneath him right now. Instead he removes the filthy cap from his head and roughs up his caramel brown hair.

"So, you want to sleep with her?"

"Yes." He drops his hat back on his head backwards. It's a momentary distraction. He might be a worthy opponent after all. He seems to be well equipped with his own bag of tricks.

"And you want me to do what exactly?" I ask, focusing on his face again. Not that it's any safer here. This man knows how to work a dimple to his advantage.

"Get me in a room with her. I can do the rest," he says with a smirk that curls the hair of his mustache on the left side of his face.

"I don't understand why you need me. I doubt you have any problems getting a girl alone." He has a certain...reputation on campus.

He flashes his dimpled smile proving my point. "You're right. Usually I don't. Charlie, however, has been difficult to track down."

"Have you actually tried?" I have a system for organizing my closet and Charlie has a system when it comes to dating and getting a man's attention. I stopped trying to figure it out sophomore year. I do know it will take more than a bicep flex to get her to notice a man.

A backwards hat and a nice smile will not work on her.

"Yes?" he says, fidgeting in his seat. "I've been busy with practice and...other things. Not other girls."

"I didn't say anything." I hold up my hands.

"You didn't have to. Your face speaks volumes." He rolls his eyes. "We were both distracted at the Halloween party and now she's playing hard to get."

"Right. That's what she's doing," I deadpan.

He scowls back at me.

"Look," I start before he can correct me. "Charlie dates. She doesn't sleep around. She wants to find a husband. Unless that is something you are also interested in, I don't think I'll be very proficuous in your endeavor." I grab a pen and put a tally mark in my planner.

"Did you just word of the day me?" His eyes narrow in suspicion.

My head tilts. He follows the word of the day too?

"Maybe. I like to use the word at least once per day. I saw an opportunity. I took it." I shrug.

He peers at my notebook. "That's your third checkmark."

"It's been a good day."

His intense gaze holds mine, making me uncomfortable. I clear my throat. "I'm sorry I can't help you with your...situation."

He scoffs. "You can. You just won't."

"Twist the narrative however you wish. The answer will still be no. I'm not a matchmaker."

"What do you want in exchange for your help?"

"You're bartering now? Why is this so important to you?" Girls are a dime a dozen to guys like Wyatt. What is it about Charlie?

"It just is. Will you do it?"

"No." I check the time. "Your tutoring session is over. I hope it was to your satisfaction." This time when I start packing up my things he doesn't stop me.

"Hardly," he murmurs.

"Feel free to file a complaint and I'll throw it away for you."

"You're a strange bird, aren't you, Wren Ellington?" he asks, watching me put each pen, pencil, and highlighter back in their proper place in my bag.

My movement falters. This time he's the one who hit the mark.

"Good luck," I say my parting words, throw my crossbody bag over my shoulder, and walk away with the heat of his stare at my back.

2

WYATT

"You got any plans tonight?" Koa asks me and Hart as we walk through the parking lot after our practice.

They have been brutal lately with our first game around the corner. I spend more time soaking in an ice bath or wrapping my shoulder than I do anything else these days. We aren't playing around anymore. Not that coach let us dick around to begin with in the off season.

"I have a few errands to run," I vaguely answer his question. I don't need them in my business. *Not about this.*

"Lauren and I are going to watch a movie," Hart says smiling.

Watching a movie my ass.

"Which one?" I ask to fuck with him. It's nice to see my friend so happy. He never smiled like this until he got with his girlfriend Lauren.

"Which what?"

"Which movie?" I say slowly.

"I don't fucking know. Does it matter?"

"It does if you actually plan on watching it. You don't want to get stuck watching something without any action," Koa says.

"There will definitely be action." Hart's eyes darken to the point they're almost black.

I roll my lips to keep from smiling. They ain't watching no movie.

"You have fun. We'll see you tomorrow," Koa says.

Hart gives a final salute goodbye before walking off to his car. I need to get going too. She's only going to be at the campus bookstore for another twenty minutes.

"I'll see you later, man." I put a fist out to bump with Koa.

Koa eyes me with suspicion, before nodding and getting in his car. I know I've been acting weird the last few weeks. I'm surprised they haven't scheduled an intervention over my behavior. Normally the fuckers are more nosy than this. My only saving grace is the two of them being wrapped up with their girls. Not that Koa would admit to anyone being his girl.

It hasn't been easy balancing classes, practice, workouts, games, and following Wren around campus like a private investigator.

Wren Ellington. She isn't like other girls. *She's worse.*

I realize I'm not her favorite person. The feeling is mutual. All I needed her to do was invite me over to their dorm and let me do my thing. I would have had Charlie eating out of the palm of my hand in no time.

If I didn't need Wren's help, I wouldn't have asked. She is my last resort. I've been trying to get Charlie's attention since the night she sang herself into my brain.

I've seen her a few times around campus last semester, but she's managed to dodge me at every turn. I thought maybe going home for winter break would erase her voice from my memory but it only made it worse. It was a daily reminder that I'm not happy with the course my life is taking.

After several failed attempts of catching Charlie leaving her dorm, I thought I would have better luck getting close to Charlie through Wren. Had I realized Wren was so hard-nosed, I would have thought of an alternative option.

I still could.

I probably should.

Then I remember the look on Wren's face when I pushed all of her pencils out of order. She was mad enough to spit nails and it made me smile. And not the fake one I put on for everyone.

I know someone else's misery shouldn't bring me joy. But it did. Seeing her ball her hands into fists and huff out breaths of frustration thrilled me. That's a feeling stress, worry, and fear have stolen from me the past few years. So excuse me for not wanting to let it go yet.

I am however ready to get Charlie's voice out of my head. I need it gone. Not only is it a constant reminder of my misery, it's also affecting my headspace when I'm pitching. I can't lose focus because getting drafted is important to me. It's crucial. My family is depending on it.

If I don't get this girl out of my system, my game is going to suffer and everything I've been working to achieve, *to save*, will be lost.

That's the *only* reason I'm here at the campus bookstore on a Friday night instead of at home in bed or out at The Armory with my boys.

After a couple weeks of surveillance, I've learned Wren has habits. *Lots of them*. She has been much easier to keep tabs on than Charlie. One of her routines is restocking her weekly supply of sticky notes at four thirty every Friday at the campus bookstore. She walks each aisle systematically while checking items off her list.

If I've timed her correctly, I should find her picking out a new highlighter right about now.

I nod to a few classmates as I walk by them.

Wren's head of dark brown hair comes into view. She has it slicked back in a low ponytail. Not a hair out of place with this one. Her shirt is another daring shade of beige. At least it's buttoned up to her neck and covers her chest.

Don't need a repeat of what happened at the library. No siree. She got me. I fell for the little devil's trickery. She set the trap and I got caught looking. I may have been wrong about not missing much. Not that I would ever admit that to her.

Walking by a table display of Newhouse gear, I snag a lanyard and a keychain. I need to make this little run-in with her believable. We're just two people who happen to be shopping at the same store at the same time.

Should I whistle or would that be overkill? No whistling. Definitely too much.

She has a shopping basket of various supplies, snacks, and are my eyes deceiving me or is that a box of condoms? Well, well isn't that something? Condoms are the last thing I expected her to be needing a refill of. I can't picture her as the type of girl to be sleeping with random guys around campus.

Why am I even thinking about her like this? I shiver and shake the thoughts from my head.

Casually I walk closer, pretending to scan the shelves for what I'm looking for as I go.

"I can hear you breathing," Wren says without taking her eyes off the two packs of markers she's holding in her hands.

"You can not."

"I can." She drops one pack of markers in her basket and puts the other back on the hook. Then picks up a red marker set and begins examining it. "Did you need something?"

Yes, I do. I need you to prove to me you're not the heartless Tin Man and help me out.

Telling her she doesn't have a heart is probably not the best way to get her assistance. I'll need to convince her it's good for Charlie, that I'll be good for Charlie. Because I plan on being real *good* to her.

Some might say better than good actually. Not to toot my own horn, but toot fucking toot.

Or maybe we can come up with an exchange. I'm not discouraged by my last attempt at bartering. There has to be something she needs even if she doesn't realize it yet.

If all else fails, I'll annoy her until she has no choice but to do what I ask so I'll leave her alone. My sister Willow has said it's one of my most endearing qualities. *Or maybe she said enduring?*

"Is this one any good?" I ask, grabbing a random highlighter off the wall. It's neon green. Maybe getting her to talk about one of her favorite things will warm her up a little.

She turns her head slightly in my direction. I'm momentarily stunned by the smell of wildflowers floating in the air. It reminds me of home and playing in the fields of flowers we had growing when I was a kid.

"What are you doing with it?"

"Highlighting stuff?" I answer but it comes across more like a question.

She expels an exasperated breath and grumbles quietly to herself. She better buck up. I'm just getting started with her. I'm about to become the best friend she never asked for.

"If you need to memorize text, use yellow. If you are simply *highlighting stuff*," she twists her tone to mock mine, "then green will be sufficient."

"Golly. Thank ya kindly, ma'am." I lay the accent on thick to irritate her further.

She rolls her eyes behind her oversized glasses, tosses the red markers in her basket, and moves on to the next aisle.

I've deduced that paper products are her second favorite purchase—ranking just behind new pens.

What will it be this week? I wonder as I tail her. New note-book? Printer paper? Large sticky notes? Small ones? *Oooh maybe another set with the cute little hedgehogs on them?*

Why do I find her behavior so intriguing? That is a question to dissect another day.

Wren stops short, causing me to slam into her back. I grasp at her waist to keep her from falling on her face. I might not like the girl, but I'm not an asshole.

My fingertips sink into the slinky fabric of her pants. As usual Wren is dressed to command a boardroom rather than sit through a college lecture. She straightens her body and ends up flush against mine with her head tucked neatly under my chin.

I have to tilt my head toward the ceiling to keep from inhaling her sweet scent. Damn she smells good. Is it her perfume or her body wash? Because if her whole body smells like this...no. If her body smells like this, it doesn't matter. It's Wren for Pete's sake.

"Do you mind?" She looks up at me. If she were anyone else, I might be tempted to kiss her. She's that close.

I glance at her lips. *Not bad.* Pink and plush. Perfect little cupid's bow. I'm sure she could find someone who could stomach a few minutes of tonsil hockey with her. *Ain't gonna be me.*

Her hands cover mine on her hips. I grip her tighter. Not sure why. *Instinct? Habit?* My hands seem to be functioning as a separate entity from my body.

"Will you stop manhandling me?" She squirms attempting to break my hold.

"I'm not. I was helping you. Next time I'll let you kiss the linoleum."

"I wouldn't need your help if you would watch where you're going. You're like a bull in a china shop." She pulls hard on my hands and breaks free, then turns to face me. Somehow our fingers get twisted together. She raises our hands, shaking herself loose with a huff.

Stepping closer, I get in her face. "I wouldn't have rear-ended you if you didn't break for sticky notes." I wave a hand in front of the rows of neon and pastel squares.

She lifts her chin and glares at me. "Why are you even here? Don't you have something better to do?" I would have *someone* better to do if she would be a decent human being and help me out.

"Don't you? It's Friday night. Let me guess. After your wild shopping spree, you are going to go home and cuddle with your cats."

"We can't have pets in the dorm." Her deadpan delivery almost makes me grin.

"I was joking. You probably have at least another twenty years before cats are your only companions."

Her face turns a nice shade of red. *Is it beet or tomato?* I tilt my head, studying the way her cheeks and neck are changing colors.

"Why are you staring at me like that?"

I tilt my head from side to side. "I'm trying to figure something out. Give me a minute will ya?"

Her ears are kind of purple. Probably more of a beet red when she's angry and a tomato when she's embarrassed.

"Are you finished gawking yet?" Damn, she's fun to rile up.

"I reckon." Where were we? Ah, her impending cat collection. I glance at her full shopping basket. "Maybe," I point a finger at the box of condoms sitting on top, "you have a hot date later. Do you have a boyfriend, Wren?"

"No boyfriend. No date. I'm making balloon animals," she says without cracking a smile. She can't be serious, but that actually makes more sense.

"Is it a side gig or something? Do you moonlight as a clown at kid's birthday parties? I'm not a fan of clowns. They give me the creeps." I shiver at the thought of being face to face with a crazed clown.

Wren stares at me. Her eyes wide, mouth pinched tight. Is she trying to decide where to punch me or figure out if I'm playing with her?

"Is it really more logical to you that I would spend my weekends as a *clown* instead of being able to find a man to sleep with me?"

I shrug. "It doesn't sound *illogical*."

She winces as if she's in pain before quickly recovering, ready to rip me a new one. "Just because you don't find me worthy of having intercourse with doesn't mean other men feel the same. You're not exactly everyone's type either."

"What are you talking about? I am most definitely everyone's type," I say smugly.

"Your dick is everyone's type. Trust me. *You* are not." Wren speaks this revelation like it's the Gospel truth, then goes back to her shopping.

I do have a nice cock, but I'm insulted she thinks people don't actually like me for my personality. "At least I know how to have fun."

"It's called having priorities, goals, being an adult. You should try it sometime."

Trailing closer to Wren, I stop behind her and crowd her back. "You think you know me? You have no idea the kind of responsibilities I have to deal with," I say through gritted teeth.

No one knows the pressure I have weighing me down every day. The fact I've let my guard slip in front of her should bother me. The girl makes me irrational. I say things to her without thinking. My brain short circuits disabling my filter.

She looks at me like she knows me. Like she already has me figured out. She doesn't know shit about my life. She's too blind living off her daddy's coffers to see how the other half truly lives.

"You're right. I don't know what your life is like." Wren faces me. Her eyes shine with pity. "I'm sorry if I offended you." Fuck that.

"You didn't." I brush off her apology.

She relaxes, accepting my lie. I'm grateful she doesn't push the topic further. I will never admit her words touched a tender spot. It isn't the first time and I doubt it will be the last. If I plan on going toe to toe with her, it seems I will have to come dressed in full armor.

"If you say so. Now that we've established that you are a full fledged responsible adult and I know how to have fun, can you leave me alone?"

"No. Sorry, can't do that. See the thing is, I'm not convinced you know how to laugh and let go. Because this," I swirl my finger around the store, "is not what I call a good time."

"And what do you suggest one does to have a good time?"

I start to open my mouth to answer but Wren holds up her hand. "Not that. I've got my sexual needs covered."

"Good because I wasn't offering."

"How will I ever survive," she replies sarcastically.

"You're funny."

"I'm what?" she questions. I see the direction her brain is heading. Time to derail that runaway train of thought.

"Being funny on *occasion* is not the same as having fun. You wouldn't know what fun is if it was standing right in front of you," I goad her.

"That may be true. Do you know what else is a fact?" she asks.

I shake my head.

"I don't care." She begins to walk away but I stop her with a hand on her forearm.

"Now hold on a minute. You mean to tell me you don't itch to let your hair down?" I tug gently on her ponytail. "Have a night out when you aren't buttoned up to your neck? Forget about all those responsibilities you have? Have you ever let loose?" My eyes trail down her body. "Nah, I bet you're a good girl. Aren't you, Wren?"

"Nice monologue. I still don't care." Oh, but she does. She holds her head high, but her eyes shine with curiosity. Somewhere inside of her is a woman who wants to break free from the self-made mold she's created for herself.

"Set me up with Charlie and I'll give you a few months of fun."

Her face wrinkles in disgust.

"That didn't come out right. Just say yes. What do you have to lose?"

"Besides my reputation?"

I huff a laugh. "Hate to break it to you, but you ain't got much of one to begin with."

"It's irrelevant. What part of I don't care do you not understand?"

"The part that doesn't believe a word you're saying. I see it in those blue eyes of yours. You're scared of what's next. Of being tied down before you ever taste true freedom. Tell me I'm wrong and I'll walk away."

"No need. I'll walk away for the both of us."

"Just answer one question."

"And you'll leave me alone?" she asks.

"Indefinitely." I nod.

"Fine. What do you want to know?"

"What are you doing after graduation?" The answer should be simple. Especially for Wren. She plans everything ahead of time. She probably already knows what pair of underwear she is wearing next Tuesday. *Stop thinking about Wren's panties.*

She swallows hard. Her fingers tap against the handle of her shopping basket. Should I tell her there isn't any way she could convince me her future will be wild and crazy?

"If you must know, I'll be working for my father." Wren gives me her back to look at a pack of sticky notes. She mumbles something inaudible.

"What was that?" I take a step closer.

She side eyes me. "Then I'm getting married," she says, with a sigh.

I choke on air. "You're what? I'm sorry. I thought you said you were getting married."

"I did."

"Holy shit. So you are using the condoms for sex," I muse over the thought.

"I was always using the condoms for sex," she chastises me, slapping my bicep.

"Who's the lucky guy? Is he a student here?"

"No, he lives in Georgia like me."

"Hold up. I'm confused."

"I'm sure you are. The details aren't important. At least not to you. I answered your question. I'll be working and getting married. You know, grown up things." There she goes taking another stab at me.

"Which is why you need to have fun now. Live a little before your life is over."

"Getting married doesn't mean your life is over," she says, walking toward the checkout.

"Sure it doesn't. I mean if you love the guy. You do love the guy, right?"

"I don't see how this is relevant." She fishes around in her shopping basket and appears to be mentally checking off her shopping list, or at least pretending to.

I do a double take. "The two of you aren't in love and you're going to marry him?"

"He could learn to love me at some point." I'm not her number one fan either, but I don't like how she said that he could learn to love her. Not that she could learn to love him. No one should settle for that. "I've only met him a few times. We didn't get a chance to talk much."

"And you think he'll start to fall for you once you talk more?" I ask, attempting to hold back a laugh.

Wren snaps her head in my direction throwing a glare like a ninja star.

"I'm just saying your bedside manner needs a little work. Is there a good reason why you would agree to marry this guy without knowing him?"

"Yes." Her answer is definitive and concise, which I'm learning is on brand for Wren.

"Well thank fuck for that," I tease her. "All the more reason to kick up your boots until you're tied down with some guy you don't even know."

"Even if I did agree with you, Charlie has a three date rule. If I set you up with her, she's not going to sleep with you until you've taken her out a few times. Real dates where you pick her up and take her to a nice restaurant."

"I told you I don't date."

"I know. Pick another girl. Charlie isn't the one." But she is. I've tried hitting on other girls when I'm out at a party or The Armory, but that voice. It creeps into my thoughts and I can't even bring myself to kiss another girl. It's starting to piss me off.

"You need me—" I begin to say.

"I certainly do *not* need you." The firm set in Wren's jaw and the way her eyebrows bunch together is fucking adorable.

"Think whatever you want but deep down you know I'm right. You do the same things every week. You run your life by schedules and checklists."

"There is nothing wrong with being organized and pre-pared." She gestures toward her weekly rations.

"Meet me at The Armory this weekend. Bring Charlie." I give her a pointed look. "I will buy Charlie some hot wings and check date one off the list. Look at me speaking your language." I wink at her. "Then I'll give you your first lesson in the fine art of letting loose."

Wren stares down at the floor. You can practically hear her making a mental pros and cons list in her head.

"Fine," she agrees. "I'll get Charlie to go to The Armory."

"Thank you." *Fucking finally.*

She steps into my personal space and places a warm palm on my chest. My skin buzzes through my T-shirt where she's touching me. Her gaze is trained on her manicured finger-nails. I wonder if she feels it too.

"I'll play your little game. You can teach me all about letting my hair down since I have *so much* to learn." She pats my chest twice before dropping her hand.

"Your sarcasm is moving. What's your phone number?" I ask, pulling my phone from my pocket.

"That hardly seems necessary."

"I need to be able to contact you and make plans. It's necessary."

With a roll of her eyes, she reluctantly gives me her number and I program it into my phone.

"I'll be in touch."

"Can't wait." Wren grimaces.

Me either. A few more days and I can get Charlie out of my system and put an end to this game I keep playing with Wren.

3

WREN

What are you doing?

I just got out of practice.

You should have seen me.

I was on fire today.

Tonight is the night.

We're going out to celebrate.

The Armory has half price beers and 25 cent wings.

"Who's blowing up your phone?" Charlie asks from the living room. I'm surprised she can hear the incessant buzzing over the reality television show she is watching.

I continue to ignore my phone. I'm sitting at the kitchen island updating my to-do list for next week. I don't want to deal with him and his text messages right now.

"Wyatt Rivers." My phone buzzes again as if I've summoned him from his lair. He has been texting me non-stop over the last forty-eight hours. I knew it was a bad idea to give him my phone number.

"Starting pitcher Wyatt Rivers?" Charlie twists her body away from her show, staring at me in shock.

Starting pitcher? No idea. He's the guy who thinks I can't get a man to sleep with me. Moonlighting as a clown? *Really?*

"He's on the baseball team. That's all I know."

"I didn't know the two of you were friends. How did he get your number?"

"We aren't. He requested it," I grumble. I was the idiot who gave it to him.

"When have you been hanging out with him?"

"You are asking a lot of questions." She is going to force me to admit the whole matchmaking scheme before it even begins. "I was his tutor." For five minutes. It still counts.

"And you just gave him your number? Why didn't you tell me about this? Do you like him?" She is like a little puppy dog about to be taken on a walk. Her enthusiasm is nauseating.

"Yes. It didn't seem important. Absolutely not." Part of my lunch threatens to crawl its way up my throat. I shudder at the thought of having an interest in Wyatt, romantic or otherwise.

She studies my face looking for a lie she won't find.

"Hmm...then why did he want your number?"

I can't exactly tell her Wyatt is interested in her, not me, as she assumes, and now I'm stuck playing cupid. "In case of a tutoring emergency?" That sounds somewhat believable. "He did invite us to hang out with him at The Armory tonight."

"Interesting." She has a calculating look in her eye. She may act the part at times, but she isn't a fool—she is sharp and will out maneuver you. No doubt Charlie is scheming up a plan of her own as we speak.

"We don't have to go. I'll text him back that we have plans." I would do that with pleasure.

"Oh no, no. Wrennie, we're going. You never want to go out. Had I known I only needed to offer up a good looking specimen of a man on a silver platter, I would have tried this tactic years ago." She giggles to herself.

I spin around, my whole body facing the living room. "He is *not* why I'm considering going out tonight." It's the fact that he thinks I lack the ability to have any fun. Why that bothers me I've yet to figure out. I shouldn't care what anyone thinks of me, least of all him.

"If you say so," she singsongs. "Text him back. Tell him we'll meet him there. Maybe he'll bring a cute friend with him."

"Why would he need a friend?" I ask, then take a sip from my water bottle.

"For me, silly. You are going to be busy flirting with Wyatt. I'll need someone to flirt with too," she says, as if the answer is obvious.

I choke on my water. "I will not be flirting with him," I say, rubbing my chest. "Why don't you flirt with Wyatt if you think he is worthy of flirting with?"

She rolls her eyes. "Because I'm not interested in him. He's hot but he doesn't want a relationship. I'm looking for something more serious."

My eyes narrow. "And that makes him the right person for me?"

"Yes, because you don't do serious relationships either. You never have. I've always assumed it's because of your engagement but I'm beginning to wonder if there is another reason."

Technically, I won't be engaged until sometime after graduation. I haven't spoken to my parents about it since I left for school in August. For all I know the situation has changed. I refuse to bring it up unless they say something about it.

My mom mentioned keeping in contact with Daniel, my intended fiancé, but I have no desire to reach out to him. Even calling him that in my head sounds wrong. She's under the impression that we chat all the time. When in reality, I've only spoken to him twice.

Once when I was sixteen and a second time at our high school graduation party.

It was my mom who mentioned how wonderful it would be if Daniel and I got married. To this day I still don't understand what she saw happening between us when we were drinking punch and eating cake side by side. Nothing about that screams happily ever after to me. It was awkward and uncomfortable. I couldn't get away from him and that party fast enough.

My mom however jumped at the chance to lock down a husband for me. Our dads saw this marriage as an opportunity to link their firms together and form a partnership. Over whiskeys they devised a plan that would keep both of their businesses successful and well connected.

I should protest, but I don't see a reason to. Who else am I going to marry? I'm not exactly putting myself out there. I haven't met very many men who have been able to handle my abrasive personality or my need for control and order.

"The only reason I don't do serious relationships is because I don't want to."

"Okay, we can go with that. Since you don't do "boyfriends" and have an aversion to catching feelings for a man. He's perfect for you. Y'all could have a little fun and walk away with no harm done."

I wince. While her words are true, they still sting. I'm not naive to the fact I am a difficult person to love. I don't love easily either. I have restricted all of my relationships in college to sex only. I never let emotions get involved. If I keep relationships within the scope of my own rules, they are easier to control. I can't get hurt or let down if my expectations stay relatively low.

I will admit Wyatt and I are similar this way. The only difference being my relationships are monogamous and last more than one night. I don't sleep with a man once and move on to the next. I'm not judging him. He can do what he wants. I'm simply a firm believer in quality versus quantity. I apply the same logic to purchasing pants. The higher the quality, the longer they last. I prefer my sexual partners to last a long time.

Regardless, I need to redirect Charlie in the other direction. Wyatt isn't interested in me. He wants her. And it seems he isn't going to leave me alone until I help him get her.

"Don't dismiss him too soon. Maybe you will have a spark tonight."

She considers me for a moment. "I thought we did a few months ago. The night he came over looking for us and you hid in your room." She gives me a pointed look.

"What? I had things to do. I didn't want to go. I doubt I was missed."

"We were both missed and you know it. Don't talk about yourself like that." Charlie stands and enters the kitchen. "Anyway, Wyatt is fun and nice to look at but he can't give me what I want."

"Finding a husband is overrated," I mutter.

"Maybe for you, but I want one. I look at couples like Lauren and Hart, and I want that."

Our friends Lauren and Hart are sickeningly sweet together. "I'm sure you'll get it. In the meantime, there's Wyatt." I plaster a fake smile on my face.

"Nice try. Not happening. Not when he's right for you," my roommate, who is currently pushing her luck, says with a smirk. I try not to gag.

"Please don't say that again." I close my planner and push it aside. "How about we go out tonight and see what happens?"

Charlie looks me up and down. "Fine. I'll go, *if* I get to pick out what you wear."

"You already agreed to going. My outfit is not up for negotiation."

"Then I'm not going."

"Perfect. If you don't go, I don't have to go."

Her brow furrows in frustration. "You're impossible." She throws her hands in the air and stomps off toward her room. She stops suddenly at the threshold. "Wear what you want, but we're going."

Once she's out of sight, I smile. After tonight, I can wash my hands of this whole situation. I text Wyatt back letting him know we'll be there.

The Armory isn't the only establishment on campus to get a drink, but it is the most popular. This is where you'll find the majority of the student body who feel the urge to blow off steam, find someone to hookup with, or watch the game on the big screen.

Tonight isn't any different. While it's not as crowded as it was on Halloween weekend, it's still busier than I would like. The draw to cheap beer and wings must be too hard to resist.

"Did you text him we're here?"

"Do I need to do that?" I told him we were coming. Isn't that enough?

"Yes, Wren. How are you supposed to find him in the middle of all of this?" She throws her arms around towards the clusters of students standing in the middle of the bar and around high top tables.

ME

We're here.

"I texted him. Happy now?"

"Thrilled." Charlie's head swivels around the crowded bar. I have a sneaky suspicion she isn't looking for Wyatt. "I'm going to look in the back. Send me a text when you find him."

"Do not leave me here," I hiss. I know Charlie. The back room is where the dance floor and DJ are located. She is going to get lost in the music, the lights, and whatever guy she's managed to sucker into dancing with her.

"I'm going to do one quick spin around the back room. It won't take me but a few minutes. I promise."

"Fine." At least it's not karaoke night. A microphone and tequila shots transform Charlie into what I can only describe as what would happen if William Hung and Mariah Carey had a love child. It's something you have to see for yourself.

My phone vibrates in my hand.

WYATT

I'm at the bar.

In the front room.

Right in front of the tv.

I have wings.

Well I had wings.

I ate them all.

No big deal.

We can order more.

More texts come through as I weave my way through the crowd toward Wyatt. We are going to have a conversation about the rapid fire texting he likes to do.

He is barricaded on all sides by beautiful women. I only recognized him by the worn down Newhouse Knights baseball cap he always wears—it sits backwards on his head and his golden brown hair flows and curls slightly around the bill of the cap.

"Excuse me," I say, to one of the women standing behind him. She gives me a cursory glance before turning back around. "Excuse me," I tap on her shoulder.

"Are you lost?" she asks.

While her question is insulting, my main source of irritation isn't with her. "I am not. If you don't mind, this will only take a moment." If I can't bring Mohammad to the mountain, then the mountain will have to go to Mohammad. I hope Wyatt likes to dance.

The girl pouts, probably afraid to lose her "prime real estate" spot as Wyatt calls it, but eventually steps aside to let me get closer to him.

"Thank you. I won't be long." I steel my spine and brush my hands down the blouse and slacks I'm wearing. Clearing my throat, I take one final step toward Wyatt. He turns and does a double take. "I'm here," I say to him.

His eyes roam over me and land on my lips for a moment. While the rest of me is business as usual, I felt the need to wear my power red lipstick tonight. "Where's Charlie?" he asks, his eyes back on mine.

"Dancing or getting someone to buy her drinks," I answer honestly. It makes him wince. "I'll text her." I begin typing out a message to Charlie. I am not subtle about demanding her presence either. I'm almost finished typing when someone slams into me from behind knocking me into the back of Wyatt's chair so hard my phone slips out of my hand.

With cat-like reflexes, he catches my phone before it falls to the ground. "Watch it," he snaps at the bulldozer as he passes behind me. "You okay? He hit you pretty hard," he says, handing me back my phone.

"I'm fine." I rub the sting out of my forearm and bicep.

"If you say so." He reaches out to straighten my glasses. My breath catches with his attentiveness to me. Wyatt is over six feet tall and built like an ox—wide shoulders packed with muscle. His gentleness seems out of character for someone of his size.

I slap his hand away when I come back to my senses. "Do you mind? I don't need your wing-sauced fingers smudging my glasses," I say, making him chuckle. It's annoying that he is constantly laughing at my attempts to insult him.

"Take a seat, Wren." Wyatt stands from his chair. Then steps to the side, offering it to me. I hesitate for a moment. I didn't want to stay long.

My hope was that I could get him and Charlie talking and then sneak out without him remembering the whole *'teach me how to have fun'* part of the evening. Now I have to figure out how to get him to Charlie. This whole situation is giving me a headache.

"If you don't want it, I'll take it," the girl from earlier chimes in. She even raises her hand with a flourish. Her eyelashes flutter as she stares at Wyatt. Give me a break. What is it about this guy that has everyone wanting to barrel themselves face first into one of his various body parts?

When she starts to chew her lip, I sit down. "Sorry, it's mine," I say sharply, scooting around on the seat to get comfortable. I smile back at her, tasting the pettiness on my tongue.

Wyatt looks me over, wide eyed and grinning.

"Yours, huh?" he asks with a glint of pleasure in his eye. I glare back harder, daring him to challenge me. Realization dawns on me. My words could be interpreted as *"he's mine"* even though I'm clearly speaking about the chair. Only Wyatt and his oversized ego would come to that ridiculous conclusion.

"The chair is mine. You offered it to me," I say. Ignoring the dimpled smile on his stupid face, I turn toward the bartender and attempt to get his attention. I'm desperate for a drink.

Wyatt takes note of my failure in flagging him down. *Of course he does.* He will likely take advantage of any moment to rub my shortcomings in my face. Little does he know, I'm well aware of all of them.

Placing one hand on the back of my chair, he leans closer, crowding me. His other hand flicks in the air like he's hailing a cab. It must be a secret signal because suddenly there is a bartender in front of us clearing chicken bones off the bar and Wyatt is ordering another beer for himself and a drink for me.

I'm only slightly disturbed he remembers my drink order from a few months ago when we sat in this very spot together.

Turning my head to say thank you, the side of my face grazes his chest. *Does he really have to stand so close?* I know the bar is crowded, but damn.

His body tenses and muscles ripple against my skin. Wyatt smells like leather, amber, and someone else's bad decision.

I lean back, shifting in my seat slightly. "Thanks for that." I wave a hand toward the bartender.

"No problem." From this position I have a closeup of his face. I can admit that he is handsome in the traditional sense, except for his ridiculous mustache. His eyes are symmetrical and line up with his lips, which are fine if you like them full and well moisturized.

He should apply whatever he is using on his lips to his hands because it is working for him.

It's his nose that makes his face interesting—it has the slightest warp, making me believe it's been broken at least once. I'm going all in guessing he's been punched. I doubt I'm the only person who's been tempted to raw knuckle his nose once or twice.

I take a long sip of my tequila and Sprite once it's set in front of me and let out a long sigh. It's perfect.

"You like it?" he asks, teasing me.

"Yes." I place the glass down on the napkin and maneuver the tiny paper square until the logo of the bar is right side up and legible. Wyatt's deep chuckle has my face heating in anger. "Something funny?"

"Not a thing." He takes a sip of his beer to hide his smirk.

"You text people in excess. I like things to be evenly spaced and orderly." I gesture toward my drink. "We all have our quirks."

"Texting is not a quirk. It's called communicating. My texts are a gift. You should consider yourself lucky to be on the receiving end of them."

"I most certainly do not feel lucky. I feel annoyed." And off kilter. Each chime of my phone makes my eye twitch. It's a nuisance and unnecessary. "There's a texting etiquette."

"There is not. You are making that up. You can't create all these rules and just expect people to follow them." He takes another sip of his beer.

I stare at his Adam's apple as he swallows, imagining how much fun it would be to karate chop it in half.

"Does your brain not think in complete sentences? Is it really too much to request you type an entire thought before hitting send?"

"I can. I'll do better just for you." He picks at the label on his beer. His nails are short and surprisingly clean after playing in dirt all afternoon.

"It's fine. I'll get used to it." *What?* No I won't. There will be no more texting with Wyatt. I don't need to talk to him anymore after tonight. "You said you had a good practice today. How so? What made it so great?" I ask to cut off the rambling in my head.

The ice in my glass spins, mixing the tequila and Sprite as I swirl the tiny straw around. I'm going to need another one of these if Charlie doesn't message me back soon. I should have known she would give me the slip.

I am supposed to be pushing her to him. How did she manage to pull a role reversal on me? I need to get this back on track.

Wyatt's eyes are wide, staring at me. The mask of confidence he wears slipping momentarily out of place. He acts like I'm the first person who ever asked him something trivial about his day.

Everyone knows it's common courtesy to follow-up. It would be rude not to ask.

"I did," he says, still looking at me like a curiosity in a cabinet.

"You've given me so many details. It's like I was right there with you."

His hand grips the top of the bar a little tighter making the tendons in his forearm flex. "You have a sarcastic little mouth on you. Has anyone ever told you that before?"

The ruckus of the crowded bar drowns out the loud beats of my racing heart.

"I may have heard it once or twice." I squirm in my seat, putting some distance between us. It could be the other bar patrons crowding around us, but Wyatt keeps inching closer to me the longer we stay talking.

"You're quite *perplexing*." His grin is immediate knowing what he just did. "That's my first for the day. How many do you have?"

My eyes narrow. "You aren't playing." I pull up the notes app on my phone anyway. I keep track of my word of the day tally marks here as well as in my planner. "I have two." The satisfaction of beating him feels better than it should.

"Oh yes, I am. I like playing games with you. It's fun."

"Are you admitting another thing I like to do is fun?" I dig into my purse for the list I made earlier with things I'm willing to try in the name of having more fun. There's no way I'm giving him that much control. "If that's the case, we should forget about the whole 'teach me' part of the evening." I hold up the slip of paper. "We can end this whole thing now."

Shaking his head, he snatches the piece of paper from my hand. "The game itself isn't fun. But getting you angry is a whole lot of fun." He reads over my list, his lip twitching with every word. "Nice try," he says, crumpling up my list.

"Hey! I worked hard on that." I wrestle with his arm, attempting to steal the paper back. He sends it flying into the trash can behind the bar before I even get close.

"Part of the fun is being spontaneous. I'll let you know when it's time to try something new. In the meantime, put my name on your scorecard and give me a mark. Whoever has the most tally marks at the end of the week gets a prize."

"This isn't elementary school, Wyatt. I don't have a treasure box full of prizes you can pick from."

"You sure about that?" His eyes sweep over my body and my face bursts into flames.

"If you're insinuating what I think you are, then fine. I have a world of wonders down there." I lean on the bar. "But that treasure is at my fingertips. Not yours." I wiggle my fingers in his face.

He swallows hard. I relish in the satisfaction of shutting him up. "Perplexing," he says, then nods toward my phone.

"That doesn't count." I practically screech. "You can't say the word by itself and expect a point. That is cheating. You have to use it in a sentence."

"Here you go with all your rules again, Wren. *You* can't have a good time when you're tying yourself down with all these limitations."

"Not everyone can be lawless like you." I surge toward him in annoyance.

"And not everyone wants to live their life like it's already over." He leans further into my space until we're practically nose to nose.

His warm breath fans over my face. Brown eyes challenge my blue ones before dropping to my lips. He inhales, siphoning what's left of oxygen between us. I'm finding it hard to breathe but I refuse to move and let him think he's won or has any kind of effect on me.

Because he doesn't. It's the tequila making me feel warm and fuzzy.

His eyes bounce back to mine. They are full of mirth and amusement. I don't know what he saw in my eyes just now, but he's wrong. I turn toward the bartender and attempt to get his attention. *Why is it so difficult to get a drink in this place?*

Beside me, he chuckles to himself. "I'm glad my frustration amuses you." My glasses slip down my nose, irritating me further.

"Hey, Tony. Can we get another round over here?" Wyatt calls out to the bartender who is mixing drinks at the other end of the bar. Tony raises his hand in acknowledgment.

"Do you always get what you want?" I ask when our drinks are placed in front of us moments later.

"If I got everything I wanted, I wouldn't be sitting here with you. Would I?"

"No, I doubt that you would." I do my best to mask the sting of rejection I feel. Which is silly, because I don't want to be picked by this man. I want him to leave me alone. "Yet, you are still here. Why? I'm not forcing you to stay. You can leave at any time. Don't let me stop you."

I turn towards the bar and pretend to be interested in the basketball game on the television. I know nothing about the sport, or any sport really, but it's better than looking at him.

Wyatt leans on the bar, angling his body in a way that puts him in my peripheral vision. "Then who would get you drinks? You'd be so thirsty without me." The innuendo drips off his tongue.

I hate him. But he's right about one thing. It is fun to verbally spar and play this little game with him. I like that neither one of us is willing to back down from the other.

"You don't think I could get someone else in this bar to get me a drink."

"Oh, I'm sure you could. But that would involve loosening the reins and having a good time. *That* is where you're going to fail."

"I don't fail at anything," I say with conviction.

"I bet you don't." His words are deep and slow. It rattles something loose in me. As if a part of myself I've been holding on tightly to is trying to break free and follow him off a cliff with wild abandon.

Before I can think too much about why I'm suddenly feeling reckless, my phone lights up with a text notification.

"It's Charlie," I announce.

"Is she coming over here?" He leans closer to read the message with me. His sudden enthusiasm grates on my nerves.

"Do you mind?" I hold my phone against my chest. He backs off but is still close enough to breathe on me like a donkey and view my screen.

CHARLIE

> Looks like things are going well. I'm heading home. Give me all the details in the morning.

Attached is a grainy photo of Wyatt and me from across the crowded bar. We are leaning towards each other and it appears as if we are seconds away from kissing. Only I know the truth, we were swapping insults. *Again*.

"You need to fix this," Wyatt says, pointing at my phone.

"I don't *need* to do anything. I will however tell her that she read the situation wrong."

"So you didn't want me to kiss you? Because in the photo it sure looks like you did," he says, with a wry smile. We can now add delusional to his list of personality traits.

"Absolutely not." I dig into my wallet for some cash. My extended stay at The Armory is over. If Charlie is going home then so am I. "I'm sorry this didn't work out for you. Maybe it's time to move on."

"This ain't over. Set up a lunch date. You, me, and Charlie." He grips my elbow as I drop money on the bar for our drinks.

"Why would I do that?" I yank myself free from his grasp.

"Because you don't fail at anything." He throws my words back in my face knowing good and well I won't be able to ignore the challenge. Especially not one coming from him.

"Fine. After this, I'm done. You're on your own."

"Deal." He extends his hand for me to shake.

Why do I feel like I just made a deal with the devil?

4

WYATT

I'm not sleeping. My game is off. Something ain't right with me.

For once it's not the thing with Charlie eating at me either. Maybe because Wren is finally helping. It's eased some of the turmoil I was feeling. Despite Sunday night being a complete disaster and a waste of time.

Instead of flirting it up with Charlie and making progress, I was stuck sparring with Wren.

And those cherry red lips. Bad Wyatt for looking twice at them.

I shouldn't be thinking about those lips because those lips are attached to Wren. And she makes me certifiable.

It must be my family that has me on edge.

My mama hasn't called in a few days. That's unusual for her and slightly concerning. Typically she's dialing my number so often, I'm dodging her calls. There are times she's resorted to calling me from random numbers to see if I'll pick up.

For the most part, my family leaves me be while I'm at school. They may not know the real reason but they know how important it is for me to get drafted. My focus needs to be baseball. Not the farm.

My family would never say nothing, but we all know the money would change our lives. I am banking on my pro salary to save our home and all our land from foreclosure. They sacrificed all of it to get me here. I'm one of the reasons we're in financial dire straits to begin with. Now, it's my turn to pay them back.

The fact that Mama hasn't called to check-in with me means something is going on and they don't want me to know about it. They think it will distract me. What they don't realize is the not knowing is just as hard.

I send my oldest brother Ford a quick message while I wait outside The Round Table—the campus sandwich shop—for Wren and Charlie to show up. It took a few days, but Wren came through.

Today's lunch will be our first date. Even though we're going dutch and Wren will be here, it still counts in my book. We're out in public and eating together. I've never been on a date before, but it sounds like one to me.

Unfortunately, I need Wren here as my wingwoman to help break the ice and get Charlie to be more receptive to my charm. I've kind of gotten used to having her around. In fact, the only thing that's going right for me this week is beating Wren in her silly word of the day game we've started.

Messing with her perfect routines brings me more joy than it should. The last few days I've been texting her non-stop, following her around on her weekly shopping trips, and over-all being a pest to her. It has become my new favorite hobby.

My mama would not be happy with me always teasing Wren, but she can take it. She gives as good as she gets.

My phone buzzes in my pocket.

FORD

Nothing to worry about. A few broken fence posts on the north pasture.

ME

If you need me to drive out there, I will.

Don't keep me in the dark on this kind of stuff.

I should be there.

FORD

You are exactly where you're supposed to be.

ME

Fine.

Tell Lenny her favorite uncle loves her and will come see her soon.

FORD

You aren't her favorite but I'll tell her you said hi.

ME

Ouch.

> This is why I need to come home.

> Remind her why I should be the favorite.

"Harassing someone else for a change?" The sound of Wren's voice has me grinding my molars and grinning simultaneously.

"Jealous?" I pocket my phone. I will deal with Ford later. I trust him to call me if he needs me. He's ten years older and took over managing the farm the best he could when my dad couldn't anymore.

"Yes. Am I that obvious?" she asks with a roll of her eyes.

"You look good by the way. It's nice to see you in a color that doesn't wash you out completely." I grin back at her.

"That's what I told her. The blue brings out her eyes," Charlie adds, complimenting her friend.

Wearing something in a color other than beige was the first thing I asked Wren to do in order to have fun and live a little. It's still her usual getup—a blouse and dress pants—but Charlie's right. Wren's eyes seem to shine brighter today behind her glasses.

"You look good, too, Charlie." I take a moment to toss her a full dimpled grin and a wink. I might as well start laying the groundwork for this date if I want it to lead anywhere.

"Thanks. You don't look so bad yourself. Don't you think, Wren?" The glare Wren gives Charlie could slice her in half.

"Sure." She can barely get the word out, her mouth is clamped so tight.

"Thank you. That's the nicest thing you've ever said to me. See, Wren, when someone compliments you, you say thank you. I'm surprised that's not one of those etiquette rules you like to throw in my face."

Charlie snickers, knowing I'm right. She's been living with Wren for years. How has she survived? They couldn't be more different—prime example of night and day, complete polar opposites.

Charlie is sunshine on a cloudy day. Wren is...well, she is the cloud.

"I do say thank you when the person is sincere. I know you aren't serious. I don't think you have it in you to voluntarily give me a compliment."

Is that really what she thinks? I've never lied to her.

"I'm not joking around, Wren. If I say it, I mean it." She doesn't look at me. Her eyes stay glued to the concrete. "Look at me."

Reluctantly she lifts her gaze to meet mine. Her full attention stuns me momentarily. She might be a cloud but her eyes are as blue as the sky on a bright summer day. The kind of sky that makes you lose track of time because you stare at it so long nothing else in life exists.

"I wasn't lying yesterday when I told you your taste in music is terrible and I'm not lying when I say you look nice today. Okay?"

"You are the one with terrible music taste," she snaps back at me. *There's my girl.* No. Not my girl. My friend. *There's my friend.*

Friend? Can I even call her that? After today, there won't be any need to communicate with each other. She will be going her way and I'll be going mine.

"Should we go eat? I'm starving and the line isn't getting any shorter," Charlie says, breaking me from my thoughts.

I nod and lead the girls inside. Wren continues to grumble about how my taste in Southern rock music is reprehensible in between ordering and waiting for our food. That unfortunately earns her another point for the day.

"You can't trash on Lynyrd. We live in Alabama for Pete's sake, Wren."

"Wren is a Georgia girl. She won't be living here forever." Charlie's words build a knot in my chest. Georgia is Wren's home. Not Alabama. She'll be leaving soon. I knew this.

I should be happy about this.

"It's not just Lynyrd Skynyrd," Wren grumbles.

"I swear to God, Wren, if you trash on Reba I will hurt you," I say as I take my seat in a booth by the front windows.

They sit across from me. This is good. I can give Charlie my full attention. No distractions. Focus on winning her over and then I can get rid of the song that has been plaguing me.

"I would never," Wren says. Thank fuck. Friendship over if she did.

Which would be fine because we're barely even friends. More like acquaintances that text and hang out occasionally. By hangout I mean, I find her on campus when she is at the library studying or walking from her classes.

I don't fully comprehend why I do this. My mama always said I was compulsive. Once I got an idea in my head I would act on it immediately. I can get so fixated on something, I can't let it go. This hyper focus helps me with my pitching. *That is until the little songbird got in my head.*

Maybe I follow her around because I'm hoping if I annoy her enough she will speed up the process of getting me closer to Charlie. And if that's the case, my plan worked because here we are. *Or maybe you enjoy her company. Nah. I mean, maybe, but nah.*

Our table goes silent as we settle into eating. I take the lettuce off my club sandwich and set it on the side of my plate. Wren lifts the top layer of her sandwich and carefully examines it. Her lip curls in disgust as she gingerly picks off a giant slice of tomato and discards it on her plate.

I don't hesitate to reach across the table and snatch it. I love tomatoes. Especially big slices like this one. Nothing beats the tomatoes we grow on our farm, though.

"Hey!" Wren exclaims as I put my sandwich back together and take a bite.

"What? Were you going to eat it?" I ask with a mouth full of food.

She purses her lips and eyes the lettuce discarded on my plate. I edge it towards her. Of course she would want more of the tasteless vegetable on her sandwich.

"You don't snatch food off someone's plate. Were you raised in a barn?" Wren continues to heckle me. Not a good look in front of Charlie.

Her question makes me wonder what type of guy Charlie typically goes for. A clean cut, polo-wearing guy? She won't find that here. I wasn't raised in a barn, but I slept in one more nights than I can count.

"Is that rule number three hundred and forty-seven? Or four hundred and ninety-one? I've lost track." I scowl back at her. Wren's eyes stare back like laser beams cutting straight to the core of me.

"Whew, your foreplay is intense," Charlie says, her eyes darting back and forth between the two of us. She picks at her salad and pops a tomato in her mouth.

"Foreplay? Really, Charlie? This," Wren waves a hand between us, "is not foreplay. It's Wyatt being..." her voice trails off as she tries to come up with the right word. Glancing up at me she must see my distress. I'm begging her not to say what she really thinks of me. I know it isn't good. "Wyatt."

"If you say so," Charlie singsongs. I don't like what she is insinuating.

"I do," we say at the same time. Charlie smirks knowingly. We are doing a shitty job at proving her wrong.

Wren kicks my shin under the table so hard I almost choke on a French fry. *What the hell?*

Say something, she mouths with raised eyebrows and wide eyes.

Like what, I ask back. Wren grunts in frustration.

I'm grateful Charlie is looking at her phone and not paying attention to us at the moment.

Wren's shoulders drop in resignation. My knee starts bouncing wildly waiting for Wren to start up a conversation.

"Charlie, did you know that Wyatt already has thirty-two strikeouts this year?"

Charlie puts her phone down and looks at Wren. Then at me. "I didn't. Is that a lot?"

"It's...decent." I stumble over my response. I don't want to come across as conceited, but it's a good number.

"Don't be so humble, Wyatt." Wren grins. It's more like a creepy grimace. "The other starter only has fifteen. Wyatt is number two in the division." Wren takes a dainty bite of her sandwich.

"That's incredible, Wyatt." Charlie beams at me. "Tell me more about your stats."

I take a sip of my drink to give myself time to think of something impressive. Nothing really comes to mind. I don't obsess over stats and rankings like some players do. I play baseball. As long as I'm pitching well and winning games, I don't care. Obsessing over numbers and rankings takes time away from practicing and honing my skills.

"He has the best earned run average and one of the highest batting averages for a pitcher," Wren speaks for me. I'm shocked she even knows this information.

Why does she know? Did she study and prepare? I laugh to myself. Of course she did. Wren doesn't do anything in half measures. I bet she has all my stats written down on one of her cute little notepads.

"What can I say? I'm good with my bat." I wink at Charlie.

"Is that so?" Charlie asks, leaning towards me. I lean in too, bringing our faces closer together.

"Statistically, yes," Wren interjects. "Some sources have reported you could be better," she says, without missing a beat. What is she doing? She's supposed to be helping me.

I flash Wren with the best *'what in the actual fuck'* look I can. She peers back at me innocently with her big doe eyes, but she knows exactly what she's doing.

"Maybe I need to see for myself. We should go to a game," Charlie says to Wren.

"It's outside," Wren says.

"You won't melt," Charlie counters.

"I don't know. Isn't that how the wicked witch finally gets taken out? I'm melting. I'm melting," I add, mimicking the line from the movie and sliding down in the booth for emphasis.

Wren kicks me again under the table. A low growl rumbles in my throat. She needs to quit that shit.

"You know what. I think it sounds like...oh what's the word I'm looking for? Fun," she says, glaring at me.

"Great," I grind out. "I'll get you tickets near Lauren and Sydney's seats."

"Yay!" Charlie squeals. "I know just what to wear too," she adds, as she collects her trash from her lunch.

I can picture her now wearing my jersey. My name and number on her back cheering for me in the stands. Her long, brown hair up in a high ponytail. After the game, I'll go back to her place and make a mess of her cherry red lips. Wait, brown hair? Red hair. Charlie has—

Wren's pointed-toe shoe hits me hard in the shin, waking me from my daydream. "What the fuck, Wren? That's going to bruise."

"Charlie left while you were daydreaming," she says, with an air of annoyance. *Damn it.* "I need to go too. I—"

"Have class. I know. Today went well."

"Uh-huh," Wren says, delicately folding her napkin and placing it on her empty plate.

"It was our first date. There are bound to be some hiccups."

"Uh-huh."

"Will you stop saying that?" I take her trash from her and clear the rest of the table.

"In what universe do you think this lunch counts as a first date with Charlie? You didn't ask her to come. You had me do it." Wren continues to point out all the ways I'm messing this up before I even get started.

I usher her outside, my hand gliding against the smooth silk of her blouse on her back. For once she doesn't shrink away from my touch.

"It's close enough. You're talking semantics. It doesn't matter."

"It matters to Charlie. Therefore it needs to matter to you." She pokes me in the chest with her finger. I grab her hand and squeeze it briefly before releasing my grip.

"What's with all the poking and kicking? I'm fragile." I frown.

"Sure you are. I need to go. But good luck with...everything." Wren starts walking away toward her next class.

"Why are you acting like I'm not going to see you again?" I tag along behind her.

"Our deal was to get her to lunch. I did that. You failed. Not me."

"Wait a minute." I jog ahead and block her path. "You're going to the game. We need to talk about that."

"I don't think so. You get the tickets. We'll show up. That's the plan." She huffs in frustration when she can't get past me.

"Maybe we need to do something else first. The game won't give me an opportunity to make my move."

"That sounds like a you problem." She attempts to push past me again.

"It might be my problem but you are going to help me solve it. I'll text you later," I say, then salute her and walk away. I'm not giving her time for rebuttal. The last word is mine.

She isn't done with me until I say she is.

WYATT & WREN

WYATT

I was just thinking.

WREN

Don't do that. You might hurt yourself.

WYATT

You are a terrible wingwoman.

You didn't even give me her number.

WREN

Oh, I'm so sorry. I didn't know that was my job.

WYATT

It was implied.

WREN

I'm not going give you her number without asking her first.

WYATT

Then ask her.

WREN

I don't want to.

WYATT

Can you come over tomorrow after my practice?

WREN

I have homework.

WYATT

Bring it.

You can do it over here.

After we talk.

WREN

THAT COULD HAVE ALL BEEN ONE TEXT.

WYATT

I thought you said my texting was fine.

WREN

I lied. Leave me alone. I just saw you. I'm done with you for the day.

WYATT

Just for the day? You say.

I rhymed.

See you tomorrow.

WYATT

How was class?

I just sat through a 45 minute lecture on dirt.

And now I get to write about it.

WREN

Fascinating. Tell me more.

WYATT

Are you asking me to talk dirty to you?

5

WREN

Why can't I say no to him? It's a simple word. It should be easy.

I keep allowing him to get under my skin. He's like a bad rash that won't go away.

I can't believe I let myself get tangled up in this situation. Wyatt is a big boy. If he wants to get Charlie, he is more than capable of doing it on his own. But he read me right and dangled the carrot of competition in my face.

I won't give him the satisfaction of thinking he has me beat.

I'm doing my part. He is the one who is botching the whole ordeal. Do you know how long I spent studying his stats? *Hours*. I made color coded index cards and memorized as much information as I could to make him look good. Was he thankful? No.

He makes inappropriate jokes instead about being good with his bat.

Now I'm here waiting for someone to answer his front door because he thinks we need a game plan. I don't need anything. *Then why are you here?*

I knock again. A little louder this time to work through my frustration.

Suddenly, the door swings open and Wyatt's roommate Nash is standing there with a game controller in his hand.

"Hey, Wren." Nash gestures for me to come inside. I about jump out of my skin when I notice the giant sitting on the couch playing a video game. "That's Eli. Don't let him scare you. He's a teddy bear. Eli, this is Wren. One of my sister's friends."

"Hi," I greet Eli. He doesn't say anything, just nods and goes back to shooting someone on the television screen.

"He's kind of shy. What are you doing here? Did you need something?"

"Wyatt," I say.

"You need Wyatt?" Nash asks with a smirk.

"No. That is not what I meant. I'm here to see him. He asked me to come over."

"Interesting. He's downstairs in his room." Nash points towards what I'm guessing is the basement door as he takes a seat on the couch and starts playing his game again.

"You want me to go down there." I stare at the door in question. My face scrunches up in disgust. I do not want to be in the same room where Wyatt brings women and does Lord knows what. I thought we would meet in the kitchen to study and figure out a plan.

"He doesn't bring girls here if that's what you're worried about."

"I find that hard to believe."

"Well, it's true."

"Why?"

Nash lip lifts in an evil grin. "You'll see. Good luck."

Hesitantly, I leave the safety of the living room and head towards the basement door. I glance back at Nash and he nods and waves a hand for me to keep going. I'm not sure I want to.

The air is significantly cooler as I make my way down the stairs and enter the open den. Minimal furniture decorates a small living area. A pub style table is positioned in the far corner beside a black leather couch. It screams bachelor pad.

"Wyatt?" I call out towards the hallway of doors. No answer. He never makes anything easy for me.

I knock on one door. Again no answer. I open it up and it's the bathroom. I pass another door on my right that is slightly ajar. A bedroom. The bed is unmade. There is a picture on the dresser of Nash and Sydney. I'm guessing this room belongs to Nash then.

Only one door left. I knock with no response on the other side. There is country music playing. Maybe he can't hear me. I try the knob and it turns easily. "Wyatt?" I call out to warn him before entering his room. I do not want to walk in on anything that will scar me for life.

Dear mother of God.

I blink hard and adjust my eyes. I was not prepared for the sight in front of me. And no, it isn't Wyatt naked. That would be a welcome visual compared to this.

"Hey. You're here. Come on in. I was just starting my paper." Wyatt pops up from the chair at his desk where his laptop barely fits around all the clutter surrounding him. How is he able to get any work done with his desk in this condition? I scratch the itch at my neck.

"Were you raided? Did your room get tossed?" Or maybe he started cleaning out his closet and got distracted. It's very easy to become a victim to memorabilia that's been lost and buried in a closet.

Wyatt has clothes everywhere. It's not just clothes. It's books, papers, shoes, belts, hats, weights.

I glance into his open closet. My knees threaten to buckle. My throat gets scratchy and dry. His closet is a hoarder's paradise. *Close your eyes and look away. Pretend it doesn't exist.*

"No, I wasn't raided. This is how it always looks."

I gasp. "You're kidding," I say as I tiptoe around his room, avoiding random objects like land mines. Wyatt lifts my backpack off my shoulder and places it on his bed.

"It's not that bad. I'm busy. I don't have time to clean. Okay?"

"I'm not judging you." I glance around his room, trying to keep my face neutral. Internally I'm having a moment.

"You are. It's what you do," he says casually as if this is information I'm already aware of. I stare back at him open-mouthed, not really sure how to respond. "Oh come on, you had me figured out the moment we met."

"I form opinions based on what I observe. If you don't want me to think of you a certain way, act differently."

He nods thoughtfully. "You're okay with people assessing you based on the same criteria?" he asks, gathering all the clothes from his bed.

"Yes. I know how I come across. I am who I am. People can think whatever they want about me." I watch in horror as he tosses everything onto the floor. "Were those clean?" I can't stop myself from asking.

"Yeah, I pulled them out of the dryer twenty minutes ago." He shrugs like it's no big deal.

"Those are going to wrinkle."

"It's workout gear and T-shirts. It's fine. I'm not worried about it. Make yourself comfortable." He gestures toward his bed. "We can do our homework first. That way I can have your full attention later." I ignore another one of his innuendos. He has no filter. It's a side of him I'm becoming more accustomed to.

"In here? I don't think I can be comfortable in here."

"I'll sit on the bed. You can have the desk."

I understand now what Nash meant about Wyatt bringing women down here. There is no way you are entertaining anyone in this room. *Why does that make me feel relieved?*

"That's not the problem." I scratch at my chest again. *Great.* I'm going to break out in hives if I don't do something about this. Wyatt pulls out the desk chair for me. He's moved his laptop, but the piles of books and miscellaneous items remain cluttering the surface.

"Sit," he commands. I glance up at him. His hand goes to my shoulder, applying the slightest amount of pressure, forcing me into the chair. I feel the same tingle I felt yesterday when he placed his hand on my back. Instinct told me to flinch away, instead I relaxed into his touch.

"Can I just...I need to..." I glance back at his laundry.

"Seriously?" he asks, his head tilts and eyebrows rise toward his hairline. I can't explain my need to organize and clean his space. I know it will gnaw at me until the task is complete. I won't be able to concentrate on anything else until it is taken care of.

I stand up and place my hands on his chest. His eyes focus on where we're connected. The tips of my fingers buzz like I'm touching a live wire. I ignore it. "It will only take a few minutes."

"Fine. If it will make you feel better." Wyatt backs away, leaving my hands hanging mid-air for a moment. He collects all the laundry he dropped moments ago and throws it back on the bed.

I eye the clothes in front of me and start mentally sorting everything into categories. "Do you fold your shirts?"

He looks at me like I have two heads. "You could call it that." Wyatt grabs a shirt off the bed and walks over to his dresser. With his eyes on me he opens the drawer and stuffs the shirt inside. I squawk or maybe I squeal. "Just don't look at it, Wren," he says, attempting to calm me.

"Is that how your mom taught you to do laundry?" I tease as I pass him walking to the dresser. I snag the shirt out of the drawer and lay it out flat on the bed. "Ignoring things doesn't make them go away. I should know. I tried with you," I say with a wry smile.

"You're hilarious." He watches me attentively as I pinch the top of the shirt near the shoulder with my left hand and in the middle of the shirt with my right. Looping my left hand around my right, I pinch the end of the shirt and then untwist my arms.

Giving the shirt a quick shake to even it out before placing it flat on the bed and folding in half.

"How the fuck did you just do that?"

His astonishment makes me giggle. Wyatt's eyes catch on mine. There's a satisfied grin on his face for making me laugh. He should be. I don't do it often. The fact that he made it happen so effortlessly should be a concern.

"It's pretty simple once you learn how. I'll teach you." I lay out another shirt. "Pinch here and here." I slow my movements and I put my hands in place and grab the end of the shirt. "Then, wallah," I say as I pull the shirt taut. "It may look like a legerdemain but—"

"Motherfucker. Seriously? You set this up just to get a point." His words come off as angry but there's a smile on his face.

"I did no such thing. I can't stand disorder. My brain." I gesture to my head. "It can't function when things are out of place. I know. I sound crazy."

Shaking his head he says, "Nah, you don't. I get it. I mean, well, obviously I don't feel the same." He smiles sheepishly looking around his room. "Needing structure and order has never been appealing to me."

"Really? I never would have guessed." I smirk at him.

"I'm not that bad, am I?"

"It doesn't matter if it's bad or not. It's your room. You're busy and have a lot on your plate. It's easy to let a few things slip." *Or a lot of things.* I'm not usually one to cut someone slack, but Wyatt looks like he could use some.

I silently work on folding all his shirts. Most have the sleeves cut off with large holes down the side. They would be more useful as rags, yet, he's hanging on to them for dear life.

His phone dings in fast succession, cutting off the music he was playing. Probably for the best. I keep having to stop myself from singing along.

"Does everyone text like you?" I ask as he grabs his phone off the side table.

"Most people like texting."

"I prefer texting to talking on the phone like the next person. What I don't understand is one word or one sentence texts. Put it all together."

I would never admit it but there are times I find myself looking forward to his texts. I'm trained like a puppy to jump when my phone chimes. I know it will be him because they always come after I leave class or before one of my tutoring sessions. Wyatt apparently knows my entire schedule. Another thing I should find concerning, but feel quite the opposite for some reason.

"That's called an email. This is my family chat. It always blows up. I should add you," he says, with an evil gleam in his eye.

"I will actually kill you. How many family members do you have?" I ask as his phone continues to ping. "Can you do something about that?" I gesture toward the phone in his hand. The one that he has yet to look at and check the messages.

"I could."

"I swear, Wyatt."

He chuckles at my annoyance. "To answer your question, I have three brothers and a sister."

My jaw drops. Five children. It sounds loud, overwhelming, chaotic. All the things I hate. Yet, I find myself a little jealous deep down that my upbringing was lonely and not wild like his.

"Let me guess. Your sister is the baby."

He looks up at me from his phone. Brown shaggy hair frames his face. "No, I am." He smirks. "They couldn't stop until they had perfection."

A derisive noise slips past my lips. "That must be why my parents stopped with me too."

"Yeah, that must be it," he says dryly. I whip his thigh with the pair of shorts I was in the process of folding.

His eyes travel slowly from his leg and back to me. "You shouldn't have done that."

"Why's that?" I taunt him.

"Because." He reaches for the gym shorts I'm holding and attempts to yank them out of my hands. He didn't anticipate my firm grip and pulls me along with the clothing. I fall forward and slam into his chest.

He steadies me with a hand on my hip. It reminds me of the time I almost fell on my face at the campus store. *My body remembers that moment too.*

For the second time today, I place a hand on his chest. I tell myself it's to keep from pressing up against him. I'm not convinced it's the only reason. My other hand wrestles him for the shorts. With each tug, he pulls me closer and closer.

With no space between us, I feel everything. Including his growing erection. My gaze slowly floats up to meet his. My stomach does a little flip. I will chastise myself about that later.

This is Wyatt I'm dealing with. It doesn't mean he's attracted to *me*. He said so himself that he wasn't. He probably walks around campus half-mast ready to spring into action.

"Why shouldn't I have done that?" I ask breathlessly. I wonder if he realizes his grip is getting tighter on my hip. I'm not a small girl yet his palm spans the width of my waist. His stare is intense like he's attempting to do long division in his head. *What are you thinking so hard about?*

Suddenly he yanks his shorts hard, throwing me off balance, and I stumble backward onto his bed. "Because this is going to hurt," he says roughly, spinning the shorts around until they are as thin as a rope. I squeal and scramble towards the middle of the mattress out of his reach.

"Please don't. I didn't hit you that hard." I hold up my hands placating him. He doesn't seem to care. I crawl further across the queen sized bed. Before I can make it to the other side he snaps his handmade whip across my upper thigh.

On all fours, I stretch out my back, hissing at the sting. "Damn it, Wyatt. That hurt." I glance at him over my shoulder with anger coursing through my veins.

His focus is on me. More specifically my ass that is currently up in the air. His eyes glaze over and his hands flex at his side.

I am confident in my own skin regardless of my size. However, his intense stare is making me feel self-conscious in this precarious position. I spin around and face him.

The tension is making the air thick and hard to breathe. His silence is unsettling. Unsure what to do, I slide off the bed and continue folding his laundry. I need to do something to quiet my brain. Because right now it's running wild with thoughts of Wyatt and why he would be looking at me the way he is.

His chest presses against my back. I'm reminded once again of how perfectly his body frames mine. He tosses the shorts on the bed. His fingers graze from the top of my forearm down to my fingers, causing the hair on my arm to rise, and he takes the clothing I'm holding out of my hands.

"Come with me," he demands. He grabs my backpack and walks out of his bedroom. *Where is he going?* I follow him down the hall until we reach the den area. He drops my bag on the bar top table. "Sit."

"I wasn't finished in there," I argue.

"Do not test me right now." He grits the words out with clenched fists. Is he angry? What has him strung so tight? He's the one who made me fall onto his bed, if that's what he's so mad about.

Once I'm sitting in a chair he walks back toward his room. I start pulling out my supplies, books, and laptop. I guess we're studying now. He enters the room with his laptop and phone.

"Everything okay?" I ask.

"Yep."

His reply is unconvincing. He's not even looking at me. His nose is buried in his phone.

"If you say so." I hop out of my seat to plug in my laptop. I find the slow draining battery signal distracting and panic inducing. The closest outlet is behind the furniture. Not very convenient. I have to bend all the way over the side table and stretch my arm behind the couch. He curses behind me.

"I'm going to get snacks," he announces. "When I get back, you better be sitting in that chair."

The commanding tone in his voice sends a tingle down my spine. It also makes me want to push him a little and see what he'll do if I defy him.

6

WYATT

I open the pantry door and immediately slam it shut. Why is there nothing to eat?

I'm not even *that* hungry.

I needed to get away from Wren.

I'm a man. It doesn't take much to turn me on. I've never met a woman who didn't get my dick at least a little excited. She, however, shouldn't be one of them.

Wren in her cream linen pants and striped blouse.

Wren pressed up against my chest.

Wren on her hands and knees on my bed.

The last straw was her bent over the side table.

I slam another cabinet door.

"You okay in there?" Nash calls out from the living room.

"We don't have any food!" What's a guy gotta do to get some chips around here? Fuck, I'd take a saltine cracker at this point.

"Check the fridge. Hart brought home some kind of chicken and pasta dish Lauren made last night. That shit was good."

"Must be nice to have a girlfriend that cooks all the time. I bet he never goes hungry," I mutter to myself as I pull out the leftovers. I open up the lid and groan. It smells fucking amazing.

I grab two bowls from the cabinet and scoop a few heaping spoonfuls in each one. While I wait for the pasta to heat up, I catch up on my family group chat.

They managed to get the fencing fixed but now one of the stable roofs is leaking and the big tractor broke down. Translation: the farm is falling apart.

Everything my family has spent generations working to build is turning to complete horseshit and there's nothing I can do about it.

Ford would remind me that I'm doing my job. Getting my degree and following "my dreams" of getting drafted. It's not where I want to be. If it wasn't for the promise of a big payday, I would quit playing. My heart isn't in baseball anymore. It hasn't been since high school.

Playing professional baseball was never the end game. I want to be at home helping my family fix our legacy and make it into something that will carry on for generations.

But I'm stuck here. I'm wasting days on women I'll never remember and playing a game that doesn't mean anything to me.

When the microwave dings, I grab a couple of forks and throw them on a tray along with some napkins and the bowls of food. *Shit, they're hot.* Not as hot as Wren looked on my bed. "Damn it." I've got to stop thinking about that. I shake out my hand to relieve the burn. I find two bottles of water in the fridge and tuck them under my arm.

Taking a few deep breaths, I mentally prepare myself to be in Wren's presence as I walk down the stairs. There is no reason for my body to react to her the way it is. She's here to help me get in good with Charlie for fuck's sake. My dick needs to get with the program. She is not an option.

When I reach the bottom step, it takes me a second to realize the den is empty. I leave the tray of food on the table and check the bathroom. Maybe Wren is in there. The door is cracked open and the lights are off. I bang my head against the door frame.

I can't handle seeing Wren in my room again. As it is, I know I will be going to bed with her wildflower scent lingering in the air. Big mistake on my part inviting her over. I've completely underestimated her. I won't be doing that again.

Standing by the door, I watch as she flies around the room like a little bird. *My little birdie*. She's managed to fold all the laundry on the bed, organize my shoes that were all over the room, and now she appears to be moving my weights to the corner of the room.

Wren has one of my fifty pound weights in her hands and is attempting to waddle it across the room. The damn thing is probably close to a third of her weight. When the dumbbell almost slips out of her grasps I jump into action.

"Damn it, birdie. Give me that." I take it out of her hands. "Where are you putting it?"

"Over there." She points to the opposite wall. "In the corner by your desk."

"What are you doing in here?" I ask as I pick the other weight off the floor and move it to the corner with the first one. It's actually the perfect spot for them. I can watch my new favorite murder documentary Lauren has me hooked on and do my reps.

"I couldn't focus knowing what was hiding behind the door." Wren's hands are clasped together in front of her and she nibbles on her lower lip. *She's lying.* She wanted to see what I would do to her if she wasn't sitting in that chair like I asked.

"I told you to wait for me out there." I step closer and she fidgets under my stare. "I made dinner." Placing my hands on her shoulders, I spin her around and escort her out of my room.

"You cooked?"

"I heated it up. Lauren cooked," I say, taking my seat across from her. I hand her a fork and place a bowl of pasta in front of her.

"Looks good." She takes a dainty bite and chews methodically.

"Are you counting your chews?" I shove a large bite in my mouth and almost swallow it whole. I barely taste it as it slides down my throat.

"It's better for your digestive system if you chew your food at least twenty times," she says meekly. I hate that she's shying away from me. I don't like this Wren. I like it when she battles me back. I like it when she is feisty and breathing fire.

"Uh-huh." I take another bite of my meal.

"You did a really good job heating this up," she says without a trace of sarcasm. It makes me laugh. A genuine compliment about heating food in the microwave. "What? I'm serious. It can be difficult to get even heat distribution in the microwave."

"I know you're serious. That's why I'm laughing." I take another bite of food. She hasn't taken her eyes off the bowl. "The key is to keep the food on the edge of the glass plate so it spins around." I twirl my fork in the air.

"Good to know. For next time."

We eat in silence until my phone starts making noise again. Her eyes twitch with each notification of an incoming text. *Is this how she reacts to my texts too?*

I respond to my brothers. Damn, I hate not being at home. This time of year is really busy. We are preparing the fields to plant and moving everything from the greenhouses. The equipment breaking down isn't making things any easier.

All the work falls on my family and anyone willing to break their back for a homemade pie baked by my sister, Willow. She makes a mean pie, but I'm not sure it's worth the price of spending hours in the sun.

"Are you sure everything is okay? Your face is really wrinkly."

"You always say the sweetest things to me, birdie."

"I wish you wouldn't call me that."

"Why?"

"It's not my name," she says. I wonder if there is another reason. Nicknames are more intimate. They're personal. Wren doesn't do intimate. I shouldn't either.

At least I shouldn't want to with her, but for whatever reason I'm doing it without thinking of the backlash.

Ever since we've started this makeshift friendship, I find myself craving her dry humor and sharp comebacks. I've become accustomed to people on campus sugar coating their words to make a good impression on me in order to get something from me.

Your dick is everyone's type. Trust me. You are not. I still find myself amused by that one. It was an insult but also the truth. I know why I'm popular with the women on campus.

Wren is right. Most people only get to know me on a surface level. Her opinions are probably accurate based on what I've given her to work with, but there's more to me than good looks and fun times. At least I like to think so.

"It is now." I smirk at her. "You can give me a nickname too."

"You don't want me to do that." She takes another bite of her dinner.

"Why not? I bet you even have something in mind."

"The names I call you in my mind aren't very nice," she says, her focus locked in on creating the perfect bite with her fork.

"I don't believe you."

She shrugs. "Believe what you want. Either way, you won't be getting a nickname."

"Whatever you say, *birdie*."

She scowls. "Stop."

"Nah, I don't think I will." I can't. In the middle of all the problems my family is facing at the farm, having this woman get angry at me makes me happy. It's a feeling I don't want to stop chasing.

My phone lights up again with a new text from Colt. It has me frowning.

"You're getting wrinkly again. What's going on?" Her voice is laced with concern and that unnerves me. I don't want her to worry about me or my family. Regardless, I find myself opening up to her.

"Have you ever heard of the small town Rivers Bend?" Wren shakes her head in response. "It's a couple hours from here. It's where I grew up. My family owns a farm out that way." And most of the land surrounding it.

We used to own the whole damn town.

"Our farm. It's failing and falling apart," I explain. She pushes her bowl out of the way and leans on the table. Of course she would want a front row seat for my turmoil. "We should be plowing and planting but nothing is going right. We're getting behind schedule. I should be there."

"But you can't because you have to be here and you don't want to be." She says the words I've left unspoken. "Are you going back home after graduation?"

"No. I'm going into the draft."

"Why? If your family needs you, why play? You'll have your degree in agricultural science. Go home and put your degree to good use," she says. My eyebrows raise in question. "It popped up when I was researching your stats."

Nothing about my life at Newhouse is a secret. It's all available on my player bio. Last semester the Newhouse social media team conducted interviews and made a full dossier on each player. If you want to know something about me, you can find it.

"When I'm done playing I will." I've already collected a few notebooks full of ideas that will help us with long term sustainability. We are currently doing what's necessary to scrape by. If I was there every day, I could...still not get it done because we don't have the money to do anything.

"That could take years. It's going to feel like a jail sentence because you don't want to play. You want to be with your family."

"Stop telling me what I want when you don't know me. I do want to play."

She laughs. It's a mocking laugh. Nothing like the giggle she gave me earlier. The sound had me second guessing myself. There was something about the trill at the end that was familiar, like I've heard it before, but I can't quite place it.

"Now it's my turn not to believe you," she says.

Wren is too smart for her own good. I didn't realize she was so accurate at reading people but I am too. It's what makes me such a great pitcher. I can tell what a batter is thinking by the way he grips his bat or how he digs his cleats into the dirt.

We all have a tell. I've figured out a few of Wren's. Like when she's lying she scratches at her wrist or when she's nervous her eyes dart around wildly. What I don't know is why she is preaching to me so passionately about my future.

"It doesn't matter if you believe me or not. I have to do it. There isn't a choice."

"There is always a choice."

"Is that so? Is that why you're getting married? Because you are choosing to marry someone you don't know and don't love?"

"My personal life isn't up for discussion."

"How convenient for you. We've both made our choices then."

"Seems we have," she says and sits back in her seat. "You can always change your mind and pick differently."

Are we still talking about me playing baseball or something else? Why would she care if I play or if I stay home with my family?

"We should probably talk about Charlie," I say, changing the subject. "That's why you're here." I'm reminding myself more than I am her.

"Right. That's why I'm here. What did you have in mind?"

"I think you should plan a movie date at your dorm and invite me." This is what I wanted to do weeks ago when I first approached her but she refused.

"Fine. I'll set it up." She doesn't hesitate this time. That raises my hackles.

"It's that easy? Why are you being so agreeable? You were giving me such a hard time before."

"Do you want me to set it up or not?" Her words are clipped.

"I do." I need this whole situation to be over with already.

"Then don't ask questions. I'm agreeing to do what you want. You should be happy."

She's right. I should. Yet, I'm not sure that I am. "When are you free?" I ask.

We go over our schedules. Wren pencils in all my practices and games into her planner. The image sparks something deep inside of me. Having my name written on the pages of a book that is her entire world makes me feel like I'm a major player in her life.

That we have a real friendship starting.

That there's something happening between us beyond this scheme.

A feeling I can't put my finger on shifts around in my gut. It makes me question the decisions I'm making.

She looks at me across the table and her electric blue eyes rattle me further. There's a slight hesitation hidden in their depths. Wren is holding back. That isn't something she does.

What are you hiding from me, birdie? And why does this interest me more than getting together with Charlie?

7

WREN

The campus cafeteria is bustling as usual. I weave my way through students congregating around tables until I reach the line for my favorite Mediterranean cuisine.

The Newhouse cafeteria is set up similar to a mall food court but on a smaller scale. They have everything from pizza to Asian fusion. After three years here, I have a favorite dish at each restaurant and keep them on a rotating schedule.

My phone buzzes a few times in my bag while I'm waiting in line. What does he want now? I've been attempting to put some distance between Wyatt and me the last few days.

Not that he took the hint.

There was something about the last conversation we had that left me feeling out of sorts. I know Wyatt isn't attracted to me, nor am I him. He isn't my type.

But I can't deny the way I feel around him. My body begins to hum below the surface and becomes hyper aware of his proximity.

The fact that he is interested in Charlie should be reason enough to shut down these irrational thoughts. Not to mention that I find him annoying and reckless.

Then I see the way he stresses over his family and I wonder if I've misjudged him some. It makes me want to help. But helping will bring us closer together.

That's the last thing we need.

Once my lunch order is ready, I secure a table in the very back of the dining area. It's much quieter in the corner away from the main thoroughfare and the students who prefer to socialize over eating.

I remove all the food from the tray and pull my planner out of my bag. My phone continues to buzz. I'm not ready to see him. As it is, I have to plan a movie day for him and Charlie. He will be in my personal space this time, and I don't know how I feel about that.

"Did you leave your phone at home?" Wyatt drops into the seat across from me. His tray is loaded with a giant cheeseburger and a basket of French fries. "I've been texting you."

"How did you know I was here?"

He rolls his eyes. "You eat in the cafeteria every Thursday. Mediterranean this week. Nice. Here." He pushes the basket of fries to the middle of the table so I can reach.

Wyatt shakes pepper on to the fries, while I squirt ketchup into the side of the basket.

"Do you think it's weird you know my schedule?"

"No. You know mine too." He waves a fry in my direction.

"You gave it to me. I didn't follow you around campus like a weirdo memorizing it."

94

He tilts his head. "That's not what I thought you'd say. I'll take it."

"Why are you here?" I dredge a fry through the ketchup and take a bite.

"Lunch."

"There are a million other tables. Why are you *here*?"

"A million? That's a stretch, don't you think?" He eats a fourth of his burger in one bite.

"You're going to get indigestion eating that fast."

"I appreciate your concern, but I've been eating like this since I was five years old. Ain't nothing going to bring me down." He takes five French fries and stuffs them in his mouth whole. "I'm here because I have something fun for us to do after we eat." He wiggles his eyebrows.

He's not wearing a hat today. He looks...handsome. His hair cascades in layers down the side of his head until it blends into the longer hair in the back. Without the bill of his hat getting in the way, I can see his eyes more clearly. They are brown, but every now and then they catch the light and transform into a warm caramel.

"What is it?" I ask.

"It's a surprise. Trust me. You'll like it."

Funny enough. I do trust Wyatt.

We finish eating our lunch and he escorts me to his pickup truck, which seems to be on its last legs.

When he parks the truck at our destination, I stare at him. "We're at your townhouse."

"I know. Come on."

He opens my door and I hesitantly take his hand and allow him to help me down. Pride wants to take over and push him out of the way. I've always done things on my own.

Maybe it is the only child in me. I never had a sibling to partner up with or even a close friend to lean on. Charlie is the closest thing to a best friend I've had besides my dad. I sometimes wonder if it's by default, that maybe if she wasn't my roommate freshman year, she never would have given me a chance.

We stuck together over the years because, why change what's working? Lauren and Sydney are my friends because of the same reasons. We were all together on the same floor in the dorms our first year. We've stuck together ever since.

Then there's Wyatt. A man who has been pursuing my roommate for a couple of months. He's getting what he wants in a few days. Yet, he still texts about random things that have nothing to do with the whole Charlie situation. He also shows up out of nowhere to walk me to class or eat lunch.

What will happen once he gets what he wants from Charlie?

You get to have your life and your personal space back. Why does that thought make me feel sad and empty?

"Don't be scared. I promise you'll like this," he says as we enter the house. Nash and his behemoth of a friend, Eli, are eating at the dining table while they study. Wyatt says hello then excitedly ushers me downstairs.

I follow him down the hall toward his room. It looks a little bit better than when I left it a few days ago. There's a new pile of laundry forming, but the weights are still in the corner and his shoes aren't scattered all over the floor anymore.

"Ta da!" he yells, gesturing toward his closet which is practically bursting at the seams.

"I don't get it." I stare at him blankly.

"I'm going to let you organize my closet."

"Why would you do that?" I realize to some people this would seem like a punishment. To me, it's a dream. I walk inside the small space and run a hand over the shirts he has hanging up. His cologne sits on a shelf which explains why his scent is stronger here.

"I knew you would like it. I also thought it was time to get rid of some of this stuff. I'll be moving out before I know it. I need the head start," he says, picking up a plastic cowboy hat that's covered in glitter and placing it on his head.

"Are you sure you want to do this? It's going to take a few hours."

"I know."

"Once we start, we can't stop until we're done." I take a step in his direction.

"I know."

"You will have to throw things away or donate them." I take another step.

"I *know*. I'm ready."

"Great. We'll start with this." I snatch the hat off the top of his head.

"Absolutely not. I wore that to my first costume party. It has memories."

"Wyatt, you do not need to remember the time you dressed up as a disco cowboy. If anything, we should be offering free therapy to anyone who had to witness you wearing this."

"Fine." He pouts, looking longingly toward the hat. "But we're donating it. It's not garbage."

"Sure. I would hate for someone to miss out on the opportunity to strut through town wearing that monstrosity."

"I guess this means I need to donate the matching silver chaps too."

"Dear God. Why don't you grab a few trash bags and I'll get started pulling everything out and sorting it into piles." I push him out of the closet.

He nods and walks toward the door. "Don't throw anything out without my approval."

"I wouldn't dream of it," I say. He nods again accepting my answer. I wouldn't do that to him. "Hey, Wyatt," I call out to him before he slips through the door. "Thanks for this. It was a good surprise."

He smiles, but it's different. His dimples barely register in his cheeks and his lips aren't turned all the way up. The smile is shy and unsure. *Sweet almost.* "You're welcome."

While he runs upstairs for supplies, I pull the sheets and comforter up on his bed. This will be our sorting area. Then I move all the clothes from around the floor and pile them in the corner. I'm assuming they're dirty, but you never know with him.

It's been a while since I've tackled an organization job this large. I'm a little giddy over it. I think it's best to clear it out in small batches. Then sort everything into piles. Keep, toss, and giveaway.

I pull down an armload of clothes he has hanging in the closet and toss them on the bed. Sorting through the stack, I realize he has a lot of nice dress shirts, but I've never seen him dress up like this before. My fingers glide over the fabric of the sleeve as I place it in a neat pile.

"We have to wear those for away games. Coach likes us arriving sharp."

I bet he does look sharp in this. And handsome. And sexy. I've been around men in suits most of my life. But there is something about *this* man, who answers to no one and typically only wears jeans and T-shirts, wearing a suit and tie that makes it sound even hotter.

Stop it, Wren. I scold myself. He likes Charlie and I'm getting married. *Maybe.*

"They can start the keep pile."

"I would rather give those away and keep the chaps." He pouts.

I roll my lips to stop myself from laughing. "I'm sure you would." I pat him on the arm.

Wyatt helps me sort through the rest of the clothes on his bed, then goes back to get more. We are able to cycle through this portion of his closet quickly. He's been doing a good job letting things go, and I'm in my element color coordinating everything to be placed back in an orderly fashion.

"I've been looking for these," he says from the back of the closet.

Curiosity has me walking in there to see what long lost treasure, or trash, he's discovered. Wyatt is sitting on the floor with a feather boa wrapped around his neck and giant glasses on his face.

"You look ridiculous." I lean against the door frame with my arms crossed.

"What are you talking about? I look fucking incredible."

"If you say so."

"I'll have you know Elton John night at The Armory was a hit. Here, I found one for you too."

"Why do I need a feather boa?" I ask, as he drapes it over my shoulders and around my neck.

"Because." He places large pink sunglasses over the glasses I'm already wearing. It's a little awkward, but it would be anyway considering their size. "We are going to go upstairs and serenade Eli and Nash."

"We will do no such thing." I start to remove the boa. Wyatt's hands clamp down on mine, stopping my movement.

"We are. Come on. We need a break and this will be fun."

"They're going to laugh at me."

"So what if they do." He shrugs one shoulder and pulls me out of his room. I drag my feet, attempting to delay our progress. "It's just Nash and his football buddy. I bet they'll even join us."

Wyatt pauses at the bottom of the steps. "Let your hair down, birdie." He reaches up and pulls the elastic band out of my hair, unspiraling the tight bun I had my hair twisted in and shakes it out with the pad of his fingers.

My eyelids flutter and I have to bite my lip to keep from moaning. He slides his fingers down a strand of my hair, grazing the top of my breast. His eyes raise to meet mine and gauge my reaction to his touch. Maybe it's the rose-colored glasses I'm wearing, but he looks very kissable right now.

He exhales a slow breath before encouraging me upstairs again.

"I'm not singing. I don't sing," I say. I don't like singing in front of people. Not anymore.

"At least say the words. You know *"Bennie and the Jets?"* That's what I sang for the karaoke party. It's the only one I know."

"I know enough," I answer, once we reach the top of the stairs. I'm crossing my fingers and toes that Nash and Eli left the house. My face and chest are warm to the touch. Sweat is building in my under arms, and I alternate waving a hand under each armpit.

He chuckles. "You'll be fine. Relax. It's all for fun. I'll start us off. Follow my lead."

Easier said than done. I wipe my hands down the back of my shorts. Wyatt nods to Eli and Nash, who are still sitting at the table. Nash does a double take, a slow grin spreads across his face.

Wyatt takes my hand in his, gives me a nod. I nod back. I'm not really sure what I'm agreeing to exactly. Suddenly, Wyatt is sliding across the kitchen floor on his sock covered feet, pulling me along for the ride.

"Hey kids..." he starts off singing. I don't know the words well enough to sing along to the verse. Not that I would be able to anyway with Wyatt spinning me around, pulling me close, then pushing me away. He has us dancing around the entire kitchen.

When the chorus hits, he jiggles my arms encouraging me to sing with him. I'm not that brave but I do say the words. It will have to be good enough.

Wyatt beams at me while he sings. I realize I'm smiling too. By the second verse Nash and Eli have given up on homework and joined our impromptu dance party. Nash takes the boa off my neck and throws it to Eli. Then he steals Wyatt's from him too.

I pass Eli my glasses. When he puts them on, he transforms into full performance mode. His voice is amazing. I look at Wyatt and his eyes are as wide as mine.

Nash grabs my hands and spins me around. Laughter spills out of me. He passes me over to Eli, who sings, while we do the twist. There's no music. Just the guys singing acapella. It's enough to make me forget where I am and *who* I am. I'm not the girl who dances carefree in the kitchen. I'm the girl who believes the kitchen has one purpose—to prepare food.

I don't know where that girl is, but she isn't here right now.

Dropping Eli's hands, I jump around and let everything go. I close my eyes and twirl and twirl until I'm dizzily falling into Wyatt's arms. He's taken his glasses off. His brown eyes dance over my face, taking in every detail.

"I like seeing you like this," he whispers.

Like what? How do you see me?

"I'll admit, you were right. It was fun," I say, catching my breath. His hand slips to the curve of my back. I clear my throat. "We should, uh, probably finish cleaning downstairs or you won't have anywhere to sleep tonight."

"Yeah, we should," he says in a way that makes me think there is something else he wants to do instead. His eyes drift to my lips for a moment. I step out of his hold. We are too close. Not that I think he would kiss me in front of Nash and Eli. Not that he would kiss me at all. *What am I even thinking? Get a grip.*

"Nash, Eli, thank you for joining our fun. You can keep the accessories. They look good on you."

"Hey, I wanted to keep those." I ignore Wyatt's protest and walk toward the basement door. "I want everything back," Wyatt says. He tells Nash something else but I can't make it out from where I'm standing on the basement stairs.

The next few hours we dig through more memories of Wyatt's first years at Newhouse. While I found him irritating at times when he would get distracted by a costume or a crazy hat he had stuffed in a corner, I also laughed more than I have since I was a child.

Is it wrong for me to hope that he doesn't sleep with Charlie? Because if something happens between them, and Charlie gets hurt, I'll lose him as my friend. I can't believe I'm actually saying this, but I don't want that to happen.

Wyatt is quickly becoming someone I can't live without.

WYATT & WREN

WYATT

What are you wearing?

Is he there yet?

Send me a picture

WREN

[IMG ATTACHED]

WYATT

Damn birdie.

Dressed to impress.

You'll have him drooling

WREN

He's met me before. He didn't seem very impressed back then.

WYATT

Is he blind?

105

WREN

I don't think so.

WYATT

That wasn't a real question.

If he can't see how beautiful you are

He's blind.

WREN

Oh. Thank you.

I'm nervous.

WYATT

Say the word

I'll come get you

I'll fake an emergency

Or something

WREN

Thanks. I'll keep that in mind.

My dad's here.

WYATT

Good luck.

Remember to smile.

But not your creepy one.

8

WREN

My creepy one? I don't have a creepy smile. I had braces for two years and wore a retainer at night for years after that. My smile is perfect.

"Wren," my dad says, pulling me into a hug.

"Daddy." I wrap my arms around him and breathe in his familiar scent. It is calming and reassuring, and brings me back home.

"I've missed you." He looks me over. "You're happy?" he questions.

"Yes," I answer, without hesitation. I am happy. I have good friends, albeit one annoying one at times. I've always kept my friend group small. Even back home, there were only a few girls that I spent time with outside of school on occasion.

While I love both my parents equally, I can admit I am my dad's little girl. I chose to spend any free time I had with him. He understands me in a way no one else does because we are similar. He has the same social and mental struggles I do.

He's taught me to use them to my advantage and be the best version of myself. I don't know who I would be without him.

Wyatt calls me strange, but to me, it's how I grew up. I've adopted all of my dad's quirks. We both thrive on order and structure. Although lately it seems Wyatt has been testing my limits and my willingness to bend my rules.

I search the bar for Mr. Abbott and his son, Daniel.

"I sent them ahead to the table. I wanted a moment alone with you. Daniel is a nice guy. He will be an asset to the company once he graduates. But if he isn't the right fit for you or you aren't interested in more, this marriage doesn't happen. Or if there is someone else in your life—"

"There's no one else," I cut him off before that idea can get planted and start to grow. There will never be anyone else. I'm not cut out for intimate relationships.

"Leave it to your mother to make an offhand comment years ago in front of Fred and have it escalate to this. She's under the impression he would be a good match for you."

When I was a teenager I overheard my mom talking on the phone talking to a friend about my dad. She said, *"he's hard to love, but I do it anyways."* It could have been in jest. The thought wormed itself into my head regardless of its validity. I'm so similar to my dad. I put two and two together and decided I must be hard to love too. The notion has stuck with me ever since.

My mom doesn't think Daniel is a good match for me. She thinks he is the only option for me to find a husband. It's a fair assumption. I've never shown much interest in dating. I know that has always bothered her.

She grew up in a world where a good marriage doubled as a status symbol. Me showing more interest in pursuing a career instead of marrying a man goes against everything she was groomed to do. I know she wants the best for me. However, wanting and knowing what's best are two different things.

"Maybe he is. We already know we are like minded when it comes to work and business. We could match up on other things too." I bet Daniel doesn't have a closet full of costume horrors like Wyatt. His clothes aren't likely to be left in piles on the floor to wrinkle. They are starched and as stiff as his personality.

"That would make things easier. The choice however is yours. This is your life. You get to decide what you want."

"What do you mean it would make things easier?"

"If you had more things in common. It would be easier," he says without looking me in the eye. Why do I get the impression he isn't telling me everything? "Remember none of this is worth sacrificing your happiness, Wren."

"It wouldn't. I never planned on getting married. It makes sense to try with Daniel."

"Let's see how things go tonight before we make any decisions."

My dad leads me to a table near the back of the restaurant. I had zero preparation time for this. It was a last minute invitation. Mr. Abbott, Daniel, and my dad were passing through Montgomery and got delayed overnight.

They felt it would be the ideal time for Daniel and me to mingle. It wasn't. I had to cancel my plans with Wyatt. He seemed fine with it. Probably relieved actually.

I press my hands down the front of my dress. It is a simple black cocktail dress with a cinched waist. It's conservative but accentuates my figure while still being classy.

Both men stand from the table as we approach. Daniel is handsome with his blond hair and boy-next-door appeal. He has filled out since the last time I saw him. Not quite the gangly teenager I remember. He looks refined and polished in his tailored suit and tie. Like a shiny new toy to play with.

"Fred," my dad says. "You remember my daughter, Wren." He gestures toward me.

"Of course. It's been a few years."

"Yes. I believe it was our graduation party." Our parents had thrown us a joint party at the country club. It was as pretentious as it sounds. "Nice to see you again, sir."

"Please, call me Fred," he says, with a gentle smile. I nod. "Daniel," he urges his son forward with a small push on his back.

"Wren." Daniel takes a step toward me and cradles both of my hands in his. "You look beautiful," he says, leaning down to kiss my cheek. His assertiveness surprises me. I recall him being quite shy and maybe even a little awkward.

"Thank you. You too." Heat rushes to my cheeks. He does look handsome. He looks exactly like the trust fund, country club guy I typically hook-up with.

Daniel pulls out a velvet blue chair for me. Then takes his seat beside me. With everyone situated at the table and being the center of attention, my heart begins to race.

Linen napkin. I place it on my lap.

Dinner fork. Salad fork. Soup spoon. Knife. I straighten them and space them evenly on either side.

Water glass. Wine glass. I straighten them as well.

The process calms me enough to take a look around the dining room. It's decorated with rich wood tones and moody blues. The lighting is low creating an intimate setting.

The waiter comes and takes our food and drink order, breaking up a little bit of the tension and unease I'm feeling.

"How is school going, Wren?" Mr. Abbott—Fred—asks.

"Great." I smile. *Is this the creepy smile Wyatt is talking about?* I try a different one, the one that I've practiced and perfected. The one that hides everything.

"What about you, Daniel? Are you looking forward to graduating?" my dad asks, rescuing me. He knows I won't want to elaborate or talk about myself for too long.

"More than ever," he says, with his eyes on me. I reach for my water with shaky hands. His attention is unexpected. I was under the impression he was agreeing to see me, to marry me, because it would be good for business.

My phone chimes in my purse. For once I'm relieved by that annoying noise. It's a welcome interruption.

"I'm sorry. I forgot to turn off the notifications before we sat down," I say when my phone chimes again. I already know it's Wyatt. He's aware I'm having dinner with Daniel. Why is he texting me right now?

WYATT

How's it going?

Did he like your dress?

I fight the urge to roll my eyes and instead send a quick response.

ME

It's fine. He didn't say.

Not about the dress anyways.

He said I looked beautiful.

"Is everything okay?" Daniel asks.

"Yes. It's a friend."

"Maybe you should tell her you're busy," Fred says. His words are sharp—the opposite of his friendly demeanor he was exuding earlier.

"*He* knows I'm here. He's checking on me because he's worried." I'm not sure why I said that. Wyatt isn't really concerned. He's texting because he likes to get under my skin and annoy me.

"Is this your friend with the farm?" my dad asks. I briefly mentioned Wyatt's situation a few days ago and asked him for advice. This is what we do after all. My dad has been breathing life into failing businesses his entire career. If anyone knew what I can do to help, it would be him.

"Yes." I give him a pleading look to not discuss this topic further. I don't want to bring up Wyatt's situation in front of the Abbotts. They don't need to be involved.

Wyatt didn't give me very much to go on, but his situation isn't far off from other projects my dad has taken on in Georgia. I can't silence the voice inside my head pushing me to get more information and try to help him.

"Very well. Now is not the time. We have other matters to discuss."

"We do," Fred agrees. "Do you plan on coming home right after graduation? Or do you need to tie up loose ends?" he asks me. By loose ends he means ending a relationship.

Another reason why I've always kept feelings out of relationships. In the back of my mind, I knew that getting married to Daniel was always a possibility. Allowing myself to get attached to someone else would only end badly for everyone involved.

I glance briefly at Daniel before answering. "I will be coming home as soon as graduation is over. I'm ready to start working."

Fred gives me a calculating look and continues to question me. "Where do you see yourself fitting in with your father's company?"

I'm not entirely sure why he is so interested, other than I know he's been trying to become business partners with my dad for the last few years. My dad has consulted on several of his projects and ever since then he's been attempting to sink his teeth in deeper and take a bite of the pie.

Is that his motive behind the marriage? If I'm married to Daniel, then he'll automatically have a stake in the company.

"We haven't discussed it in entirety yet. I think my skill set is best served in consulting and focusing on business development." I enjoy finding problems and solutions. It is satisfying work.

"I look forward to having you on board," my dad says with a smile. Then takes a sip of his wine. "We have several new projects starting up I think you will find interesting."

My dad and Fred discuss the new strip mall Fred has acquired. He's brought Ellington Business Solutions on board to consult with the existing businesses that are leasing the retail space. These are exactly the kind of projects I want to drown myself in.

Fred is a greedy man, but he's also smart. He purchases run down pieces of commercial real estate using his development firm. Then hires my dad's company as the consultant. I can see it in his eyes. He is looking forward to double dipping and growing his financial portfolio with this marriage.

He also expects my dad to extend the same courtesy and use his real estate firm when needed. I don't think my dad has that on his agenda, which has been brewing tension in their professional and personal relationship.

Dinner is served and I silently eat my salmon and rice while absorbing every detail of their conversation. I don't miss the hint of hostility in Mr. Abbott's voice when my dad says he is taking one of his projects in a different direction.

After we finish eating, my dad and Mr. Abbott excuse themselves and head toward the bar. I try my best to look appreciative for the privacy they've offered us.

"You're really interested in this," Daniel says to me, leaning back in his chair. He's assessing me. I don't know how I feel with his sharp eyes on me.

"I am. You aren't?"

Daniel shifts his body closer to me. "I have been working alongside my dad every summer since I graduated high school. He's taught me the benefits of clean slates and starting over."

"You think it's better to force business owners to quit their dreams instead of offering them the tools to succeed?"

"Businesses fail every day. He believes we are doing them a favor by saving them from years of being in debt."

I shake my head. "I disagree. You are letting them drown. Saving them would be throwing them a lifesaver, and showing them where they can improve and stop the bleeding." I take a quick sip of my water. "You said that's what he believes. What about you?"

He glances at his father who is deep in a conversation with my dad at the bar. "I want to throw them a lifesaver."

"Is this why you are agreeing to the marriage?" It would make sense. It's a way for him to work with my dad without insulting his own. It's a dramatic approach instead of simply standing up to his father and telling him he doesn't believe in his business practices.

"Not entirely. Please don't take this the wrong way. I'm sure you're great." His smile seems genuine enough. "My dad is holding my inheritance ransom. If we don't get married, I lose access to my trust. I need that money to start my own venture."

That is a glaring difference between our parents. I had access to my trust the day I turned eighteen. The stipend was small in the beginning and has increased over the years. I have been saving most of the money.

Besides the occasional splurge on office supplies, I don't have the need for much beyond food, gas for my car, and clothing—all of which is budgeted every month.

"Can he do that?" I feel Fred watching me out of the corner of his eye. I move closer to Daniel and stroke the top of his hand with my fingers. Daniel jumps in surprise. "He's watching," I whisper.

Daniel's hand curls around mine. He leans in closer. The scent of his aftershave wafts over me. It's clean and refreshing. It suits him, but I don't feel that same high when I'm lost in a haze of Wyatt's familiar scent. "He can do whatever he wants. It's his money. I can think of worse fates for the two of us."

"Is that a compliment?"

"All I'm saying," his thumb grazes against my wrist, "is we could make it work. At least long enough for me to get my inheritance. I'm sure there is something in this for you too."

"There isn't. It could be good for business." Other than making my mom happy by seeing her little girl get married, I can't think of any personal reason why this is a good idea for me.

"Good for business, but bad for you. My dad is skilled at manipulating people into believing a deal favors others more than it does him. I promise whatever story he has sold to your dad, it isn't at all what it seems."

"They have been working together for years. Friends for longer. Why would he try to pull one over on him?"

"Money," he says with a shrug. "Power. Men have done worse for less. He's been trying to purchase a piece of your family's business for years. If we are married, he can use the family card to get what he wants." I smile. Pretending what he said doesn't send bouts of rage through my body.

"You are not selling yourself very well if you actually want me to walk down the aisle." I refuse to play a part in some rich man's game.

"What I want is my freedom."

"Interesting that you are seeking that while acquiring a ball and chain. Some might say you are trading one jailor for another," I joke.

"I like you. You aren't the same quiet girl I remember. I think I might enjoy this more than I thought I would."

"I haven't agreed to anything. If what you say is true, I should be warning my father against this whole arrangement." I keep my voice low even though I know they can't hear me.

"You might. Or we can beat my father at his own game."

"What are you suggesting?" My instincts are telling me I can trust Daniel. However, he is still the son of a man who may be trying to hurt my family.

"We go forward with the engagement. Give me time to talk to lawyers and find a way to work around my father. If we break this off now, I don't stand a chance."

"This seems very beneficial to you. I would do better cutting my losses and walking away."

"A favor for an old friend?" He flashes a boyish grin. "After graduation, I'll get down on one knee. You say yes and we spend the summer trying to stick it to the man."

I can't think of any reason for me to say no.

Except for the way I felt dancing in the kitchen with Wyatt. And the way his eyes would flicker with delight when he caught me looking at him.

But he's not interested in me. Wyatt likes Charlie. And I'm the one who's going to help him get her. I shake my head in a lousy attempt to erase the memory of his hands against my skin.

"Yes," I say and lift my glass.

"Cheers, fiancée."

A weight lands heavy in my stomach making me feel like I'm making the wrong choice. But that can't be right because there is only one real option.

9

WYATT

"You never told me about your dinner with your *fiancé*," I tease, throwing a bag of chips into our shopping cart. Wren and I are shopping for snacks for my movie date with Charlie.

"He's not my fiancé yet," she mutters.

"I thought it was set in stone. A done deal."

She consults her shopping list on her phone and lets out a sigh. "He's not who I thought he was. I don't know. He..." her voice trails off as she picks up a bag of plain popcorn and puts it in the cart. I immediately take it out and exchange it for white cheddar.

"He what?" I stand in front of the cart, stopping her forward progress. The metal of the cart cuts into my hand since I'm gripping it so tight. If he said something to her, or worse, did something.

"Don't get your boxers in a bunch," she says. I would tease her about knowing what kind of underwear I have but she's the one who's been organizing my laundry. "It's nothing. He was nice. We had a good conversation about our future."

"So you're going to marry the guy?" My fingers flex around the cool metal of the cart. Why does this bother me? I can try to fool myself all day long saying it's me being concerned for a friend. That ain't it and I know it. I'm just too afraid to say it out loud.

I throw a few more bags of chips into the cart before we move on to the cookie and candy aisle.

She hesitates before answering, "Yes?" The word comes out more like a question and that little inflection in her voice offers me hope.

Hope for what? You are going over to her place to attempt to hook up with her roommate, you idiot.

"I still don't see how you can say yes to marrying someone you don't even know, let alone not in love with."

"Is that your plan? Marry for love?"

"Yes," I say confidently.

"The trail of broken hearts left in your wake makes me wonder if you're capable."

"I may not act like it now but I do want that someday." I want what my parents have. I've watched them fall in love over and over again every day. They fight and argue, but they love hard. Even through the tough times they find a way to still laugh together.

Wren grabs a couple bars of dark chocolate and I pick up a bag of chocolate peanut candies.

"Not everyone is suited for that kind of relationship. I'm being practical."

"Practical," I scoff. "Love should be wild. So wild it consumes every part of you," I say, stepping closer to her. "Yet, rooted deep enough in your heart it won't be ripped away when the weather gets rough. There's no room for practicalities in love."

"Maybe I prefer being sensible." She lifts her chin in defiance.

"You mean settling. You're willing to settle for some guy that isn't going to be loyal to anyone but himself. You are setting yourself up to live a very lonely life." Her eyes turn to stone and she huffs an angry breath. Too bad. She needs to hear this.

"You can keep pretending that it's what you want. That you prefer a life of solitude. I've watched you, birdie. You light up around other people when you give them a chance."

I saw it when she was dancing around the kitchen. Witnessing her drop her guard and not worry about who's watching or what anyone is thinking, it was a revelation. An awakening occurred in my soul. Seeing Wren come alive set off a stirring inside of me that's impossible to explain.

It's tempting to pull her close to me again. I like the way she felt when she was wrapped up in my arms while we danced in my kitchen.

Without the pretense of dancing, I'm not sure how she would react. Instinctively I step closer. Her eyes scan my body and she bites down on her lip. Her grip tightens on the shopping cart.

Why are you so tempting to me?

"I'm not pretending." Her jaw tenses. "I've always been better on my own. My teachers even wrote it on my report cards growing up. *'Doesn't play well with others. Better with independent studies.'* Can we drop it? We should focus. We still need a few more things and Charlie is waiting. Are you going to push or do you want me to?"

"I'll push. You hop on the back." I gesture toward the end of the cart.

"You're kidding."

"I'm not. Get on. Prove those teachers wrong and play with me."

"One aisle," she says, stepping on to the rail at the end of the cart. "Don't go too fast either."

"It's cute how you keep making all these rules for me to break," I say before sprinting down the empty aisle. She shrieks when I take the corner hard and fast. "Having fun yet?" I ask as we zoom down the next aisle and back around to where we started.

"So much," she says sarcastically, with a slight curl to her lips.

Hopping off the cart, she reaches on her tiptoes to grab a bag of cookies on the top shelf. Even at five-nine she can barely get her fingers to graze the side of the packaging.

Her shirt rises just enough to expose a sliver of her skin. It's barely an inch, but with her it might as well be a mile. That tiny bit of skin is enough to give me a slight chub. *Damnit.* This girl teleports me back to middle school every time we hang out.

"A little help would be nice," she grunts, as the cookies get pushed further back with her efforts.

Standing behind her, I slide a hand around her waist. I allow myself one touch to see if her skin is as soft as it looks. And it is. Of course it is. I know I'm tempting my fate as I stroke my thumb over her.

Her skin breaks out in goosebumps, but any other reaction is hidden behind a solid poker face.

"Might as well eat sawdust," I say, backing away and passing her the plain animal crackers. "These aren't even real cookies."

Wren elbows me in my side. Son of a bitch. "You really got to stop hitting on me, birdie."

"You've really got to stop calling me that. It's juvenile."

"Says the woman who enjoys eating crackers in the shape of little animals."

"Make fun all you want. They're my favorite."

I hold up my hands in surrender. "Get whatever you like. Don't come crying to me when you want something with a little flavor."

"You are the last person I would ever go crying to." Her words are spoken with conviction, strong and steady as always. But her eyes flash with an uncertainty that tells me she doesn't believe what she's saying any more than I like hearing it.

We make quick work of the rest of her list. I'm glad to see everything I texted her made the cut. I had a good time texting her one item at a time. By the eighth item she decided to video call me.

125

We ended up talking for over an hour. By talking I mean I would say something and she would make a smart ass comment about it.

Later that same night Charlie's voice filtered through my dreams again but it wasn't her. The image was blurry but I know it wasn't Charlie. I barely got any sleep. I was a wreck at practice and Coach was pissed.

I've got to get this situation wrapped up so I can move on and get back on my game. You'll never hear the words leave my mouth, but I will miss spending time with Wren when it's all over. I don't care what her teachers said. She gets along with me just fine.

"What's that?" I ask Wren as she whips together cool whip, vanilla yogurt, and cake mix.

"Ooh that's Wren's special dip she makes. It's so good when you dunk animal crackers in it," Charlie informs me from the living room where she's setting up the movie.

"Wyatt doesn't like animal crackers," Wren says, smiling. *The little devil.*

"I might."

"No. You don't. Tastes like sawdust. Remember?" She pushes up her glasses with the back of her hand.

"I might like them with that." I nod towards the bowl of white whipped topping that smells like straight sugar.

"Too bad you'll never find out because I'm not sharing this with you." She moves the bowl out of my reach.

"Don't be like that. Give me a taste." My words register in my brain as one thing but somehow the translation gets twisted when it gets to my dick. It's twitching in my jeans at the thought of tasting Wren. Which is bad. *Very bad* because I'm here to see Charlie.

A slight flush covers Wren's cheeks and neck. Is her train of thought as dirty as mine? Because I am currently having a lot of thoughts about her that I shouldn't. And if she's thinking the same as me...*stop.*

She changed into something more casual when we got back to her place. Her hair is tossed up in a high ponytail that appears relaxed but is still perfectly put together. She threw on a pair of black leggings and a long sleeve shirt that keeps slipping off her shoulder exposing a thin strap of a tank top underneath.

It's distracting me from my mission. Charlie and her haunting voice. That's why I'm here. *Focus man.*

Wren has all the food spread out on the countertop in matching bowls and serving platters. She is quite the little hostess. I spy the animal crackers and snag a handful. Popping one in my mouth, I regret it immediately.

The cracker absorbs all the moisture in my mouth and turns into a gummy paste. Wren slides the bowl of whipped yogurt and cool whip closer to me. Her arms cross over her chest as she waits for the verdict.

I swipe the cracker through the dip getting a hearty spoonful. As soon as the sweet mixture hits my tongue, I brace myself on the counter and drop my head. I'll be damned if I let her see the pure ecstasy on my face. *Fuck,* this stuff is good and addictive. I already want another bite.

"Not bad," I say, once I finish chewing. Wren laughs. The sound pokes holes in the defensive walls I just forced myself to put up.

"More for me then. I wouldn't blame you if you go back for more. I know it's hard to resist." Wren dips a cracker in the fluffy white goodness and pops it in her mouth. "So good," she moans.

Son of a bitch. That sound. She's doing this shit on purpose. She thinks she's being cute rubbing it in my face that I was wrong about the damn animal crackers. Meanwhile, I'm hard as a fucking rock. No one should be laughing about that.

I scrub a hand down my face to wipe my memory clear. "Should we head in there?" I ask.

"Yes. Do you remember the plan?" she asks once she's close enough to whisper. I nod.

We're going to start watching the movie. After a few minutes, Wren is going to come up with an excuse to leave which will give me an opportunity to be alone with Charlie. Simple and straightforward.

"Good," Wren says with a nod.

We both grab a bowl of snacks off the counter and walk into the living room. Charlie is already sitting comfortably on the couch with a blanket covering her legs. I'm not sure where I should sit.

There are two armchairs on either side of the couch and the whole right side of the couch is available. I opt for the right side of the couch leaving an empty space in between me and Charlie.

It would be weird if I plopped down next to her. I need to ease into it. This is not my typical hookup situation. Usually if I'm walking into a girl's dorm, it's already been decided that we are going to hook up. The question is when are we going to give up the pretense of watching a movie and have sex.

Wren places her drink on a coaster, *naturally*, on the table beside me. "Can you scoot over? I like sitting here. It's the optimal seat to watch a movie."

"Why would I give that up then?" I get more comfortable, resting my head on the back of the couch. She's right. It is a nice spot. I can see the television perfectly from here without straining my neck. I have the table beside me and the arm of the couch to lean on.

"Because you're nice and you want me to have it."

"Am I though?" I question her. "If this is the best seat then I think I should have it as your guest."

"Wyatt," Wren snaps, losing her temper. She raises her eyebrows in Charlie's direction. Oh. *Oh*, she's helping me. *Why do I find that irritating?*

"Sure, you can have this seat. I'll just scoot over here." I slide over to the middle cushion and attempt to get comfortable again. I already miss the armrest. But I am closer to Charlie. That's all that matters. "Hi," I say to her. "What movie are we watching?"

Charlie smiles. Her eyes sparkle just like the first time I met her. "*The Proposal* with Sandra Bullock and Ryan Reynolds."

"I love this movie! It's my favorite." I shift in my seat and get cozy under a blanket they had folded on the back of the couch. I didn't expect the girls to pick out a movie I actually liked.

"I know. Wren picked it out. She said it was your favorite. I love Sandra Bullock. *Miss Congeniality* is one of my favorite movies." Charlie beams.

Wren quietly eats popcorn as Charlie and I run through all of Sandra's filmography. She did this for me. She picked my favorite movie knowing it would give me and Charlie common ground.

Leaning toward her, I grab a handful of popcorn from the bowl she has resting in her lap. "Thank you," I whisper close to her ear. Her wildflower perfume fills the space between us. I forgot how good she smells.

"No problem. I'm just holding up my part of the agreement."

She is, but she's going above and beyond. Why? Maybe this is just how Wren is. Her ability to observe and retain the minute details makes her a thoughtful and caring person underneath her stoney exterior.

The movie starts and the three of us settle in. I've watched this movie a thousand times. I start silently mouthing the lines along with the movie.

"Do you mind?" Wren asks.

"Mind what?" I take a handful of popcorn from the bowl and pop a few pieces in my mouth.

"Your mouth is moving. It's distracting."

"You're distracting," I snap back without thinking. Her head slowly swivels to me. She stares, trying to understand the meaning behind my words.

I'm distracted by both women sitting beside me. Charlie because she keeps squirming on the couch trying to get comfortable and Wren because my body is hyper aware of hers. I can feel her presence without having to touch her. There is this electric buzz that flows between us.

I can't explain it, but it's almost like two magnets hovering over each other. You can only keep them apart for so long before they're forced to come together.

"I forgot how much I love Margaret," I say in a weak attempt at ignoring this pull I feel towards Wren.

"Me, too," Charlie agrees. "She kind of reminds me of you, Wren. You have a similar style and personality."

"Is that a good thing?" Wren asks. "She's kind of a bitch, isn't she?"

"She's direct. Nothing wrong with that. She knows what she wants and goes for it," I tell her. Wren is a lot like Margaret now that I think about it.

"She's also a big softie deep down. She just needed some-one to bring out that side of her. You know, tell her to not take everything so seriously," Charlie adds. I turn to Wren. Her eyes are focused on the bowl of popcorn.

"Good thing you have me, huh?" I say it low enough that only she can hear me.

"Yeah. Good thing. Not sure how I would carry on through life without you." Her eyes slant behind her glasses and her lips pinch.

"I was thinking the same thing," I joke back, dipping my hand in the popcorn for another handful and tossing it at her.

Wren collects all the little pieces and drops them back in the bowl. "Shouldn't you be spending more time wooing?" She gestures towards Charlie.

"I'm going to. One cannot simply woo on demand." I admit, the whole plan slipped my mind when the movie came on. "Are you going to..." I make a shooing motion. She nods in response.

"Don't worry. I have an exit strategy."

A few minutes later, cool liquid splatters across my right arm and chest. *What the hell?*

"Damn, it. I'm so clumsy. It just slipped out of my hands," Wren says. Her acting is atrocious. Don't quit your day job. She stands up, wiping water off her face. Her sweater is drenched and droplets of water are covering her glasses.

"Are you okay?" Charlie asks.

"Just embarrassed. I'm going to change. I'll be back."

"Do you want me to pause the movie?" Charlie reaches for the remote.

"Oh no." Wren waves her hands in front of her. "You can fill me in when I get back. Don't wait for me. I'll only be a few minutes."

Wren's eyes catch mine one last time. There is a trace of melancholy to them. I'm not sure why but whatever it was, it didn't last long. She brings her empty glass to the kitchen and walks down the hall toward her room.

It's just me and Charlie. Exactly what I wanted. I clear my throat. She glances up at me. Is this my chance? Do I kiss her now? Should I say something first? Do I ask her if she wants to make out? Do I want to make out with her?

I cross my arms over my chest and pay attention to the movie. But I can't focus. Margaret is running around the backyard with Kevin the dog. It's one of my favorite parts, but all I can think about is how I don't want to be sitting here anymore.

I want to know what Wren is doing. *I want to be where Wren is.*

"I'll be right back," I tell Charlie. "Keep watching the movie. Quick bathroom break." Except I don't go towards the bathroom. I trace Wren's steps back to her room.

Knocking lightly a few times, I wait for the door to crack open. "Did you screw up already?" she asks, still wearing her wet clothes.

"I wanted to check on you. You okay?" I step into her room. No surprise it's pristine down to the perfectly fluffed pillows.

Her bedding is a mix of creams and whites. This should also surprise absolutely no one.

"Why wouldn't I be?" She fiddles with the sleeves of her sweater.

Because you are beginning to question this whole scheme like I am?

Because the idea of me hooking up with someone else bothers you a little?

Because everything about this feels wrong and it would be nice if you were on the same page.

"I don't know," I say instead, picking up a picture of Wren and her parents sitting on her dresser. Wren is the spitting image of her dad except she has her mama's eyes. "Cute." I place the photo back down. I fully expect Wren to straighten it once I leave.

"That was my first day at Newhouse." Wren moves toward her closet. "You should go back out there. Charlie's going to get bored. She probably left already." Wren picks out a new shirt and lays it out on her bed.

I shrug. I was a little bored myself without Wren out there with me.

"If you blow your chance, don't say I didn't warn you," she says. As much as Charlie's voice haunts me at night, I'm not sure she's who I want anymore.

"Consider me warned," I joke. Wren shrugs then rips her sweater and tank top off in one go.

My eyes about fall out of the sockets. It's not like I've never seen a girl naked before. I never thought I would be lucky enough to see Wren. "Damn, birdie. You've got to let a guy know before you flash the high beams."

With a roll of her eyes, Wren turns her back to me. "They're just boobs. Don't tell me you haven't seen any before." She looks at me over her shoulder as she adjusts the shirt she's pulled over her head.

I had no idea Wren was so comfortable in her own skin. I would have pegged her to be more of a prude and reserved when it comes to taking off her clothes in front of other people.

But nope. Here she is half naked in front of me without a care. Why do I find that so attractive?

"I've seen plenty of boobs," I say smugly. None as phenomenal as hers. They're full and round. *Fuck they're pretty.* "I would even consider myself a *connoisseur*."

"Damn it, Wyatt." She yanks her ponytail out of the neck of her shirt. I chuckle at her. "I'm still up by two this week," she says, turning to face me. My laughter dies on my tongue.

Lord, have mercy. I scrub a hand down my face.

She might as well take the shirt back off the material is so thin. Saran Wrap would offer her more coverage. Her dark nipples mock me. You can go ahead and pencil in jacking off to the memory of her tits to my evening festivities.

I shouldn't because I'm supposed to be here for Charlie.

But fuck, if she doesn't get my rooster crowing.

Question is, what am I going to do with this new development?

At the moment, I'm not sure I should or could do anything. She thinks I'm into Charlie. There's no way she would understand my sudden shift of interest. Is it sudden though? Or has she been slipping slowly under my skin?

If I miscalculate and move too fast, I could ruin our friendship. I can admit that I like having her around. I didn't think this would ever be the case. She is opposite me in almost every way. Being in her presence steadies me. Knowing she has everything in control makes me feel like I can spin out and she would be there to hold me together.

"Still think you didn't miss much?" she sasses, before opening the door.

"I think I'm missing out on a lot of things." My admission has more truth in it than either one of us is willing to dissect.

10

WYATT

"If you keep throwing heaters, I'm going to need a new glove," Koa says, removing his catching gear. We just retired the side and are waiting for our turn at bat in the dugout.

I'm already dreaming of icing my shoulder when I get home. It's hurting like a bitch thanks to all the fast balls I've been throwing today—they are my go to pitch when I'm irritated.

And boy am I irritated.

Wren and Charlie are at the game today. I royally messed up last week at their place. I let Wren get in my head.

And she's doing it again today.

Because what is she wearing?

Thomas, our second baseman's jersey.

Not mine. Her best friend.

Yes, I'm claiming that role. We text, FaceTime, eat lunch, do laundry, and study together. We do everything together. Not everything. Because if we did everything I'd probably be a lot happier at the moment.

Most of her free time is spent at my place organizing something and leaving sticky notes all over the place. And she has the audacity to show up in his fucking jersey?

"Sorry, man. I'll switch it up next inning," I lie. I'm too mad to throw anything else.

"Don't worry about it. I know you're trying to impress Charlie. She's here because of you, right?" Koa leans forward, attempting to get a glimpse of the girls in the stands. It's almost impossible to see them from this angle.

I can't really see them when I'm pitching either, but I can feel them. I can feel *her*.

"Yup. That's what I'm doing." Do I sound convincing? I don't even believe the bullshit that is coming out of my mouth anymore. I don't expect my friends to either. They know me better than that.

Hart scowls in my direction. "You need to pick," he says once he's done assessing me.

"You need to get ready to bat." I ignore his statement completely. There's nothing to pick. It's painfully obvious Charlie isn't interested and Wren...she was never an option. She's practically engaged to another man.

"Who is he picking between?" Koa asks, his brows furrowed under the rim of his ball cap.

"Wren and Charlie," Hart answers.

"But I thought he liked Charlie? What does Wren have to do with anything?" Koa and Hart continue to talk about my life like I'm not sitting here.

"Wren's been coming over to the house almost every day. You wouldn't know because you haven't been around much, have you?" Hart's accusatory tone doesn't faze Koa.

"Where have you been?" I ask.

"Nowhere you need to worry about," he grumbles.

"No need to snap at me, Mr. Sensitive." I wish he would tell Nash he's in love with Sydney already so he'll stop being a grouchy asshole. I've known these guys most of my life, and Koa has always had eyes on that girl.

I would be surprised if Nash didn't already know. If Koa and Sydney think they are being secretive, they're idiots. It's probably why Nash keeps reminding us Syd is off limits. Because he isn't blind or stupid.

Oh goody, Thomas slides up next to Hart and taps him on the shoulder. "Who are the new girls sitting with Lauren and Sydney?" he asks.

Hart doesn't answer him.

"The cute brunette is wearing my jersey. Think she's into me?"

"Absolutely fucking not," I say with a scoff.

He turns toward me. "How would you know?"

"Because she has more than two brain cells in her head." I scowl at him.

"That's too bad. She looks fucking phenomenal with my name on her back." He smirks. *Fucker*. He won't be smiling when I put super glue in his body wash.

"Choose," Hart says, as he puts on his batting helmet and leaves the dugout.

Thank fuck he takes Thomas with him.

Does Hart know something I don't? Is Wren talking to Lauren? They do have their weekly lunches. Maybe I need to crash one of those again and get some intel.

Koa stands and grabs his helmet. "When did you become the dating type anyway?"

"I didn't. Hart don't know what he's talking about. And if you think you're going to give me advice on my love life, be prepared to hear my thoughts on yours."

Koa frowns and grunts before leaving the dugout to go wait on deck. *That's what I thought.*

"Rivers," Coach Lawson calls out to me.

"Yes, Coach?" I walk over to where he's standing near the dugout entrance.

"How's your arm holding up? Do you have another inning in you?"

"I'm good."

"There are a few scouts in the stands," he says, never taking his eye off the field.

"I'm aware, sir." Despite my focus being split between the game and Wren, I haven't lost sight of the bigger picture. Making a good impression with the scouts is vital.

Thomas ends up striking out, *sorry not sorry*, leaving Hart and Koa on base and ending the inning. Time to get back to work.

On my walk out to the hill, I keep my eyes locked on Wren. She's sitting up straight with her hands clasped in her lap.

She's looking up at the scoreboard where my photo and stats are on full display.

The breeze blows a piece of hair out of place and she tucks it back behind her ear. Charlie whispers something to her and Wren's attention moves to the field. *To me.*

I clasp my mitt under my arm and readjust my ball cap. My hair is starting to get long enough it's becoming more of a nuisance than a good luck charm. I rake my fingers through the waves and tuck everything back into my hat.

I put my glove back on my hand and run my thumb over the elastic band I wear on my wrist. I haven't taken it off since the day I removed it from her hair. With one last look at Wren, I turn back to the batter and get in the zone.

I have a girl, I mean *scouts*, to impress.

Sydney, Lauren, Charlie, and Wren are all waiting for us outside the stadium. This is the first time I've had someone waiting for me that wasn't a blood relative or a cleat chaser. I didn't think I wanted it, but seeing Wren bobbing her head around the crowd looking for me has me walking on water.

As soon as Lauren sees Hart, she runs and jumps into his arms. "*Cariño*," he says into the side of her neck.

"Congratulations!" Charlie cheers. "It was a great game."

"Thanks, Charlie. I'm glad you had a good time. What did you think, Wren? Did you have fun at your first game?"

"I did. I can see the appeal." Wren smirks and all four girls start laughing.

"Is that so?" I know exactly what they find appealing. Hart has overheard Lauren and Sydney more than once talking about our *'equipment'* when they would come to our practices.

"Yep. I might be persuaded to come to another one."

Not in that shirt you won't.

"What's everyone doing after this? Anyone want to grab a bite to eat before Lauren and I have to go to work?" Sydney asks with her eyes on Koa.

"When are you going to quit that place?" Koa practically growls. Someone pass me the popcorn because Syd's about to hand Koa his balls on a plate. I move out of their way and bring Wren with me.

"Trust me, you don't want to get in the middle of the two of them arguing," I say when she tries to fight out of the grip I have on her wrist.

For a moment, I'm tempted to slide my hand down and hold her hand. How incredible would that feel? And why am I getting hard at the thought of holding a girl's hand? *Because it's not just any girl.*

"Whenever I'm damn well ready to." Syd crosses her arms over her chest and dares him to say something else. Koa's a smart man and keeps his thoughts to himself.

"Well, I would, but I was going to ask Wyatt if he wanted to go out," Charlie says to the group. "What do you say, want to go on a date with me to celebrate your win?"

My vision blurs momentarily. *A date?* Is she serious? This is what I wanted. A date with Charlie that leads to a night with Charlie. I should say yes. I should want to say yes. Then I glance at Wren and my gut plummets.

Would she even care? She's not making eye contact with anyone. Her eyes are glued to the gravel below her feet. The movie date was an epic fail. No one's fault but my own. I didn't anticipate Wren tripping me up the way she did.

Maybe that's the problem. If Wren is out of the picture, I can concentrate on Charlie. Would Wren care? Wren isn't exactly objecting to the idea. Why do I want her to tell me not to go? Or to ask to come along like she always does. Instead, she's avoiding me.

"Sure, Charlie. Let's do it."

"Great. I rode over with Wren. Do you mind driving?" Charlie takes a few steps in my direction, pushing Wren further away. The new arrangement makes me feel uneasy.

"Yeah, of course," I say. Charlie takes my hand in hers. Where is this coming from? Did Wren say something to her? I don't understand. The last time I saw Charlie she barely took the time to say goodbye.

After the movie ended, she grabbed a bag of chips and went to her room. I must have done something right, because now the girl I want is holding my hand. *Keep telling yourself that.*

And Wren is staring at it with a mix of shock and hurt in her eyes.

"Why don't you go to my truck? I'll meet you there," I say to Charlie.

"We'll walk with you," Lauren says.

"Catch you later, bro." Koa fist bumps me.

Once they're all out of ear shot, I can deal with my little birdie.

"Any idea why Charlie is suddenly asking me out on a date? Seems kind of out of the blue. Did you say something to her?"

"I'm as shocked as you are. Maybe she bumped her head and has amnesia. She's forgotten how annoying you can be." The side of her mouth curls slightly.

"Funny." Damn, I like it when she's mean to me. There has to be something wrong with me to get turned on by all the strikes she sends my way.

"I thought so." She lets out a sigh. "You better go. It's rude to keep her waiting."

"Of course it is." Wren and all her rules. "Thanks for coming today."

"No problem. That's what friends do."

"Wait, are you admitting that we're friends?" I feign shock. She rolls her eyes.

"It seems to be the case."

"I agree. And as your friend, I have to tell you that I hate your shirt," I say. Then start walking backward toward the parking lot. "It's hideous." Wren looks down at her clothes in confusion. I hope she doesn't put two and two together and figure out I hate it because it isn't my name on her back.

Charlie pushes her plate to the edge of the table next to mine.

We've kept ourselves entertained with small talk about our classes and Sandra Bullock movies.

If this is what dating is like, it isn't terrible. I can't help myself from wishing Wren was here instead. Charlie is nice to talk to but it's like talking to myself. Every time I say I like something she says '*me too*'.

In theory, it's cool to have things in common, but I miss the verbal battle. I miss the glares and the cheap shots. I send Wren a quick text under the table.

ME

Charlie hasn't picked on me once.

It's nice.

She actually likes the same things as me.

WREN

Good to know you both have terrible taste. You're made for each other.

I chuckle in my head but I can't stop the smile from etching my face.

"How is she?" Charlie asks. I must look confused because she says, "Wren. You're texting her."

Oh. She noticed.

"It's fun to annoy her."

"Right. You like her. Yet, you're sitting here with me. Why?"

I huff a laugh. Wren asked me the same thing weeks ago. She wanted to know why I was still sitting with her instead of chasing after Charlie like I wanted.

Now I'm sitting with Charlie wishing I was with Wren. *Oh, how the tables have turned.*

"You asked me out. I wanted to give it a shot. We're having a good time."

"Is that why you're texting Wren? You're having so much fun with me? Come on, Wyatt. You and I do not have chemistry. We're admittedly good looking people, but there is no attraction. No spark. Every time we've hung out you've had your eyes on Wren. So, tell me again, why are you here with me?"

I drop my head and sigh. "I can't get your voice out of my head. I thought if we hooked up your voice would be gone and my brain would function normally again."

"My voice?" Her eyes are wide in shock.

"Yes, your voice. I heard you singing, and it re-coded my brain." I wave my hand dramatically around my head.

"When did you hear me sing?"

"Months ago, when I came over to get you and Wren for Syd's game night, but I only left with wine."

Charlie's smile grows manic. "That was Wren singing. I can't carry a tune to save my life, I'm afraid."

"No, it was you. You were the only one home."

"You know Wren better now. Probably better than I do. What do you think she did when she knew someone was about to force her to leave the comfort of her room and be social for a night?"

She hid. Of course she did.

It dawns on me.

"It's been her the whole time," I whisper.

"It's been her the whole time," Charlie agrees.

"I'm sorry."

"I'm not. You're good for Wren. She's been different since the two of you became friends. But Wyatt." Charlie's face drops. "She's still supposed to be getting married."

"I'm aware."

"I don't like it either if it makes you feel better."

"It doesn't." I sigh.

"What are you going to do about it?"

What am I going to do?

Isn't that the golden question?

There is only one option.

I've got to figure out a way to make her mine.

11

WREN

"Do you know what I think would be fun?" I ask, spinning around in Wyatt's desk chair. I just wrapped up an online tutoring session at his place while I waited for him to get home from baseball practice.

It's odd how comfortable I feel being in his private space. Well, after I started getting it organized for him. It took a few days of cleaning for me to be able to enter his room without feeling itchy all over.

"Let me take a wild guess. Color coding my sock drawer."

"That wouldn't be fun. They're all white. Organizing them by size and style on the other hand." I mentally add the task to my to do list.

"That makes me sad for you." He frowns. "I already told you we're going out to do something." He bops me on the nose like I'm a child.

I huff a breath of annoyance. I have no idea what he has planned. If I had to guess it's going to be something where my humiliation is imminent. Worst case scenario we are spending the day outside. My only hint was Wyatt texting me to dress casual and comfortably.

His exact text was, *"If you wear anything that requires dry cleaning, you'll be going naked."*

I don't do casual well. I managed to find a pair of olive green pants that are casual enough. I paired it with a white tee and comfortable footwear. Wyatt still managed to tease me about it. *Because he's so fashion forward.*

All he wears are jeans and T-shirts. He'll claim his wardrobe has variety because all of the logos are different. I'll give him that. Wyatt advertises everything from the Newhouse Knights to farm supply companies on his chest. It doesn't however give him authority to be the fashion police to me.

"Can't wait." I pout.

"Give me a few minutes to get ready and we'll get out of here." He grabs his clothes—jeans and a T-shirt—and heads toward the bathroom down the hall.

"He's going to make me do something awful. I just know it. I'm going to look like an idiot," I grumble to myself.

Too antsy to sit still, I start to organize his desk. I've been dying to get my hands on this thing. There is no way he does anything productive in this mess. I set his phone to the side and begin gathering up all the writing instruments.

I only have a few pencils in my hand when his phone starts buzzing. I do my best to ignore it. He's always texting with his siblings in their group chat. I can't help but wonder if it's Charlie, though. He hasn't mentioned anything about their date.

I haven't asked either. I'm not sure I want to know what happened.

It's been a few days. If he wanted to talk about it, he would. I asked Charlie how it went when she got home and she just grinned. I figured that meant it went well.

Which is good. I'm happy for them. They make a good couple. They are both happy go lucky people who enjoy going out and letting loose.

I bet Charlie wouldn't have sweated through her clothes at the thought of singing and dancing in the kitchen with Wyatt. She would have led the way.

It makes sense that he would like her.

Wyatt's phone buzzes again. I glance at it even though I shouldn't. But I have to know. Unknown number. *Stupid spam.* I decline the call for him. Before I can drop all the pencils and pens in a cup, his phone is lighting up again. *Read the room.* I decline the call again.

Wyatt's phone lights up for the fourth time with an unknown number. *Seriously?*

Phone in hand, I walk to the bathroom. "Hey," I say, knocking on the door. "Your phone keeps ringing. Do you want to answer it?" I ask through the door.

"Nah, it's probably just my stalker."

I inhale a sharp breath. "Your stalker?"

"Yeah, they call all the time. I can't get rid of them."

"You're serious?" I need to see his face. He has to be lying. Who would be stalking him? A fan? A classmate? I'm tempted to open the door but he said he was getting dressed. Not something I want to walk in on. *Now who's the little liar?*

"What are you doing in there?"

"Shaving."

His phone rings for a fifth time. Another unknown number. I've had enough of this. I swipe right and answer the call.

"I don't know who you are but you need to lose this number. Stalking is illegal. And creepy." The door clicks open. Wyatt's staring at me with shaving cream and a big grin on his face. He needs to take this seriously. Someone could be trying to hurt him. "Don't call this number again. If I find out you are still bothering my friend, I won't hesitate to get the authorities involved," I say, hanging up before they can reply.

Taking a calming breath, I straighten any hair that got ruffled in between my threats.

"You really took care of them. I doubt they'll ever call again." Wyatt barely gets the sentence out before his phone is ringing.

"Unbelievable. Give me that." I hold out my hand.

"I got it," he says, pushing my hand away and answering the call. My eyes travel down his body and I realize for the first time that he's shirtless. How did I miss that? I must have blacked out while I was reprimanding the unknown caller.

My eyes zone in on his chest and abs. I find myself leaning toward him and counting each row of packed muscle. Eight. *Is that how many you're supposed to have?* I don't think I have one. I'm going to make a note and ask my doctor about it.

"Hello." Wyatt's deep, southern twang pulls my attention back to his face. Which appears to be quite satisfied with the fact that I was checking him out. "Hold on a second," he tells the person on the phone. "See something you like?"

I cross my arms over my chest. "I was looking for research purposes."

"Research purposes?" He laughs and places the phone on the vanity.

"Will you just deal with that please?" I point towards the phone. He's so infuriating sometimes.

He puts the caller on speakerphone. Good, I want to give them a piece of my mind. I was too nice before.

"Are you there?" he asks.

"Who was yelling at me?" a woman on the other end of the line asks. She sounds older. Really, lady? Get a life.

"Mama, that was birdie," he says, grinning at me.

"Your mom?" I ask aghast. "I'm going to shave your mustache off while you sleep. I would keep one eye open if I were you," I warn.

"You wouldn't," he says, smoothing his mustache down with his hand.

"Watch me." I snag the phone. "Ma'am."

"Please. Call me Faith."

"Oh, okay. Faith, I want to apologize. Wyatt said he had a stalker and I let my instincts take over. Taking charge seems to be my default setting. He led me to believe he was in danger." I glare at him.

"Honey, I'm not mad. You stuck up for my boy. Not very many people would do that. It's my fault I'm afraid. I call him from random numbers hoping he'll pick up the phone."

"I do pick up the phone, Mama."

"Not every time," she grumbles. "I'm glad he has someone like you on his side."

"It was the right thing to do. I would do it again," I say honestly, with a quick glance to Wyatt. The razor stills in his hand momentarily before continuing to shave away the last twenty-four hours of stubble.

"It's one of the many reasons Wyatt likes you so much." Her words feel sincere, but I question their truth. I find it hard to believe he speaks to his mother about me. The red tint to his cheeks and ears makes me think he might have at least mentioned me once.

"Mama, did you need something?" Wyatt abruptly changes the subject.

"I hate to ask on your only weekend off."

"What is it this time?"

"The planter broke down again. Colt is working on fixing it. I'm counting on it being ready by the time you get here. It will be all hands on deck to get the field prepped for planting. Birdie, that means you too."

"Wren. My name is Wren."

"She doesn't like my nickname for her, Mama," Wyatt informs her.

"She will one day. I'll see you both in a few hours."

"Bye, Mama." Wyatt hangs up the phone. Then he wipes his face with a towel. His skin is smooth and free of hair except for his upper lip.

"You missed a spot."

"Where?"

"Your entire mustache." I tug on a few of the hairs on the corner.

He frowns. "You don't like it?"

I briefly think of what it might feel like scraping against my inner thigh. "It's growing on me better than it is on you. Maybe you should take care of it now. Save me the trouble of doing it later. Your stalker? Really, Wyatt? I just yelled at your Mama!"

"It's fine. It's something we'll laugh about in ten years." The statement makes my heart flutter. He's probably saying that we will laugh about it as friends in ten years, but my heart hears it will be a funny story to tell our kids. "You really don't like my mustache? It's my good luck stache."

"Serial killers have nicer ones."

He pulls a shirt over his head. I take advantage of his temporary blindness to ogle—yes ogle—his body. *Again.* My eyes get stuck on the band of his underwear and the way his jeans sit on his waist. It's a tease. I want to grip his hips and run my thumb under the ridge of his bone.

I wonder if he's sensitive there. Would he like it if I touched him there? Or *kissed* him there? *Why am I even allowing these thoughts into my head?*

"That's not very nice," he says once his head pops through the neck hole. Huh? What's not nice? Oh, right we were talking about his facial hair.

"I'm not here to feed your ego. I'm here to tell you the truth."

"You take your job too seriously," he jokes.

"I'll try to be nicer."

"Don't. I like you mean." He grins. I think he's being serious, but I'm not certain. Why would anyone like someone being mean? That doesn't make any sense to me. "We need to get going. It's a two hour drive back home."

"You actually want me to come?"

"If Mama said you have to be there, then you have to be there. Don't worry, I'll still show you a good time." He smirks at me. I know that look. He's definitely up to something.

"We're going to be outside. I'm going to get dirty, aren't I?"

"Oh, we'll definitely be getting dirty," he says, his eyes trained on me. A spark of fire spreads over my skin. "Don't worry. I'll take care of you, birdie."

That's exactly what I'm afraid of.

12

WYATT

"Do we need to get gas?" Wren asks, as I back out of the parking spot. I've got one hand on her headrest as I look behind me. The urge I have to run my fingers through her hair or touch the back of her neck is troublesome.

I itch to have a hand on her all the time. Is that weird?

I glance at the gas gauge on the dashboard. A little under half a tank. "We've got plenty to get us there." I shift the truck into gear.

"What about the way back? It would be better if we had enough gas to get us there and get back home. It will be late and we'll be tired. We won't want to stop. Your truck is also older than my grandfather. I don't know if we can trust the accuracy of that gauge."

"Can I do anything right in your eyes?" My tone is light, but sometimes I wonder if I'm a complete fuck up to her. And I don't want to be.

"Yes. Of course you can. What kind of question is that?" She asks as if I've offended her.

"I don't know." Now isn't the time to get into it. I'm not in the mood to sit in the car with a pissed off Wren. That's like being trapped in a trash can with an alligator. "Fine. We'll gas up but only because I want to get something to eat too."

My mouth is already watering thinking about the fried cheese and beef taquitos they have at the gas station about ten miles down the highway. I stop there every time I head back home.

"Wait in the car," I say, as I pull up to the gas pump and shut off the engine.

"I want to pick out what I want."

"I'll get it. Lock the door. I'll be back."

"You are extremely bossy today," Wren scowls. She can complain all she wants, but she needs to learn how to shut her brain off and let someone else take care of the details for once. "I want—"

I hold up a hand signaling her to stop talking. "I know what you like. I'm serious. Don't move."

"Fine." She balls her hands into fists. "But if you don't get the—" I slam the door before she can finish the sentence.

I get the gas started before running inside to grab everything. I even manage to get it all without a list. I doubt she will find it impressive, more like irresponsible.

With two grocery bags full of taquitos, chips, and chocolate that I wanted, plus the almonds, Starbursts, and the nasty yogurt covered raisins she likes so much, I finally leave the store. If she thinks I forgot gagging the last time she ate those nasty things at lunch, she would be mistaken.

Wren hops out of the truck when she sees me coming. I have to fake a scowl because she looks damn good standing by the open door of the cab.

"Thought I told you to stay in the truck."

"You look like you could use a hand. I'm trying to be helpful." Wren takes one of the drinks and a bag of snacks. Then climbs back inside.

"I know a better way you could be helpful with your hands," I mumble as I round the hood of the truck.

I place my drink in the cup holder and leave the other bag of food in my seat. Then finish up the gas. Through the back window, I watch as she digs into the bags of food. Her eyes light up and a small smile spreads over her face. *Told you I know what you like.*

"You ready?" I ask as I start up the engine.

"As I'll ever be. Thanks for this." She holds up her bag of goodies. "What did you get? It smells really good."

I drop the bag in her lap. "They're taquitos. Pass me one. You can have the other one." Good thing I bought two.

"You sure? I don't want to take your food." Wren pulls everything out of the bags and organizes the food in the space between us. She has it all lined up and a pile of napkins within reach for both of us.

"I'm sure. Go ahead." I nod toward the food.

"So, what is your family like?" she asks before taking a bite. "Oooh, this is really good."

"I know. That's why I bought it." I wink at her and take a hearty bite. When I'm done chewing I say, "My family is loud. Nothing is private. They are always in my business."

"It shows they care about you." Wren twists in her seat and leans her back against the door.

"Right. We can go with that and not the fact they are nosy and up to no good. Ford, my oldest brother, has a little girl. Her name is Lennon. She's a pistol. He lets her run wild on the farm." Lenny's mom left a few months after she was born. My whole family pitched in to raise her, and she has each and every one of us eating out of the palm of her hand.

"She'll be there?"

"She will. Everyone will."

Wren nods. Her glasses slip a little and she pushes them back up on her nose.

"You don't need to be nervous. Everyone's going to like you. My mama already does."

"She thinks I'm crazy."

"Nah. And if she does, you'll fit right in. I promise. Relax. Enjoy the ride." I flip the radio station on. "What do you want to listen to?"

"You're going to let me choose? Isn't it a rule that the driver controls the music?"

"From now on the only rule is there are no rules. What do you want to listen to?"

"This is fine." She nods toward the dash. I have my favorite country radio station playing. I'm not convinced I could find another station to work even if I wanted to. My truck is old.

Wren isn't wrong about that. It used to be my granddad's—he gave it to me when I was fifteen.

"You don't look like a country girl to me."

"Looks can be deceiving."

That they can. I try not to think about all the ways she is changing the way I see her.

The scenery slowly changes from busy city life to open stretches of highway and country roads. Secretly I keep waiting for a song to pop on the radio that she can't resist singing along to. I still can't believe the voice that's been haunting me belongs to Wren.

Not sure it mattered if it really had been Charlie at this point. I was kidding myself if I thought I could go through with hooking up with Charlie. It only took hanging out with Wren a few times to know there was something between us.

Mainly irritation and annoyance. There's something that happens to me when I'm in the same room as Wren. I can't stay away from her. She lures me in, insults me, and all I can do is wait for her to do it again.

We do a good job depleting our food stash. My bladder is about to burst from my big gulp, but we're almost home.

"This is part of our land." I nod towards the fields coming up on her right. Her eyes go wide as she looks over the rolling hills and green pastures.

I turn on to the dirt road that leads to the main house. I expect my mama and Willow will be waiting for us on the front porch. They will be quick to turn Wren's visit into a spectacle. Colt, Mason, and Ford are likely down at the main barn fixing the planter still. I'll go check on them once I get Wren settled.

"All of this is yours?"

I nod. "We had more. It's been parceled off here and there to other farmers. We've kept around five hundred acres or so."

Her jaw drops in disbelief. It is a lot of land. My siblings and I have a vice grip on a dream to make this place something to remember. Every year we talk about selling a few acres and making it work with less. Every year we can't do it. Even knowing the sale of the land would change our current financial situation we can't seem to bite the bullet.

The tires on the truck kick up dirt and gravel, announcing our arrival. Right on cue, the front door opens and my entire family steps out onto the wrap around porch.

I hop out of the truck and salute them as I make my way to Wren's door. She hasn't moved since I put the truck in park. "Hey, you're gonna be fine." I give her thigh a reassuring squeeze then unbuckle her belt for her.

With a nod, she slides down gracefully from the cab of the truck. I take her hand in mine. I expect her to deny me. Instead she twines our fingers together and squeezes. The gesture makes me a little dizzy.

"Whatever you do, don't look anyone directly in the eye. That's how they weaken your resolve and get you to spill the beans. If you do get caught up in their web, know that anything you say will be used against you later."

"Thanks for the tip."

"There's my boy," my mama yells from the porch. She rushes down the steps to greet us.

"Hey, Mama." I give her the best hug I can while still holding on to Wren's hand. "Mama, this is birdie."

"Let go of her. Let me see her." I drop Wren's hand so my mom can give her a proper hug. "Nice to meet you."

Wren is stiff in her arms, but gently pats my mom's back. I don't think she's used to genuine affection from strangers. Or maybe anyone.

"Mama, let her breathe." I tug on Wren's shoulder and release her from my mom's hold. "Do me a favor and introduce her to everyone. I'll be right back."

I run toward the house with Wren scowling at my back. "Sorry, birdie, nature calls."

I handle my business as quickly as I can. I don't trust my siblings to keep their traps shut. If I don't hurry, they'll be telling Wren embarrassing stories about me before she even has a chance to shake their hands. They are sweet and vicious creatures. Every last one of them.

"You brought her home. She's the one you've been texting me about." My sister leans against the wall outside the bathroom door with her arms crossed over her chest.

"Jesus, Willow."

"Mama said you were bringing your girlfriend home. I didn't believe her. Yet, here she is in the flesh. Your texts made me think it wasn't serious. I didn't even think you liked her."

Do not make direct eye contact. Do not make direct eye contact. Do not make direct eye contact.

"We're friends. We were together when Mama called," I say, staring at the faded floral wallpaper above Willow's head.

"And of course she told her to come on down with you. Just friends, huh? You want me to find out if she likes ya?"

"Do you want me to tell Mama how you really feel about her *famous* lemon cupcakes?" The glare my sister gives me could cut glass. "Wren is my friend. Don't make this into something more than it is."

"I would never do such a thing. You may want to get in there. Colt was just about to tell her about your buckaroo stage."

Panic flares through my body. "He sent you to distract me," I snap. Colt and Willow have always been thick as thieves. They are the closest in age and have a special bond.

"I admit nothing." She doesn't have to. Her grin says it all.

I race down the hallway toward the living room. Skidding to a stop, I scan the room for Wren. My dad is sitting in his favorite chair with his bad leg propped up on an ottoman.

Ford has Lenny sitting in his lap on the other side of the room. Mason is standing behind them. In the middle of the couch is Wren, absorbing every tall tale Colt is telling her. It's almost worth being the butt of the joke to see Wren smiling the way she is.

"Colt, shouldn't you be fixing the planter?" I ask. My arms are crossed over my chest with my hands clamped into tight fists to keep me from pulling Wren away from my brother.

"Already done. I was just getting to know your friend, birdie, here."

"Wren. You call her Wren," I say between gritted teeth. My mom rolls her lips to keep from smiling. Ford chuckles, knowing full well what Colt is doing. And that it's working.

Wren's eyes bounce between the members of my family trying to figure out what is going on. She doesn't know that we don't bring girls home. Not since Lenny's mom bolted. She doesn't know that having her here, even under the pretense of being a friend, has triggered every wild thought in my mama's mind.

She walks across the room and stops in front of me. "Are you alright? You look a little tense." She at least has the courtesy to whisper. Not that it matters, since I swear my entire family was born with sonic hearing.

"I'm fine. Are you going to be okay in here with my parents and Willow? We need to get started plowing the field."

"Wasn't I supposed to help with that?"

"Do you want to be outside sweating and getting dirty?"

"No. I suppose not." She glances around the room. "I'll be alright. I like them."

"Of course you do. They like the same things you do." Wren's brow bends in confusion. "Ragging on me."

"It is kind of fun. But if it bothers you—"

"It doesn't," I say, cutting her off. "Don't believe everything you hear. Colt likes to stretch the truth."

She places her hand on my forearm. My eye drifts to where we're connected and the electric pulse I feel pumping through my veins. "So you didn't run around the farm in only a cowboy hat and boots, buckaroo?" Wren's lips tilt up. "You don't have to confirm. Your mom is going to show me pictures. Have fun outside." She winks.

Before she can walk away, I grab her arm and pull her back into my chest. "Remember whatever you plan to do to me with this information, I will make you pay ten times over for it."

Her eyes drift over my body and back to my face. "I look forward to it."

What in the actual fuck was that?

"Come on, little brother," Ford says, slapping me on the back while I'm stunned speechless. "We've got work to do. Lenny, are you coming or staying here with Grammy?"

Lenny places a finger on her chin. Her eyes go to the ceiling. "Are you going to question Uncle Wyatt?"

"Of course." He pretends to be offended that she even had to ask.

"Then I'll stay and get what I can from the new girl."

Oh for fucks sake. I would apologize to Wren if she wasn't busy trying not to laugh at the little sleuth.

"We'll meet after dinner in the treehouse for ice cream sandwiches and compare notes."

"Deal," Lenny agrees with her dad and shakes on it.

"Dad," I plead as I pass him on the way out the door. He knows what I'm asking. We all call on him to keep the others in line.

"I'll do the best I can, son." His face is full of mirth. I already know he's going to turn on the baseball game and let Willow, Mama, and Lenny have their way with Wren.

I glance at Wren one last time. She shrugs with a smile on her face.

"Let's get this done so you can get back here and rescue her from the vultures," Mason says, dragging me out the door.

13

WREN

Wyatt gives me one last glance before walking out the door with his brothers. I'm not sure what was going on in my head to say something like that to him. *I look forward to it*. Look forward to what exactly? What am I hoping he'll do?

The way his eyes dilated and narrowed on me. A man has never looked at me the way he does. I don't understand what is happening between us. There is this constant draw I feel towards him.

Every grin, every bad joke, every twitch of his silly mustache makes me even more attracted to him. I don't know what to do with all these...feelings.

Wyatt's mom, sister, and niece stand together in a solid formation. I told him I would be fine, but seeing them banded together against me is making me sweat.

"What are your intentions with Uncle Wyatt?" Lennon asks, not wasting any time on her interrogation. Her arms crossed over her chest.

"What? Nothing. No intentions. We're friends," I stammer through my answer.

"Friends, you say. Is that why you are at his house every day? What are you doing over there?" She pushes like a seasoned cop.

I look at Faith and Willow. Surely I'm not expected to answer to a seven year old. Both women stare back at me expectantly. "Nothing special. Study. Eat."

"You're hiding something. I can see it in your eyes," Lennon says, pointing a finger in my direction. Wyatt warned me. He said not to look directly at them. Is this why? I attempt to blink away whatever she thinks she sees.

"Mama?" Willow asks, keeping her eyes trained on me.

"Yes, honey?"

"When was the last time Wyatt brought a girl home?" Willow's eyes are calculating. Her lip lifted in a slight smirk. I take a step away from her. She's beginning to scare me.

"Well, let me see." Faith runs a hand through her long blonde hair. There are a few gray highlights blended in with the blonde, but she still looks young and spry despite having five adult children. "I don't think he's ever invited a girl home before."

"I'm not his girlfriend. He didn't ask me to come today. I'm here because you invited me. Wyatt said I had to be here because you said so."

"Isn't that lucky? Mama handed him a reason to bring you home on a silver platter. He didn't have to come up with an excuse of his own to get you here," Willow explains.

"He wouldn't have asked me to come. We aren't really meet the family kind of friends."

"You are now," his mama exclaims. "Come in the kitchen. Jack will have the game on soon and we won't be able to talk over that noise."

I glance back at Wyatt's dad. He's resting back in a leather chair half asleep. His leg is propped up on a matching ottoman. I don't think he plans on moving any time soon.

"Wyatt said you're a business major," Willow remarks as we make our way through the kitchen. It's a large, open kitchen with two toned cabinets and butcher block counters. Lennon's artwork covers the fridge along with grocery lists and coupons.

"I am." Wyatt did tell them about me. I wonder what else was said besides my major and the fact I hang out at his house all the time. He doesn't have much of a filter. Combine that with their interrogation skills. He was set up for failure.

"Have a seat." Faith gestures toward their dining room table. It reminds me of a picnic table with benches on either side and a chair on each end. "We're working on plans for the new season."

Blueprints of what look like different fields are spread over the table. I straddle a leg over the bench seat and get comfortable. I glance over the papers without disturbing anything. There are a few sketches of buildings, but mostly it's empty plots of land with notes on what to plant where.

Faith brings over sweet tea for everyone. I pull a napkin from the holder in the center of the table and fold it in half. It isn't the most ideal solution for a coaster but I would hate to ruin the table. I take a quick sip before putting it down.

All three women are staring at me. "It's delicious. Thank you."

"You're welcome, honey," Faith says. "Now, while the boys are out there preparing the fields, it's up to the Rivers women to decide what we're going to do with them."

I should feel uncomfortable sitting here discussing family matters. Yet, a warm feeling floods my chest with Faith including me as a *"Rivers woman."* I wonder how Wyatt would feel about that.

"We have enough growing in the greenhouse to fill two fields for a late spring harvest," Willow says, pointing to a smaller field on the large blueprint. "Cabbage, broccoli, and some of the lettuce will be ready to pick this month. Lennon and I have more seedlings started to take their place. They should be ready to plant in a few weeks."

"How do you sell what you harvest?" I ask.

"We have a monthly membership program. It runs from May through October. Members get a portion of that month's harvest for a fee. They don't know what they will be getting. However they can make requests," Willow says.

"We do our best to give everyone what they like and what they'll use," Faith adds.

It's a smart plan. This way you don't have product going to waste. Everything gets sold as long as the membership is high with good customer retention.

"Do you have a storefront?" I search the map of the property looking for a store where customers can shop.

Willow glances at her mom. "No. It's something we want to do eventually. Along with a million other things."

"Daddy wants more horses and cows. He says Pumpkin is working too hard and she needs a friend," Lenny says. She takes a long sip of her sweet tea.

"Well, your daddy is going to have to wait. Pumpkin is our dairy cow. We had more, but we had to sell them last year," Faith says to me.

Questions form like rapid fire in my head. I want to know if they sell the milk. Do they have other animals? How big is the property? How many customers do they have? What is your plan to make a profit and not get further behind?

I don't ask anything. Instead, I listen while they go over plans for beans, five different varieties of lettuce, cucumbers, collard greens, tomatoes, green beans, and the list goes on. They map out the location for each plant, the timelines of harvest, and what to do with the surplus.

They discuss the wildflower and hay fields, chickens, and goats. I wonder how they manage it all. It's no wonder Wyatt feels like he needs to be here. There is so much involved in the day to day operations.

I also understand why he's trying so hard to save it. I hear it in their voices as they speak. This farm is their heart's work.

I start making my own mental notes on how I can help. What resources do I have access to? Can Ellington Business Solutions help? Would Wyatt let me?

There isn't much I can do without seeing their financial records. I doubt that's something they would willingly hand over to a stranger.

Is that who I am to them? It doesn't feel like it as I sit at the table with them. Even though I've spent most of the day in my own thoughts, I feel welcome here. I feel like I'm a part of whatever they're doing.

Even more so, I want to be a part of it.

Too soon the front door opens and Ford is walking through, followed by Mason, Colt, and Wyatt.

His shirt is soaked with sweat and dirt. His jeans are dusted over with soil along with his boots. A cowboy hat sits on the top of his head. I have to grip the edge of the table to keep myself from slipping underneath it.

Seeing Wyatt stride through the door covered in the two things I make a point to avoid, has me second guessing my stance on dirt and sweat.

Wyatt's lip twitches and his eyes dance with delight. What is he up to? He rushes towards me and wraps his arms around me. I fight his hold as his sweat begins to coat my skin. It's a natural instinct even though I like the heat of his skin transferring to mine.

"You can fight me all you want, but I see the way you're looking at me," he says close to my ear.

"You don't know what you're talking about. I was staring at you in disbelief because you came inside your mama's house like that," I lie, fighting my way out of his arms and gesture toward the dirt he's left on the floor from his boots. "You're going to bring the whole farm inside the house at this rate."

"Well, if that's the reason," he says, heavy with sarcasm. "You don't need to worry. We've been trailing dirt in this house for years." Wyatt reaches over me and picks up my glass of sweet tea. It's a little watered down. He doesn't seem to care as he chugs the entire glass.

"We sure have, haven't we, buckaroo?" Colt says from across the kitchen. Wyatt glares at his brother, but Colt just laughs him off.

"Daddy, did you get any good info from Uncle Wyatt?" Lennon asks, giving Wyatt a new member of his family to throw daggers at. She gets up from the table and walks over to Ford. "The way he came running in here, I know something is going on. New girl was pretty tight-lipped. I couldn't get much out of her, especially with Grammy and Aunt Willow yapping so much."

"You're going to have to wait until our meeting later tonight. I'm not going to share all my intel in front of every-one," Ford tells his daughter.

"Don't y'all have something better to do?" Wyatt asks.

"Not really." Mason smirks back at his brother.

"I wish Shelby was here. She'd put you in your place," Wyatt mutters quietly but loud enough it makes a few people in the room gasp.

"Don't talk about her," Mason says through gritted teeth.

"That's enough. Willow, help me get supper started." Faith hugs Mason as she passes him. Whoever this Shelby person is, the whole family seems to care about her.

Wyatt moves deeper into the kitchen to wash his hands. He shares a few private words with Colt and Mason before coming back over to me.

The whole room clears out suddenly except for Willow and Faith a few feet away in the kitchen. I wonder if there is anything I can help with. I've been sitting here most of the afternoon not doing much of anything but listening. I've only gotten up once or twice to use the restroom.

I scrap the idea when I feel Wyatt's eyes on me. "How did everything go out there?" I ask in hopes of getting him to stop staring.

"Nothing broke down again. We got the fields plowed and ready for next week. There's still a lot that needs to be done." He taps his fingers on the table.

"I can tell. Listening to them talk about all their plans for the next few months and the future..." My voice trails off when Wyatt frowns.

"We can barely get enough crops for our customers. Their plans and ideas are pipe dreams. They ain't ever going to happen until we're out from under all this debt."

He truly believes getting drafted will solve all his problems. I glance at the lists and blueprints. If there was a way I could help him carve out a future here instead of leaving to play baseball, I would do it. I would do anything.

If someone told me months ago that I would bend myself backwards to help Wyatt Rivers, I would have laughed in their face. Over the last month or so he's become a staple in my life. He's become one of my closest friends. A friend I would go to extreme lengths for.

"Let me help." I place a hand on his thigh. His gaze drops to his leg then follows my movement as I remove my hand and I tuck it between my thighs to keep from touching him. Great. Now he's looking at my thighs. *Give me strength.*

"I'm not sure there is anything you can do to help. You don't like dirt, going outside, the heat, bugs. I'm going to go rogue and add farm animals to the list too," he says, grinning.

"True. I don't like many of those things. But I'm good at analyzing." I tick off with my fingers. "I can take a look at the finances, current operations, and figure out where we can make more profits and cut the losses."

"*We*," he repeats quietly, almost to himself. Wyatt removes his cowboy hat and rests it on his knee. His hair is matted down with sweat and I want to ruffle my fingers through it. "Why would you want to do all that?"

"Why wouldn't you want my help?" I counter. Too scared to tell him the truth. That I want to help him because I care about him.

"I never said I didn't. I'm not convinced it would make a difference." *Oh.* He doesn't think I'd offer value. "I don't know what you're thinking but I guarantee you're wrong. It has nothing to do with you and everything to do with the farm.

It's bleeding so much money. I'm not sure how we can turn things around without financial help."

"I understand. I'd still like to try."

"Didn't mean to eavesdrop," Willow says, walking toward us whipping something in a bowl.

"Sure you didn't," Wyatt snarks.

"I didn't. Honest. But if you can help, Wren, you should come back with Wyatt for spring break," Willow says.

"I'm sure Wren has plans with her own family."

"Do you, honey?" Faith asks from where she's standing by the stove.

My eyes dart between Wyatt and his sister.

"Real plans. Not going back home to sit around and do nothing but hanging out with your folks. You'll have plenty of time for that later," Willow adds.

"My parents are going to Greece," I offer.

"Oh, that's wonderful. It's so pretty there. You'll have the best time," Faith says over her shoulder.

"You have to do one of those photo shoots with the flowy dresses. I saw one online once. It's stunning," Willow says.

"I'll be sure to tell my mom. I won't be going with them."

"Oh no. Why?" Faith asks, expecting the worst.

"I don't enjoy flying very much."

"What are you talking about? Birdies love to fly," Wyatt jokes.

"Not this one."

"It's settled then. You'll come back home with Wyatt for spring break. Help us figure out what we can do around here to get things moving in the right direction."

"Willow, stop pushing," Wyatt warns.

"You seem to be the only one who's pushing me." I turn on him. "You're pushing me away. If you don't want my help just say the word and I won't." It's a lie. I feel it the moment the words leave my lips. Whether he wants me to or not, I'll be helping him and his family figure a way out of this mess.

"It's not..." Wyatt drops his head and shakes it slightly. Almost as if he's talking himself out of saying something. "You know what. Fine. You can come back with me. If that's what you really want."

"It is. Thank you."

"Don't thank me yet. You're going to have to get your hands dirty this time. No way around it if you're here for a whole week. I was able to save you this time."

I look Wyatt over again. He's in desperate need of a shower. One I wouldn't be opposed to joining him on. Help him clean all his hard to reach places. *No. Just stop. Remember he likes Charlie,* I scold myself.

"I can handle anything you throw at me."

"We'll see about that. Throwing curveballs is kind of my specialty." He winks before getting up from the table. "I'm going to go clean up before dinner. Are you good here?" I nod in response and he squeezes my shoulder.

"You need anything, honey?" Faith asks a few minutes later. I'm still feeling Wyatt's touch on my shoulder, wishing he would come back.

Do I need anything? What I *need* is a lobotomy if I'm going to keep naked thoughts about Wyatt out of my head.

WYATT & WREN

WYATT

Do you have any allergies?

Willow wants to know.

WREN

No allergies

WYATT

Favorite foods?

WREN

I'm a guest. It's rude to request a certain menu.

WYATT

Forget I asked.

I told her what you like.

WREN

Did I leave my blue pen at your place?

WYATT

Which one?

You have a lot of pens.

WREN

My favorite one. The one you keep stealing with the polka dots on it.

WYATT

[IMG ATTACHED]

Oh, you mean this one?

WREN

Take that out of your mouth right now. That's mine.

WYATT

I licked it. It's mine now.

WREN

Now who has the stupid rules?

WYATT

It's the golden rule.

WREN

That is not the golden rule.

WYATT

Hart asked me again about going to Ray's to celebrate when midterms are over.

A full sentence in a text? Are you turning a new leaf?

Absolutely not.

Are you going?

It could be fun.

14

WYATT

I have exactly fifteen minutes to get across campus before Wren leaves for her study session at the library. I managed to slip out of the locker room before Koa or Hart could question my plans for the night.

At the moment, I'm not sure what they are. Even as I stand in front of Wren's door, I don't know why I decided to come over here. I'm simply desperate to see her.

Once again, I'm struck by her voice filtering through the room. I've yet to catch her singing in front of me, but I've heard her occasionally in moments like this when she doesn't know I'm listening.

It hits me even harder than it did the first time. Now I know the woman behind the voice. It isn't just the melody or the lyrics anymore. It's her making me feel something. *It's Wren.*

I knock a few times. The singing stops abruptly. I wonder if she knows the walls are paper thin and everyone can hear her. She has to. She's complained multiple times about the girl who lives next door having sex—she claims it's one of the reasons she's been studying more and more with me at my place.

Grinning at the peephole, I wait for the door to crack open.

"Hi," Wren greets me. "What are you doing here? Charlie isn't home."

"Okay. Are you going to let me in?" The door is only opened wide enough to see a partial silhouette of Wren's body. She's wearing shorts and a loose blouse in the same fabric. A material that most likely has to be dry cleaned.

"I guess. I was about to head out the door." She says this as if I didn't already know her entire schedule.

"Change of plans. You're hanging out with me the rest of the night. We'll go do something fun, grab a bite to eat, maybe watch a movie."

"I can't, midterms."

I should have seen that one coming.

"Forget the movie. We'll study instead. But you have to eat and doing something fun will reset your brain. You'll retain more of the study material with a clear head."

"I don't know how true that really is. We can study here and order pizza."

I eye her outfit one last time and mask my face of how I really feel about her showing more skin than usual. She is all legs. I long to run my palm over her thick thighs and wrap them around my waist.

"Do you have jeans? Boots? Gloves? Are you *prepared* for spring break?" As soon as her eyes start bouncing around the room I know I've got her.

"I've made a list of items I think I'll need according to the short amount of research I've been able to do." She pads over to her planner that's sitting on the small peninsula in their kitchen. She fishes out a piece of notebook paper and hands it to me.

"Let's go shopping. We'll get all of this and a few other things I think you'll need," I say after reading over her very detailed list. "We'll have a good time."

"Shopping for clothes is never a good time."

"That's because you've never gone with me."

"I thought we were going shopping for clothes," Wren says, as we pull in front of the farm supply store. It's the best place to find clothes and everything else she needs under one roof.

"We are. You'll have to trust me." I get out of the car before she can start talking. I've figured out this is the best way to handle Wren. I open her door and offer her my hand. "Come on."

"There is a giant iron cow statue on the sidewalk."

I glance over at the six foot metal cow wearing a cowboy hat. "I know. Isn't it great?"

She doesn't get one foot through the door before she is holding her nose. I chuckle at her as I grab a shopping cart.

"What is that smell?" she asks. It comes out nasally with the way she has her nose pinched.

"That is poultry and stock feed *eau de parfum*." I attempt a French accent. "You'll get used to it after a while." I lead her to the back of the store where they have all the clothing and shoes. There is also a small dressing room if she needs to try anything on.

"I don't remember it smelling this bad on the farm."

"You were outside for all of five minutes. Trust me. It smells worse." Once you get used to it, it smells like home. "Alright. Here we are." I gesture to the racks of clothing and the back wall of jeans and pants.

She pulls her list out of her purse and starts to look it over. Glancing around the store then back at her list, I can see her mentally plan out the most efficient way to shop. It's fascinating.

I've always gone into things with guns blazing. I get in, get it done, and walk away. If we were shopping for me, I would haphazardly throw things in the cart and hope for the best. Wren walks around the store methodically checking items off her list one at a time.

"Do you want to try those on?" I nod toward the jeans she dropped in the cart.

Her eyes dart toward the small dressing room. "No. They should be okay." She throws in a second pair then moves on to shoes. "Is there anything else you can think of that I need?"

I pick a random cowboy hat off the rack as we pass and place it on her head. Her eyes slant in annoyance, but fuck me if she doesn't look like a dream. Even without the jeans and boots, she is a vision that will haunt me for years to come.

"It doesn't really go with my outfit," she jokes. A shy smile covers her face. This is the first time I think I've ever seen her look unsure about something.

"It looks good on you, ."

"As long as you think so," she says, then tosses the hat on top of her pile of clothes. She walks away from me in the direction of the shoe department like she didn't just say something important.

As long as you think so. What did she mean by that? Does she want me to think she looks good? She could be joking but it didn't have her usual deadpan delivery. It was lighter, happier.

The thought stays with me while we finish shopping and drive back to her dorm.

Wren is sprawled out on the floor highlighting index cards and making additional notes on notebook paper. I've spent more time watching her than I have been studying. The thing is, I know agriculture. It's been my entire life. It's in my blood.

What I don't know enough about is her. Wren is something I could study for the rest of my life and never reach the bottom of her depths. There is too much to learn and too many layers to uncover.

I like knowing what she's afraid of and what motivates her. Or that I can bring her a fresh pack of sticky notes and make her smile. And that she keeps Starbursts in her nightstand so Charlie doesn't eat them.

There's a knock on her door. She barely notices, completely lost in her own little world.

"I'll get it." It's probably our pizza. I don't need her answering the door in the tiny bike shorts she changed into.

"There's cash in my purse."

"I've got money."

She stands, grabs her wallet off the counter, and hands me enough cash for the pizza and a tip. "I know, but you paid last time. It's my turn."

"I bought you a hot dog from the cafeteria on my meal plan. Hardly the same thing."

"It's the same to me." She snatches the cash out of my hand. "I'll pay him then."

Her thighs flex as she strides toward the door. The bottom of her sweatshirt sits perfectly on the curve of her ass. "Give me that." I grab the money and maneuver her to where she is standing behind me when I open the door.

I don't want the guy to have an opportunity to look at her. It shouldn't matter. She is completely covered, but no other man sees her like this. They see her in linen pants, silk blouses, and slicked back hair. I get her in bike shorts and T-shirts, her hair a mess on the top of her head, and old sweatshirts from her high school mathlete team.

That's my Wren and I want to keep her to myself.

Fuck, do I want to keep her.

Behind the door is a pimple-faced teen. He looks over my shoulder as he pulls our pizzas out of the warmer. For fucks sake. Wren is setting the table and bent over the damn thing. The kid probably just jizzed his pants. *The little shit.*

"If you want to keep your balls where they are, I suggest you stop staring at my girl," I say low enough only he can hear.

"Yeah, man. Uh, sorry. Here." He passes me the two large pizzas we ordered.

"Keep the change." I slam the door in his face.

"That was rude."

I ignore her and walk into the living room and set the pizzas down on the empty side of the coffee table. I stack up my textbooks and laptop and put them under the table. "Come in here and eat with me."

Wren's eyes dart between the dining table and the living room before she grabs some napkins and sits beside me on the floor. I slide the pizza boxes over until they are side by side and flip the tops open.

We inhale at the same time, both wanting to breathe in that cheesy, greasy, aroma. She giggles and I bump her shoulder with mine.

"When I was a kid my mama would do pizza picnics on the floor every week in the summer. Dad worked late in the field back then." I serve Wren a piece of pepperoni and the basil mozzarella she likes. "I guess it was her way of giving herself a break and making it fun for us at the same time."

"I used to love eating at my dad's office when I was little. We would order sandwiches from the deli in his building and eat in the boardroom." She takes a bite of her food and chews slowly. "There was a giant white board," she adds once she swallows.

"I bet you loved that."

"I did." She smiles and I have to look away before I make it awkward by staring at her. I've always thought Wren was pretty since the first time I saw her eating lunch with the girls.

I didn't give her a second look because of her indifference to me. She made it clear she was not my biggest fan. But when she smiles at me, the sight hits me like a hammer to the head. I forget where I am and struggle to find the right words to say.

"What about your mom? You don't talk about her much."

"She's around but she tends to enjoy society life more now that I'm grown and away at school. Her social calendar is busy with lunches and charity work. I don't think I was the daughter she was hoping for."

"What do you mean? It sounds like you've been the perfect daughter growing up." It's obvious she would do anything for her parents. Her whole life has been spent trying to make them proud of her. I would be surprised if making them happy isn't her biggest motivation for getting married.

"I was well behaved. I followed the rules. I didn't have the same interests as my mom. She liked to socialize and be the life of the party. I wanted to be like my dad. I love her and she loves me. We just aren't really close. I think she wanted me to be her little doll and wear dresses. I preferred to wear pants. I didn't want to date or get married. I wanted to work. Save businesses like my dad."

"Yet, you're getting married now," I point out.

"Agreeing to marry Daniel serves a purpose," she says. Her words feel significant and deliberate.

Daniel. He sounds like a tool. How about Dan or Danny? Daniel sounds so formal and boring.

"Let me guess. You're doing it for the sex. It sounds like the kind of guy who could make you scream," I joke. "Does he know you are sleeping with other people?" I haven't stopped thinking about the box of condoms she bought and who she uses them with.

I'm not sure when she would find the time to hook up with some random guy. If she isn't in class, she's tutoring. If she isn't tutoring, she's with me.

"He doesn't get a say in my life until he puts a ring on my finger. I'm sure he's enjoying himself just as much as I am."

"You deserve better." *Me. I'm better*. Wren tries to read my face and figure out what I'm really trying to say.

I've never done relationships before and I've made my stance clear—I hookup. I mess around and I don't get attached. If she wasn't set on marrying someone else, could we have something real?

I'm always asking her to bend her rules for me. Can I break one of my own for her?

"I've never had a relationship with someone I liked. Attracted to? Sure."

"Are you attracted to Daniel?"

She gives me a look that I can only describe as annoyed. "He's like the guys I usually sleep with. But I wouldn't say he's my type." She shifts her body. *Interesting.* What kind of guy is your type? *Perhaps long hair, mustache, tall, muscular, and has a fucking amazing personality?*

"You're not attracted to him then. Yet, you plan on him being the last man you ever have sex with. There is something really wrong with that." I gesture towards her with my slice of pizza before I take a bite.

"I would have thought out of all my friends you would be the most understanding."

"Why, because I've slept with random women in my past? Sure, I've slept with a generous handful but I found every one of them attractive in some way." How I felt about the women in my past is microscopic. A fleck of dirt in a hundred acre field. Nothing compared to what I feel when I do something as mundane as sitting beside Wren eating pizza.

"*Generous handful.*" She scoffs. "How many sexual partners have you had?"

"Let's see. There are three hundred and sixty-five days in a year. I lost my virginity at fifteen. So that's..." I pretend to do the math in my head. It's nowhere near that many but it's worth it to see the look on her face.

"Fifteen?" Her eyebrows jump to her hairline. "Was your dick even full size back then?"

I cough to cover up a laugh. "It was proportionate to my body. Still is, if you're wondering." I smirk at her.

"I'm not," she deadpans. Her fingers reach out to scratch the soft skin over her wrist. She's lying. She starts to scratch on the inside of her wrist or her neck when she's not telling the truth. She is definitely wondering about the size of my cock.

"My number is less than you think."

"I'm not going to judge you. I'll answer first. Make you feel more comfortable," she says. Hearing about how many guys have touched her will make me anything but comfortable. It will make me furious. That's an inside thought I should examine later.

"Go ahead, birdie. What's your number?"

"Six," she says. My eyes bulge. I expected more with the surplus of condoms she has in stock.

"Does that include the guy you're sleeping with now?"

"I'm not sleeping with anyone right now. I haven't been with anyone in...awhile."

"But you bought condoms."

"I like to be prepared." She shrugs. "Well..."

"Well what?"

"What's your number?"

I sigh. "I honestly don't know. I never kept track. I could tell you the first girl and last. That's about it." I'm not ashamed about sleeping around but it's not something I want to talk about in detail with Wren.

"And the next one. You could tell me the name of the next girl you're going to sleep with," she explains. Does she know I want to have sex with her? I guess I haven't been hiding my attraction to her as well as I thought. "Charlie. You're still trying to hookup with her, right?"

Charlie? Is that why she told me she wasn't home earlier? Damn it. I never told Wren. I haven't thought about Charlie like that in over a week. If I was being honest with myself, she was off the table after the first time Wren came over to my place and started cleaning up my room.

"Charlie and I aren't going to happen."

Wren dips her head and stares at the box of pizza in front of her. "I'm sorry. I know you liked her."

I wipe my hands with a napkin then toss it into the pizza lid. Leaning back on my hands, I watch as she consolidates the leftover pizza into one box.

"I didn't though. Like her that is. I didn't even know her."

She laughs. "Because you've gotten to know every girl you've slept with."

"And you have?"

"Yes, I have. I might not know their mother's maiden name or their favorite cereal but I knew enough," she says, pointing out a few things she knows about me. "I didn't want to know more than necessary. Those relationships were only meant to be sexual and nothing more. I'll never let myself get involved like that."

This is not what I want to hear her say The more I think about it, the more I want to be involved with her like that even though I know it will only set me up for heartbreak when she goes back home to Georgia.

"Why?" I ask.

"Because I know how it ends." She stands and collects the trash and puts the leftover pizza in the fridge.

"What does that mean?" I follow her to the kitchen. When she closes the fridge door, I'm right there waiting for her.

"It means I know I'm a lot. I'm bitchy. I say what's on my mind without thinking of the consequences. I have quirks." She motions towards the hallway where she has sticky notes all over the wall. "I know that once they get to know me, they'll get tired and it will end. Instead, I choose to not let my relationships get that far in the first place."

I crowd her against the countertop, careful not to touch her. If I touch her it will be over and I won't be able to stop. I'm not sure she is ready for that.

"You're a smart girl. I don't understand where all these foolish ideas are coming from." I tip her chin to where she's looking at me. "You're not too much. Don't settle for someone who makes you feel like less. Wait for the man who will get on his knees and beg for more of you."

I kiss her forehead and walk away before the temptation to pull her into my arms and start kissing her takes over.

15

WREN

The girls talk around me while we eat lunch. I can't seem to focus on anything they're saying. My mind is back on Wyatt and the way he crowded me in my kitchen. I take a small bite of my sandwich. I should at least pretend to pay attention to their conversation.

It's a beautiful day. One of the few days I don't mind sitting outside for lunch. There is a nice breeze and the shade to keep me from sweating through my clothes. I appreciate my friends' love for nature and fresh air, but personally, I like it just fine looking out a window in an air-conditioned room.

"I have to put together a charity event. *From scratch*. Do you know how much work that is going to be?" Charlie asks.

"That's your final?" Sydney pops a chip in her mouth.

"You say that as if it's a simple task. Yes, this is the final. It's basically the only grade for the semester. Professor Jim—"

"It's so weird that you call him that," Lauren says, smiling. She's not wrong.

"He looks like Jim from *The Office*." Charlie shrugs. "Anyway, Professor Jim is breaking the final up into smaller assignments. I'm grateful it isn't a pass or fail situation."

"What are you going to do?" Lauren asks.

"I'm not sure yet. It needs to be epic. I'm thinking about something physical. Maybe the proceeds can go to Royal Oaks?" Royal Oaks is the trailer park on the other side of town where Lauren lives during summer and semester breaks.

"That would be incredible. The summers are the hardest for the kids without school lunches. I know they would appreciate it," Lauren says.

"Maybe you can do something the kids can get involved in. Something fun," Sydney suggests.

"Like a fun run or a mud race?" Charlie asks.

"Why do they call it a fun run? There is absolutely nothing fun about running in this heat," I say, finally joining the conversation.

"It's fun because you're outside enjoying the fresh air and raising money for a good cause," Charlie explains.

"It's deceptive advertising. There is nothing fun about being outside." Then they want to add running too? No thank you.

"Then why are you spending your entire spring break on a farm? Huh?" Charlie teases.

"Back it up. I missed something. You're spending spring break on a farm. Where?" Sydney asks.

"Wyatt's family farm," Charlie answers for me with a slick smile on her face.

"Our Wyatt?" Lauren asks. No, *my* Wyatt. "Hart mentioned something was going on between the three of you. A sordid love triangle. I thought he was joking."

"There is no love triangle. Wyatt is my friend," I say. It's the truth. That's all we are. Friends. Just because it didn't work out with Charlie doesn't mean he wants something with me.

I thought he was going to kiss me the other night. He got so close to me in my kitchen, but he had pulled back seconds before I was going to push forward.

We studied into the early morning and he ended up sleeping on my couch. If the situation was different—if he actually liked me like that—he would have forgotten all about studying.

The things he said to me make me want that. He makes me believe he could be that man who begs for more of me. When I close my eyes, I can still feel the forehead kiss he gave me.

"There's no love triangle because Wyatt isn't interested in me," Charlie says.

"Because you turned him down," I state.

"I turned him down because he didn't want me." I know for a fact that isn't true. "My God, Wrennie. Read the room. The boy is obsessed with you."

If by obsessed you mean, I'm going to hound you until you help me get into your roommate's pants, then yes he is that. Actually obsessed with *me*? I don't think so. We're friends. That's it. That's all we can ever be.

"It makes sense now," Sydney says, nodding her head.

"What does?" Lauren asks.

"Nash. A week or so ago when we were out at dinner. He said Wyatt told him not to get any ideas. That you were off limits. Nash said Wyatt didn't want him flirting with you anymore. What do you have to say about that?"

I shrug, but I do wonder if this is what Wyatt whispered to Nash after we had our impromptu dance party. "I don't know why he would say something like that. Sounds like the same warning Nash gave his friends about you. Maybe Wyatt sees me as his sister." The thought makes me die a little inside.

"It's not the same," Syd claims.

"Did you see the way he went feral over her wearing Thomas's jersey?" Charlie asks Sydney and Lauren.

"You told me to wear it because he would want me to wear school colors. And Wyatt said he hated the jersey by the way. You were wrong." I point a finger at her.

"Who's going to tell her?" Lauren asks. Sydney raises her hand and starts chanting pick me over and over. "Educate the woman."

"He hated it because it wasn't his name on your back. You were publicly claiming Thomas as your favorite player."

"That is the most ridiculous thing I've ever heard of. I don't even know who Thomas is, let alone if he's a good enough baseball player to call him my favorite," I explain.

"It might sound arbitrary, but Hart would lose his mind if I wore someone else's jersey to one of his games or at all," Lauren says, further cementing this bizarre jersey wearing rule.

"Are you sure there's nothing going on between you and Wyatt?" Sydney asks.

"I'm sure." I fiddle with my lunch to avoid their scrutinizing stares.

"You're at his place all the time or he is over at our dorm," Charlie states. *That was all to get close to you.* "You text all day long. You hate texting in case you forgot. You do laundry together. Eat lunch every day." I look up to argue the fact that I'm eating lunch now and there is no Wyatt in sight. "Almost every day. Whatever. Should I go on?"

"There can't be that much more," I grumble.

"You share food. You order each other's meals. You buy him office supplies," Charlie continues.

"He's very unorganized. He needed help getting his notes in order."

"My point is, the two of you are very close. You even have the little word game you play."

"That's so cute," Sydney says. It is not cute. It's frustrating. Wyatt is currently winning this week. I've been trying to think of a way to work *surfeit* into a conversation all day.

"We're friends. I don't know what to tell you." I shrug defensively.

"Sounds like the two of you are in a relationship," Lauren says nonchalantly. They don't know why he started spending time with me to begin with. If they did, they would come up with a different conclusion.

"She giggles now," Charlie tells Lauren and Sydney. They both gasp. I roll my eyes. "She's been singing more around the dorm. Wren, you're happy. I know it has to do with that man."

"Maybe it's my new vitamins," I counter. I discovered new vitamins right around the time that Wyatt started harassing me. They are made with real fruits and vegetables. Who's to say that's not why I'm suddenly so much happier?

Charlie sputters a laugh. "Sure, vitamins. And I'm going to marry a famous football player one day. Why don't we all move to Deluluville with you?"

"Okay, I'll entertain you with a hypothetical situation. Let's say Wyatt is interested in me."

"He is. Carry on." Charlie gestures with her hand for me to keep talking.

"Wyatt's interested in me. What would you have me do? I'm not just going to walk up to him and tell him to kiss me. It's too risky."

"Love is worth the risk," Sydney says.

"Is it Sydney? What risks are you currently taking for love?" I ask.

"My situation is different," she claims. I suppose. I don't understand how a man can be off limits because he is your brother's best friend. Especially since he's been your friend the whole time too. "I took a risk by dating someone new. It might not have worked out, but I'm happy now."

The lie is there behind her eyes. They don't shine as much as they used to. She may be able to trick herself into thinking that she's happy. Maybe she is but I don't believe her. It's all a facade.

"No comment," Lauren says to her best friend. Lauren would know better than me and Charlie what's going on with

Sydney. They are basically sisters after living together for years. "Lucky for you, I'm more interested in Wren and Wyatt hooking up. Otherwise we would have to give you a lesson in how to define real happiness."

"Brainstorm ladies," Charlie says, redirecting the conversation. "What should Wren do to get his attention?" Charlie pulls out her phone to take notes. I should be impressed.

"I know. I could take my shirt off and show him my boobs. Oh wait, I already did that. It didn't work." You would think if Wyatt was interested in me, he would have said something. *Done something*. He didn't. He stayed in one spot until we left the room.

"You what?" Charlie screeches.

"I flashed him my tits. It's not a big deal. I was changing clothes and he happened to be in the room." Being naked isn't a big deal to me. I'm not a modest person especially when I'm around people I'm comfortable with.

And I am comfortable with Wyatt.

"And he didn't jump your bones?" Sydney asks. I shake my head. "That doesn't sound like Wyatt at all."

"Exactly. It sounds like a guy who isn't interested." I start packing up the rest of my lunch and gathering the trash.

"It sounds like a guy who's worried he might lose someone he really cares about if he messes up," Lauren says.

I sigh. I wish that were the case. "I appreciate your advice and insight on this matter. I think it's best if I let it be."

"Fine," Charlie relents. "Tell him hi for us," she tacks on with a wink.

I wish we never had this conversation. All I can think about now is *what if*. What if I wasn't tied up in an arranged engagement? What if we gave it a chance? What if we try and we mess everything up?

16

WYATT

I straighten my new hat on my head before I exit my truck. The bill is stiff and needs working in. I know Wren will be happy I'm not wearing my old Newhouse one tonight. I've been tempted to force her into wearing it every time her little nose scrunches up looking at it.

This new hat magically appeared on the top of my dresser yesterday afternoon. I'll never stop wearing my old one, but I'll wear this one for her since she bought it for me.

Hart and I walk through the parking lot toward the front door of Ray's, a local honky tonk—Lauren and Sydney got a job here bartending last semester. Hart wasn't thrilled with the idea. I've heard him grumble about it once or twice.

But he knows Lauren is made of tough material. He learned early on in their relationship that his girlfriend can handle anything on her own. Drunk guys are a walk in the park compared to everything else Lauren has been through.

Koa on the other hand hasn't stopped getting on Sydney's case about her job. "I thought Koa said he wasn't coming?" I ask as we pass a red Camaro that looks a hell of a lot like my roommate's car.

Hart glances at Koa's car parked near the front of the lot. "I asked him if he wanted to go to The Armory." Hart smirks. "He didn't know we were coming here tonight."

"How did you know he was going to be here? Wait. Is this what he's been doing every night?" I ask, opening the front door. The music hits me like a brick wall.

Hart nods. Even with the music to hide behind, my friend will still choose silence in public places and around people he doesn't know.

"How long?"

Hart shrugs then nods towards the back of the bar. I guess I get to have my questions answered straight from the source. Koa is nursing a beer discreetly at a low top table. He bobs and weaves his head, keeping his eyes laser focused on the bar. On Sydney.

Earth to Captain Obvious.

"Is this seat taken?" I pull back a chair and sit down, not waiting for him to turn me away.

"Shit," Koa curses under his breath. "You said you were going to The Armory." He directs his statement at Hart.

"I lied."

"You're an asshole. When did you figure it out?" Koa asks.

"The day you told Sydney to do whatever the hell she wanted and stopped riding her as much about working here."

Koa drops his head. "Someone had to do it."

"Whatever helps you sleep at night. I'm going to find *mi brujita*." Hart disappears into the crowd.

A waitress comes by to take our order. I get a beer for myself and a tequila and Sprite for Wren. I'm not sure what Charlie drinks or I would have ordered her something too.

"Don't start," Koa says. I hold my hands up in surrender.

"I wasn't going to say anything. I think it's great you're looking after Sydney. I bet Nash appreciates all that you do for her."

"Maybe he asked me to check up on her." He raises an eyebrow. Like having Nash's permission to keep an eye on Sydney will negate all his possessive feelings over her, but sure let's go with that. "How about we talk about your current situation?"

I shrug. Then take a sip of my draft beer. "I don't know what you're talking about."

He smirks. "I'm talking about that." Koa points toward the door. Looking over my shoulder, my eyes bulge, my tongue rolls out of my mouth, and my heart immediately starts racing.

Lord have mercy.

Time slows to a halt. Every step Wren takes in my direction is excruciating. Her hair bounces over her shoulders and glows under the neon lights like a halo. She's wearing the jeans and boots we bought together last week and a white tank top that dips low enough to tease me with cleavage.

I knew Wren had a body under those blazers she wears. Shit, I saw her half naked with my own two eyes.

Seeing her in a pair of hip hugging Wranglers? It has my blood going south. Damn, she looks fucking hot right now.

It's going to take all my willpower to keep my hands off of her.

Charlie leans over to whisper something in her ear. Wren's eyes catch on mine. There's a faint blush on her cheeks.

I stumble from my chair. *Smooth. Real smooth.* Koa snickers behind me. I don't even realize I'm walking in her direction until I'm standing in front of her.

She's not wearing her glasses. Suddenly I can't see anything beyond her blue eyes. I've always liked looking at them behind her glasses. I know her that way. *I like her that way.* But to see her eyes unobscured in their natural state is more breathtaking than a night sky full of starlight.

I wave a hand in front of her face. "Can you see me?" I ask, more to distract her from the fact I can't stop staring at her. Saying something dumb keeps me from telling her how beautiful she looks. "Last time you didn't have your glasses on you were walking around your dorm like a mummy."

She slaps my hand out of her face. I maneuver our hands until our fingers are laced together. Wren inhales a slow breath. "It's called wearing contacts. I can see just fine." Her eyes roam over my face, down my neck and chest.

"You look good," I say close to her ear so she can hear me. I rub my nose against her hairline and enjoy the smell of her shampoo. She shivers—it's so slight that if I wasn't attuned to her body, I wouldn't have noticed it.

"You look...the same. Nice hat." It doesn't sound like a compliment but if you are knowledgeable in Wrenguistics, you would know it translates into you look good too. *You always look good.*

"My best friend got it for me." I squeeze her hand. "Thank you."

"Someone needed to save you from yourself. Is that for me?" She lifts her chin toward the table.

"It is. Come on." I tug her hand. "Charlie, what do you want to drink?"

"I'm going to go to the bar and find Lauren and Sydney," she says, grinning at Wren.

"I'll go with you." Koa greets Wren and says his goodbye in one swoop.

"You really know how to clear the room," I say, taking my seat.

"It's a specialty of mine." Wren's eyes dart around the bar as she sips her drink.

There's nothing fancy about Ray's. The bar is a horseshoe in the back of the building. The main attraction is the large dance floor in the middle of the room with flashing neon lights strobing all over the interior. None of the tables and chairs match and the floors are sticky. But the music's loud and the beers are cheap.

"So," she draws out. "Now that you have me here. What are you going to do with me?"

I lift my hat off my head and scrub my hair. It's a tactical move I've used once before on her. I need the diversion to give me time to rid myself of all the ideas that just flooded my brain.

What do I want to do with you? Where do I fucking begin?

While Wren is busy watching my biceps flex, I'm trying to figure out a way to get my blood to start circulating properly again.

"You said this would be fun. When does that begin exactly?"

The tempo of the music changes picking up to a nice dance beat. People are already lining up on the dance floor. "Right now. Down the rest of your drink." I chug my beer and wait for Wren to catch up. It only takes her a few long sips to suck down every drop of her mixed drink. It's a pretty sight seeing her lips wrap around the straw.

She's wearing her cherry red lipstick again. I have to close my eyes and picture my grandma in her bathing suit. Grandma Alice is a pretty lady but the image of her in her floral swimming skirt is a bucket of cold water washing away any thought of Wren sucking on my cock instead of that straw.

"Come with me and follow my lead."

"Where?" she asks, looking around the bar. "You can't be serious," she says, as I drag her on the dance floor. She crosses her arms as people rock stop and slide around her.

"Heel, toe, do-si-do, birdie," I joke, as I attempt to follow the moves of the person line dancing in front of me. I'm completely lost. I spin left when I should be going right. I grapevine into the girl next to me. She doesn't seem to mind as her eyes rake over my body.

"Need me to teach you a few steps, handsome?" the girl asks.

"He's good," Wren cuts in, grabbing my arm and pulling me into her chest. This isn't the first time she's acted possessive over me. I hope it's not the last. "Why don't you try following me this time?" Her lips are moving but I can't seem to compute anything with her soft curves pressed into me.

Wren maneuvers me right where she wants me. Then takes her place half a foot ahead. We take up the same amount of space on the dance floor that is typically allocated to one person.

Looking over her shoulder, she starts to direct me. Left foot. Right foot. Kick. Kick. Stomp. Wren does a half turn and we repeat the same movements. A few more rotations and I have the sequence memorized.

I'm too busy watching my feet, trying not to trip and make a fool of myself to notice what she's doing. I feel her though. She's watching me as her feet slide across the wood floor. I never would have guessed she would be the type of person to be able to keep up on the dance floor of a rowdy bar.

After a few more songs, the music switches over to something with a slower tempo. Dancers partner up for a two-step and start gliding around the floor in unison.

"Put your hand on my shoulder blade," she says, taking one of my hands in hers. My fingers scrape the bare skin of her back. I'm tempted to do it once more just to see her eyelashes flutter again. "When I step backward, you go forward." She keeps an eye on the dancers, timing their movements. "You ready?"

I nod and we begin to move. "Eyes on me. Your body knows what to do," she says, her gaze unyielding.

My body knows what it wants to do. I'll give her that. I want to find a dark corner in this place and pin her up against a wall.

By the chorus, I'm more confident in my steps and she lets me lead us around the dance floor. It's a heady feeling to have her relinquish control to me. She holds every aspect of her life in a tight grip, but she's giving me this.

Small refractions of light dance over her skin. My eyes dart in every direction chasing it like a cat. She is glowing and I want to bask in her. I want to get on my knees and worship this woman. Just the thought has me digging my fingers deeper into her back.

Her eyes shutter and she pulls me closer. It's not really that kind of dance but she doesn't seem to care. I don't either. I want Wren. So much, it's becoming a problem. I need to tell her, but how?

How do you tell your best friend you think she's the most beautiful woman you've ever seen? Not just because she's gorgeous on the outside but because you know all her insides are beautiful too.

Friends don't say things like that. Not when they're wrapped up in each other's arms slow dancing like they're desperate for each other.

Dancing like they want to say *fuck it* and not worry about the consequences.

That isn't Wren though. She weighs out every outcome. She doesn't have *'fuck it'* moments in her life.

Just once I wish she would and use it on me.

Thankfully the song ends before I can shove my foot in my mouth. I put some much needed distance between Wren and my growing erection. "I need a shot," I announce.

"Yeah, okay." She takes a step back and wraps her arms around her middle. *Fuck.* I'm messing this up.

Hope you like the taste of leather you idiot because you're going to be eating your boot.

I trudge behind her to the bar. Some guy with a black cowboy hat offers Wren his seat. I see now why Koa makes his presence known when Syd is working. This guy is creepy with his smarmy smile. He's looking at Wren like she's going to be his alarm clock tomorrow morning.

I don't think so buddy. If any man is going to be waking up to Wren in the morning, it's going to be me.

Stepping up behind Wren, I wrap my arm around her and glare at Slick Rick to back the fuck off. Wren doesn't protest. She leans into my chest and I smirk at the guy.

Once Lauren passes him a drink, he leaves and transfers his attention to a group of girls a few bar stools down.

"Can I get you something to drink?" Lauren asks, wiping down the counter in front of us.

"Two shots of tequila and two beers please," Wren requests. "What did you want?" She turns to me.

You. The word could easily slip from my lips.

"Funny," I say instead.

215

"I keep telling you I'm fun. You refuse to believe me," Wren says as Lauren drops off our drinks and scurries back to Hart at the other end of the bar.

"I never said you weren't funny. I said you didn't know how to have fun."

"Do you still believe that?" she asks.

Wren slides a shot in my direction and reaches across me to snag a salt shaker. The brush of her arm against mine makes the hair stand on end. The light touch is nothing compared to the vision of Wren licking salt off the back of her hand.

I clear all the desire from my throat. "I'm learning there is more to you than meets the eye," I say, watching her lips wrap around the shot glass and the way her throat moves delicately as she swallows.

"Your turn," she says, wiping lime juice off her lip with her pointer finger. I stare at her dazed, swiping my tongue over my lips. "Wyatt." She nods toward the salt and tequila.

Right. My turn. I would love to lick the salt right off her body. I would be satisfied with a small taste of her wrist at this point. Is this the level of pathetic I have succumbed to?

She watches with rapt attention as I lick, swallow, and suck down my shot. I grimace as the tequila burns its way down my esophagus. "How is this your drink of choice?"

"It's a nice mix of sour and sweet. Just when you think you know what you're getting it changes on you. I'm also a lot more *fun* when I drink tequila. Life of the party," she says in her usual deadpan delivery but with the addition of jazz hands.

Wren may think it's the tequila, but I've never seen her have more than one or two drinks when we've gone out before. The tequila is a smokescreen, an excuse. She doesn't need a drink to give herself some slack. She wants something to blame her behavior on the next day.

I know her. She doesn't do anything she doesn't want to do. Tequila happy or not.

"That's you alright."

"You don't think I can be the life of the party?"

"I..." I start to say. I don't want to offend her but... "No. I don't. I think you would pick a quiet night at home curled up on the couch, watching a movie, and drinking one of your flavored waters every time over line dancing at a honky tonk."

She takes a quick sip of her beer. "Dare me to do something. Anything. Dealer's choice." She turns her body toward me. Her thigh knocks against mine and my dick decides it wants to say hello. My brain is slow processing her question. The combination of her body near mine and the tequila is hindering the function of my cognitive skills.

She gives me a look that says *'Well, what are you waiting for?'*

"Kiss someone," I blurt out, clearly not thinking with the right head. If I were, I would realize that I'm giving her my permission to put the lips I've been staring at all night on someone that isn't me. Not that she needs my permission to do anything. But I wouldn't have recommended it if my dick wasn't trying to monopolize the conversation.

"Kiss someone," she repeats, her voice soft. She licks her lips. I want to do that. Instead I'm left wondering how sweet that bitter tongue of hers really is.

"Pick anyone you want."

"Anyone I want?" she questions, her eyes never leaving mine. The neon lights of the bar dance off her white tank top creating a kaleidoscope of colors.

"Yep." I glance around the bar looking for someone I could stomach her kissing. Pickings are slim. Wren stands up on the rung of the bar stool and uses my shoulders for balance.

Her tits land a couple inches from my nose and I'm desperately fighting the compulsion to shove my face in her cleavage and suffocating myself.

There's a tiny lift to her lips as she searches the bar for her guy. She knows exactly what she's doing. I need to check her ancestry report. She has to have the devil in her bloodline somewhere.

Cool air skims the top of my head bringing my focus back to Wren. She's removed my hat and is flipping it around over my head. When she places it back on my head backwards, I'm a little lost.

Wren's palms slide down the side of my face until she's cupping my cheeks. Her thumbs graze my stubble and my eyes close voluntarily, savoring the feel of her skin on mine.

Her lips press gently into mine and my whole world tilts. *Anyone I want?* Me. She picked me. She's kissing me. What does that mean? Does she want me? *Get out of your head idiot. Kiss her back.*

Wren jerks back and I blink my eyes to get out of this haze she's put me in.

"I shouldn't have done that." Wren misinterprets my stupidity as lack of interest. She drops down in the stool and covers her hand over her mouth.

"You're right," I say. Her sharp intake of breath is like a needle in my heart. I tip her chin up. "I should have done it." Wrapping my hand around her neck, I pull her towards me and softly brush my lips against hers.

Her hands find my side and she grabs hold of my shirt, pulling me closer to her. I lick the seam of her lips and get her to open up for me. When the sweet taste of her hits my tongue, I want to claw my way closer to her.

Wren tastes bittersweet with the mix of lime and tequila from her shot. Sweet and salty just like her. I need more. I wrestle her for control until she finally yields letting me explore her mouth slowly, savoring every moment of this kiss. It could be the last one I get from her. *The only one I get*.

I nip at her plush lower lip, playing with her and giving her a moment to breathe before diving back in for more.

She pulls back, her chest rising and falling as she catches her breath. I rest my forehead against her. "I'm having fun now," she says. My lips curl into a smile.

"Would you like to have more fun back at my place?" I kiss her again.

Her head reels back. "Does that line really work?"

"I don't know. Never used it before." I shrug. "I don't bring girls home."

"You can't bring girls home."

"Even if my room didn't look like an EF5 just blew through, I wouldn't. I don't like people in my personal space."

"We can go back to my dorm then."

I shake my head, pulling her closer until she is flush against me and press my dick, that is borderline begging for her at this point, between her thighs.

"I want you in my bed tonight," I say, enjoying the little whimper that escapes her lips.

"Okay. Let me tell Charlie we're leaving." She hesitates a moment. The wheels in her brain are turning. "Are you sure?"

Am I sure?

"I don't want you to wake up tomorrow morning and have regrets," she adds.

"Birdie, if you aren't in my truck in the next five minutes I'm going to throw you over my shoulder and carry you out of here. Let's tell our friends we're leaving and then you're all mine."

We find Charlie hanging out with Koa, Hart, and a couple of other guys from the baseball team.

"Oh hey you two. Having a good time?" Charlie asks. She glances down to where Wren and I are holding hands.

"So much fun we're going home," Wren says dryly. I don't bother fighting off my grin. "Can one of you make sure Charlie gets home?" Wren is asking Hart and Koa, but several of my other teammates eagerly volunteer as tribute. Charlie preens under all the attention.

"You can't leave yet. Lauren and Syd are about to do their dance thing at the bar," Charlie says. I couldn't care less about Lauren and Syd right now. "You don't want to miss the big guy watching Syd dancing on the bar, do you?" Charlie nods toward Koa who is glaring at her.

I peek at Wren to see what she wants to do. Her eyes troll up my body and get hung up for a minute on my crotch. "Five minutes, birdie. Then I'll have you screaming my name all night," I whisper in her ear.

"Fine. Five minutes," Wren agrees.

It was not five minutes. It was more like thirty minutes and two more rounds of shots for Wren. I stopped drinking so I could drive us back to campus after my second beer.

Was it funny watching Koa snarl and flash teeth every time Sydney kick-stepped around the bar with another guy? Absolutely?

Do I regret staying? One thousand percent.

Halfway through the drive home Wren passed out against the window. I should have known better. She has a strict bedtime of ten o'clock every night. Add in the extra shots she's not used to drinking, it was a recipe for disaster.

I put my truck in park in front of my townhouse. "Birdie. We're home," I say. I unbuckle her seatbelt. She groans as I maneuver her into a position where I can pick her up.

Her limbs cling to me like a koala bear as I make my way through the house and downstairs to my room. "I hate the way you smell," she mumbles half-asleep into my neck. Did I forget to wear deodorant? I know I got a little sweaty dancing. Not as bad as I do playing a game.

"Your smell. It gets stuck in my nose. And I hate it," she groans quietly. I gently lay her down on the bed and start to take off her boots. "I hate that I love it so much," she whispers. I squeeze the sole of her boot until my knuckles turn white. "I'm sorry. I'm so tired. I ruined it."

"You didn't ruin anything. Let's get you to bed." Reaching underneath her, I pull the covers down.

She snuggles into the pillow and takes a deep breath. "This pillow smells like my best friend." Wren sighs. "I wish things could be different," she whispers into the pillow before shutting her eyes and drifting off to sleep.

I stare down at her speechless. She is half asleep mumbling nonsense.

What does she mean? Different how? And if it's different good, why can't it be that way?

17

WREN

The lack of light in the room is my first clue I'm not in my dorm room. The second is being surrounded by Wyatt's leather and amber scent. *Oh crap*. I told him I loved the way he smelled. That's what I get for drinking tequila with Charlie.

My eyes feel like they are full of sand. I rub a hand over them. "Damn contacts." I blink a few times to see if that helps with the dryness. I hate wearing them. It was worth it to see Wyatt looking at me the way he did.

And that kiss.

I pull the covers over my head and squeal. I've never been kissed like that before.

"Birdie," Wyatt says, before knocking softly on the door and cracking it open. "Are you okay in here? I heard you scream."

"I'm fine. My contacts. I didn't take them out last night." I grasp for an excuse. I'm not one to squeal like an excited little school girl. He knows that as well as I do.

I'm still wrapped up in a cocoon of Wyatt's blankets when I realize the other side of the bed was left untouched. "You didn't sleep in here?"

He prowls over to the end of the bed and crosses his arms over his chest. Lust-filled eyes drink in my body. I'm in his room. *In his bed*. The thought has me rubbing my thighs together.

"Slept in Hart's bed." The muscles in his forearms flex as if he's clenching fists that are currently hidden behind his biceps.

He didn't want to sleep in the same bed as me. Why? Does he think last night was a mistake? He's not looking at me right now like kissing me was a bad judgment call.

"That sounds...*cozy*."

He smirks at me. "He stayed over at Lauren's place. You were passed out. I wasn't going to sleep in the same bed as you without your permission."

"What a gentleman." I wrestle myself out of the sheet and comforter. "Stupid sheet. Get off me." I kick my feet until I'm able to set myself free. With a huff, I push my hair out of my face. Wyatt curses under his breath.

"Birdie." My name is a warning.

"What?" I ask. He nods to my chest.

I guess my tank top twisted around my body while I was sleeping. My left boob has slipped out of the arm hole. "It's not like you haven't seen them before." I shrug and straighten my shirt.

"Birdie," he says my name again, with a growl. "I'm barely hanging on here."

"Hanging on to what?" I snap at him, my hands on my hips.

He stalks over to me. "Do you know how good you looked sleeping in my bed?" He pushes a piece of hair behind my ear. "I could have watched you sleep for hours."

"That's a little creepy," I whisper. And sweet.

His lip twitches under his mustache. "Go get ready." He kisses the top of my head.

"I need to get my suitcase and something for my contacts." Suddenly I feel out of sorts and panicky without everything I need to get ready for the day. We are leaving for Rivers Bend today and I'm not prepared.

"Picked up your stuff this morning. I had Charlie throw in something for your contacts." He nods toward the wall by his closet. "Meet me upstairs when you're ready."

"Oh, okay. Thank you." That was thoughtful. How early did he get up? Could he not sleep? I have a hard time going to sleep in unfamiliar places. I didn't struggle last night though. *That's because Wyatt is familiar*, I think as I make his bed and breathe in his scent one more time.

The routine of showering and getting ready calms the sudden rush of anxiety I feel. Routines are reliable and steady. I need that feeling to counterbalance the wild stir of emotions running rampant through my mind. The next week is filled with too many unknowns.

Too many scenarios where things could go wrong. Too many people who don't know me well and may not understand me. Too much time with Wyatt not knowing where we stand.

Breathe, Wren. This week is a job. I'm helping Wyatt and his family. I can do that. I can focus on the tasks, not the people.

Wyatt's in the kitchen cooking something on the stovetop when I finally make my way upstairs.

"Can I help with anything?" I ask. He tosses me a glance over his shoulder, and his gaze scans my body thoroughly before licking his bottom lip. I'm dressed casually today in joggers and a T-shirt. My hair is thrown up in a high ponytail.

"Do you want to toast the bread?" He nods towards the bread.

"I think I can handle that. Do you cook a lot?" I drop the bread in the toaster, then turn my attention back to Wyatt. He's expertly folding eggs to create the perfect omelet. He's cooked for me a few times but we typically get food on campus.

"Not a lot while I'm at school. There isn't enough time between classes and practice. At home we take turns making meals and cooking for the family." He slides the omelet onto a plate and passes it to me.

The bread pops up from the toaster. I spread butter on them and add them to our plates. I grab a few forks from the drawer and take a seat at the table. Wyatt puts his omelet on his toast and has half of it eaten before I even finish my first bite.

"One of these days eating like that is going to catch up with you," I tell him. Not that he will change the way he chews.

"I'm glad you care." There's a hint of mirth in his tone but also a layer of appreciation for my concern. I focus on cutting a bite of omelet to hide my blush. *He wants me to care.*

He grins, taking a bite of his eggs at the same time as me. We both chew silently. When I get to twenty, I swallow. He swallows.

I cut another bite. He does the same. I'm about to eat the bite on my fork but stop short of putting it in my mouth. He mimics me again.

"What are you doing?" I ask.

"Eating. What does it look like?"

I eat my next bite, eyeing him suspiciously. He continues to mimic me. He thinks he's so funny. I smirk at him. He wants to be cute. I'll be cute too.

I take what's left of my omelet and place it on top of my toast. It's a massive bite, but doable. I lift the entire sandwich, fold it in half, and stuff it in my mouth. My eyes begin to water as I try to choke down the toast and eggs without gagging.

Wyatt watches with his mouth agape while I chew. I raise an eyebrow and nod towards his plate.

"You're something else, Wren Ellington." The way he says my name with reverence has me slowing my movements like I'm swimming through quicksand at the same time blood rushes through my veins making me feel reborn. I want him to say it again.

"That was child's play," I say, collecting our dishes and bringing them over to the sink. "I can fit a lot more than that in my mouth," I mumble more to myself.

He passes me the dirty skillet from the eggs and pins me against the sink from behind. His warm body sends a chill down my spine. "I intend on finding out just how much that mouth of yours can take very soon." Large hands squeeze my hips. "I'm going to load up the truck. Then we can get out of here."

"Can't wait," I say, a little breathless. I would be lying if I said I wasn't nervous. At this point I'm more concerned about the close proximity to him for the two hour drive. Even more if we get stuck in traffic.

"Hey," he spins me around, "you don't have to go. I know this was all forced on you."

"Do you not want me to go? If something's changed..." my voice trails off.

He searches my eyes for an answer to a question I'm not privileged to know. "I want you there."

"I hope you will still feel that way after I pull out all my sticky notes and make you multiple to-do lists," I joke.

"I will. I love your sticky notes," he says in a tone that leaves no room for dispute. Our eyes lock and linger on each other longer than necessary. For a moment, I think he might kiss me, but he takes a step back for whatever reason.

"Go get the bags. I'll finish up here," I say, shooing him away with a spatula and saving myself from further embarrassment.

"Please stop," I beg. We're an hour into the drive and Wyatt keeps singing so loud and out of tune my eardrum is about to burst.

"I told you I'm not going to stop until you sing with me."

"And I told you, I don't sing." I cross my arms. He gives me his I know you're lying look.

"I've heard you sing, birdie."

"You have not. I know for a fact you haven't." I've been really careful not to sing when I'm around him or anyone except for Charlie. I could have slipped up. Singing is mindless to me. I do it when I clean or when I'm in the shower or making something to eat.

"Just last week when you were rummaging through the pantry for snacks you were singing to yourself," he accuses me.

"I don't like singing in front of people." I never have. It makes me uncomfortable.

"Why? Your voice is incredible." He sounds outraged. It almost makes me laugh.

"I just don't, okay?" I say, ignoring his compliment.

"Tell me."

"You're like a dog digging for a bone. You're not going to let this go, are you?" He shakes his head. "Of course not. Fine. When I was a little girl my mom signed me up for beauty pageants. It was a big thing where we lived. I had fun in the beginning. It was a way for me to feel connected to my mom. I loved singing on the big stage back then. I even won a few times."

I watch the trees blur as we drive down the highway thinking back to how proud my mom was of me as she watched me perform.

"You mean I'm in the presence of royalty?" He gasps.

"Yes. Bow and worship me," I joke back.

"Gladly," he murmurs, his voice deep and rough. He clears his throat and asks, "What does this have to do with you not singing now?"

"Word got around that I had this talent. Soon I was asked to perform at my parents' dinner parties or social gatherings. I started to feel like a trained monkey. I was probably around the same age as Lennon. I told my mom I was finished with pageants and stopped singing altogether. That's when I started spending more time with my dad."

"I'm sorry, birdie. I won't ask again." He pats my leg and I desperately want him to keep it there.

We drive for miles in silence. The radio plays quietly in the background. His thumbs drum on the steering wheel. When one of his favorite songs comes on, he turns up the volume. The music is so loud his voice blends into the background.

He grins at me. That's when I realize he turned up the volume for me, not him. *You're safe with me.* He says the words without having to open his mouth. A small wave of emotion hits me and I have to blink it away.

When the chorus starts, I decide to join in. I'm on a road trip with my best friend. If I can't let it all go in front of Wyatt, then who? There isn't anyone. He is the only person I feel okay being myself completely around without fear of judgment.

My voice is soft at first, but soon I'm belting out the lyrics along with the radio. His grip tightens on the steering wheel and his whole body tenses making me pause and turn the volume down on the dash.

"Don't stop." He looks at me with sincerity. He covers his hand over mine, forcing me to turn the volume back up. "Please." His plea makes me want to sing to him, only him, every day for the rest of my life. I let these thoughts settle over me. I'll analyze them later.

Time on the road passes quickly. Before I know it we are turning on to the dirt road that leads to the Rivers' farm. I try to take in the land with new eyes. There are green pastures and rolling hills for as far as the eye can see.

With the right resources and vision, they can turn this place into anything they want. They can use the land closest to the road to build a storefront. It's easy access for anyone driving by to stop and grab some of Willow's pies or home grown vegetables.

The front porch is empty as we arrive, unlike last time. I guess my novelty has worn off. I'm not sure if I should be offended or find comfort in that.

"They are all working or they would be here," Wyatt says, putting the truck in park.

"I didn't say anything." I hop out of the truck.

"Didn't have to."

"I'm not that obvious."

He grabs my hand and I freeze mid-step on the porch. He's standing one step below me. In this position we're eye level. "You're right. You aren't that obvious. But I know you. Your eyes were darting around in a panic. If you'd let me add you to the group chat, you'd already know what everyone is doing right now."

"Don't. I will still kill you," I say.

"Nah, you like me too much to do that."

"You're right. I do," I admit. It's a scary admission but the truth usually is. He blushes under my stare. I really wish he would kiss me or say something. I need reassurance that he's feeling the same way about me that I am about him. He's going to have to make the next move. I'm not brave enough to do it this time.

"Come on. Let me show you our room." He steps in front of me and opens the front door.

Did he say *our room*?

"Our room?" I ask out loud as I trail him upstairs.

"It's not exactly a big house, birdie. Colt and Mason moved to one of the old cabins on the property a few years ago. Before that we all shared a room. Ford sleeps in the old guest room and Lenny has Willow's old room."

"I see." We walk into the bedroom that used to house three boys. It's clearly been redecorated since then. The walls are white shiplap. There is a queen bed in the middle of the room with a black metal frame and beautiful white linens. Two side tables anchor the bed on either side and a long dresser sits on the opposite wall. It's simple and classic.

"What's wrong? You don't want to share a room with me?"

That's not it at all. I do. I mean, I don't care. It's fine.

"There's only one bed," I say. He nods and takes a step closer to me.

"It's kind of small." I wave a hand toward the bed. It's the same size as his bed at school but I feel the need to point out this fact because it's going to feel like a twin mattress with him laying beside me. He nods and takes another step.

The thing is, I'm not convinced he wants to share a room with me. I know what he said this morning, but I can't help but wonder if that's the truth. I close my eyes for a moment. I feel him all over me, even without him touching me.

"What's the real problem?" he asks.

"You haven't kissed me again. I'm worried you regret it. I don't want to share a room with you if it's only going to add to the list of things you wish you never did."

He crowds me further until my back is pressed against the door. "I haven't kissed you again because if I do, I won't want to stop until I have you naked and my dick buried inside of you." He rubs his nose against mine teasing me. "Trust me, birdie, I'm just getting started with you. I'm going to ruin you for that future husband of yours."

He backs off and starts nonchalantly unpacking his bag. I collect myself as I watch him take out neatly folded T-shirts and place them in the dresser.

"You better keep your hands to yourself while we're in your mama's house."

"I can't promise that. She's the one who put us in a room together anyway." He shrugs.

"You said it was a small house."

"It is," he says. "But she could have made Lennon sleep on an air mattress in Ford's room or have you room with Lennon."

"But she didn't." I open my suitcase and unpack a few things.

He watches with a smile as I remove all the jeans and sun dresses I brought with me. Once we're all unpacked, he says, "Come on, I think I smell someone making lunch. Let's go see who's made it back home."

I stop at the door looking back over our space for the next week. "Does your mama know something I don't?"

"She knows the same things we do, birdie," he answers before kissing the top of my head and ushering me out the door.

18

WYATT

"What are you doing out here by yourself?" Ford asks, taking a seat in the rocking chair beside me.

"Getting some fresh air." After dinner, my dad pulled out the Scrabble board which is apparently the equivalent to catnip for Wren. I left her side a half hour ago to come out here and think.

From the kiss last night to seeing her sleeping in my bed, my head is spinning. I want her, but she's not mine to keep, and that's worrisome. I'm not one to get caught up with feelings, but it hasn't stopped them from showing up anyway.

"You're thinking pretty hard over there."

"Wren's engaged," I blurt out. "I keep thinking that no matter what happens between us, she's getting married to another man."

"Shit. This guy doesn't care if she's spending a week with you?"

I shake my head. "Technically they aren't even getting engaged until this summer. It's some kind of archaic arranged marriage bullshit." I don't have all the details. I didn't want to be the one to bring it up. I figured she would tell me if she wanted to.

"Tell me how you really feel." He snickers but quickly stops when he sees me glaring at him. "What do you want to happen?"

Good question. I want to have sex with her. The need to be inside her is almost paralyzing. I want to feel her come around my cock and see her face when she falls apart because of me. I bet she's fucking beautiful.

Then I think of what my life would be without her snarky comments, her sticky notes and lists, her complaining about my laundry, or her getting after me about the way I eat. There's a void. I feel hollow without her.

"I want her," I admit. In every way possible.

"Can you fuck her and then let her go to live a life with another man?" Ford asks.

Can I? It's what I've done with every relationship in the past. Is she that different?

"Maybe." That's what I tell my brother, but the truth is to me she is different. She stands out in a crowd. In every room, I am drawn to her.

"She's your friend. If you only want to sleep with her, do some kind of friends with benefits thing." He shrugs. "Keep feelings out of it. You're leaving to go play baseball after graduation anyway."

I tense at the thought of not coming back home and running the farm with my family. How am I going to be able to sign a contract and stay away for another three to five years? That seems easier than keeping things casual with Wren.

"Does that kind of relationship work for you?"

Ford looks up at the stars. "I can't risk any kind of relationship. Not now. Maybe not ever. I'm not putting Lenny through that again. I don't need her thinking someone leaving has anything to do with her. She comes first."

"You don't think it would mess up our friendship?"

"Set up ground rules. Make sure you are both on the same page. Hell, have a safe word." He chuckles. "Pick an end date and know that you can stop at any time and go back to the way it was before. Put her in charge."

"She'll love that." I grin thinking about Wren writing up all the rules to this arrangement. I was ready to dive in dick first last night, but maybe setting up some parameters is a good idea. "Thanks, Ford."

"Not sure I said anything helpful but keep it down tonight. I don't need Lenny asking me what all the animal noises are inside the house again."

"That was Colt, not me," I say, pointing a finger at him.

"What was me?" Colt asks, stepping onto the porch to join us.

"The guy who had sex with the girl who sounds like a dying cow when she's fucking," Ford answers. "Lenny had so many questions."

"She wasn't that bad," Colt attempts to defend himself but he can't keep a straight face. We all start laughing. "I came out here to tell you that Wren went upstairs for bed. She was getting tired."

I shoot up from the rocking chair so fast it crashes against the house.

"Have a good night," Ford shouts, as I rush inside and up the stairs. I can hear their laughter with every step until I reach my room.

I open the door slowly not wanting to startle Wren. When I walk inside, the room is empty but the water is running in the bathroom. I sit on the bed and wait for her to come out. I could use the time to get my head on straight.

Am I really going to propose a friends with benefits situationship? Could we do it? Will she be offended if I don't want more? Because I would ask for all of her, if things were different.

Is that what she meant too when she said she wishes things were different? That we could try if she wasn't stuck with her engagement arrangement?

The bathroom door clicks open pulling me from my thoughts. Wren walks out wearing a silky blue pajama set with tiny shorts and a top with white buttons. *Fucking hell*. I groan and drop my head back to stare at the ceiling.

"Hey," she says, turning her back to me and starts messing with her phone. Is she stalling? I know she can feel my eyes on her by the way she bounces from foot to foot. Either that or she needs to pee again.

"I'm going to get ready for bed." I hop off the bed. Reaching around her, I pull some underwear out of my drawer. I run a finger along the hem of her shorts. "I like these."

I take a quick shower, take a piss, and brush my teeth. She is still checking something on her phone when I walk back into the bedroom but does a double take when she sees me in nothing but a pair of black boxer briefs.

"Why aren't you wearing any clothes?" she asks, scolding me.

"I'm wearing my pajamas."

"Those are not pajamas. These are pajamas." She gestures to her clothing. "You are wearing underwear. Those go *under* your actual pajamas. If you are trying to change my mind about messing around in your parents' house, you will have to try harder than that."

"I'm not trying anything. This is what I sleep in." Hooded eyes follow my hand as I run it over my abs and further down to readjust my cock. She is making me hard just by having her eyes on me. Her little shorts are doing a good job of spurring me on too.

She chews on her lip absentmindedly and I want to pluck it out from between her teeth. I resist the urge to step up behind her and pull her ass against me. It would be nice to ease some of the pressure. My poor dick is angry. Instead I walk over to my side of the bed and make a show of pulling down the covers.

I lay down on my back and put my hands behind my head. I'd close my eyes but then I'd miss my little bird being fit to be tied. Her chest heaves as she zones out staring at the bed. That head of hers is going a mile a minute right now.

She said I have to keep my hands to myself while we're in my mama's house but there is no way I'm sleeping next to her every night and not touching her.

I'll give her tonight. Let her get a good night's sleep. Then tomorrow we're going to have a conversation about how we're going to do this. I'll see what she thinks about a friends with benefits relationship.

It's not what I want with her, but it's likely all she's willing to give. I'm not going to get my feelings wrapped up in her any more than they already are knowing she's going to run off after graduation with another man.

But if I can have her for a little while...

"Is it really comfortable sleeping in your underwear? You don't feel weird being almost naked?" she asks, moving closer to the bed.

"Oh yeah." I rub a hand down my chest with exaggerated movements. "The sheets are soft and cool against my skin. I'm going to sleep like a baby tonight."

"Just stay on your side of the bed with all that." She gestures toward my crotch which is at half-mast tenting the sheets.

"Don't worry. I'll be a good boy."

"Good because now I'm curious." She slips her fingers into the waistband of her shorts and shimmies them down her legs.

My heart is beating so loud it's all I can hear as I start to pant.

The hem of her pajama top covers just enough of her body to make you wonder what she's wearing underneath. "I want to see if the sheets feel as good as you claim they are." She starts unbuttoning her shirt.

"Wh-what are you doing?" I panic as she continues her striptease. It was going to be hard enough staying on my side of the bed when she was wearing clothes. Now she's standing in front of me in nothing but a pair of blue lace panties. *Fuck*.

"Following your slumber party dress code. You make sleeping in your underwear sound so cozy." She shimmies her shoulders making her tits jiggle. I've just entered the seventh circle of hell. She slides into bed and I'm knocked back with a tidal wave or her delicious scent.

"Oooh this is nice," she says, burrowing further under the covers. She removes her glasses and places them on the bedside table.

"This isn't funny," I grumble.

"What are you talking about? You started it. I want to sleep like a baby too." She leans forward, letting the sheet drop enough for me to see the fullness of her breasts, and kisses me on the cheek. "Goodnight, Wyatt."

I grab her by the back of the neck before she can get too far. My kiss isn't pretty. It's punishing. This girl gets me so wound up I can't see straight and I have to force myself to pull away from her.

"Goodnight, birdie," I say, with my forehead pressed against hers. Laying back down I try to get comfortable. It isn't easy considering how hard my dick is at the moment.

"You can't kiss me like that and then roll over and go to sleep." She props herself up on an elbow. "You said you weren't going to kiss me again until I'm naked and pressed against you. I'm halfway there." She yanks the blanket down exposing her chest.

"Fucking hell," I curse under my breath. This woman is always pushing me to my limits. I mimic her stance and edge closer to her. "And you said you didn't want to do anything in my mama's house."

"I guess we both said things we didn't mean."

"I meant what I said. I'm trying to be respectful of what you were asking of me."

"I'm getting a little tired of this gentlemen act," she says, moving a little closer. I'm trying to do the right thing here. We should talk about this first. I've never been a talk first kind of guy, but with her I feel it might be necessary.

"We need to go to sleep. We've got an early morning," I say, gripping the covers to keep my hands from wandering up her thighs and caressing her tits that I've been dying to touch.

"We should." She slides over and pushes her body against mine.

"Birdie," I warn. My hand finds her hip. Instead of pushing her away, I bring her even closer. "Is this what you want?" I flip her on her back and rub my growing erection against her pussy.

Her hands grip my shoulders and she rolls her hips against my cock, causing a moment of temporary blindness.

"Wyatt," she pleads.

I capture her lips and she responds eagerly. Sliding my palm up her side, I don't stop until I've reached her breast and massage it in my hand. I have to stop kissing her for a moment to recenter myself. I'm finally touching the body that's been the star of every fantasy I've had the past few months.

Now she's here. She's real and soft and warm.

I kiss and lick her neck as I slowly make my way down to her chest. Her fingers thread through my hair as she guides my head down her body. I swirl my tongue around her nipple and rake my teeth over the tight little bud.

She grinds into me again and it sets me on the edge of an orgasm. "Shit, birdie." I lift my hips out of reach and rest my head on her chest for a moment to compose myself. "Give me a second."

I slide off of her and trap one of legs under mine.

"What are you doing?" she asks, as her fingers graze up and down my back. "Why did you stop?"

"I'm not stopping." My hand drifts down her stomach, stopping short just below her belly button. I spread my fingers and dip my pinky under the lace of her underwear. Slowly, I tease her by moving my pinky lower and lower.

"Do you still want me to touch you, birdie?" My fingers are waiting and ready to sink into her wet pussy.

"Yes. Please," she begs her eyes not leaving mine. I'm not sure how much she can see without her glasses on. It's for the best. I don't need her to see exactly how much she affects me. I'm sure I look like a mad man with how bad I want her.

Gently I dip a finger inside her tight cunt, stretching her. I graze a finger over her clit and her hips rock against my hand. Her thigh pushes against my dick and I have to bite back a curse. If she keeps it up, I'm going to come before she does.

"I knew you'd be a good girl. So wet for me." Her little whimpers and moans get louder. I kiss her to keep her quiet. I don't need Ford or anyone else in the house hearing how hot my little bird sounds when she's fucking my fingers.

"Are you going to come for me?" I add a second finger and continue to pump into her while adding a little bit of pressure to her clit with my thumb. "That's it, birdie. You look so pretty falling apart for me," I say as her orgasm crashes over her.

Her hair fans the pillow and her eyes slowly close as she continues her fall into bliss. She bites down on her lip and...*fuck*. The sight of her and the pressure of her thigh against my cock has me cumming in my underwear and seeing stars. I would be embarrassed if I wasn't so turned on.

I kiss her again before I remove my fingers from inside her. I put them in my mouth and suck them clean. Damn she tastes good. "Next time, I'm getting it straight from the tap. I'll be right back."

"You don't want me..." she gestures toward my crotch.

"You already did." I pop a kiss on her forehead then leave for the bathroom, grabbing a new pair of underwear on my way. I give her a wink over my shoulder. I didn't think she could see, but her giggles tell me she knows enough.

I'm so fucked.

Wren's hair tickles my nose. It's still dark outside, and the sun has yet to start waking up. I've been laying here for an hour, savoring the feel of Wren in my arms and her head on my chest. She found her way to me at some point in the middle of the night.

I should have called her out on it but having her warm, almost naked body draped over mine was not something I was willing to give up just to rub it in her face. Her leg is hitched over my thigh and I trace a line with my finger from the hem of her panties to her knee.

I don't want to leave her but I have to get up or my brothers will start banging on the door; I can already smell the coffee starting to brew. We have a full day of work ahead of us.

With a deep sigh, I push her hair off her face and lightly brush my lips on her forehead before sliding out from underneath her. For a moment, I think she might wake up but she settles easily on my pillow. Her breathing deepens as she inhales my scent I've left behind.

Could it always be this good? I think as I throw on jeans and an old T-shirt. Waking up early every morning with my woman in my arms. Getting to do the work I love with the woman I...

Do not finish that thought.

I glance back at her one last time. The sheets barely cover her ass exposing her bare back and one of her legs stretches out from underneath the covers like it is dying for fresh air.

I don't know if I'm in love with her yet. I've never been in love before. I don't know what it feels like. I'm willing to bet it feels something like this. But I'll be damned if she doesn't make me want to be a better man so she'll fall in love with me.

19

WREN

Heat blooms in my cheeks thinking about last night. I don't shy away from the things I want. I go after them full force. Last night I wanted him.

After the orgasm he gave me, I did sleep like a baby. It wasn't my lack of clothing that made the difference. It was being able to cuddle with Wyatt.

I was sad he was already gone when I woke up this morning. It turns me on to think I got him off last night without even putting my hands on him, but I *really* want to put my hands on him. I wanted to wake him up this morning the same way he put me to bed last night.

Sadly I woke up clutching a pillow in my arms instead of him.

The house is empty except for Wyatt's dad relaxing in the living room. I scrounge up some breakfast and make myself at home. That is one thing about being here. It doesn't feel weird to be left to my own devices. I understand everyone has a job to do. I like that they don't cater to me as if I'm a guest.

"Wren, is that you in there?" Wyatt's dad calls out from the living room. "Come in here and keep me company."

"Good morning," I greet him when I enter the living room. "Can I get you anything?"

He shakes his head. He's sitting in his usual brown leather recliner with his leg propped up again. I'm curious to know the story behind his injury—whatever happened had an effect on the entire family.

"Did you sleep okay?" he asks. My steps falter. Wyatt wouldn't have told his dad that I stripped all my clothes off and let him finger bang me, would he? His expression is blank, wrapped up in whatever is happening on the television. Maybe he's making small talk.

"I did. Thank you." I take a sip of my coffee and immediately start coughing. "What is this made with? Tar?"

His deep chuckle makes me smile. "You'll get used to it after a few cups."

"After a few cups, I'll be doing laps around the farm." I'll admit the second sip does go down a little easier than the first. Likely because ninety percent of my tastebuds are tainted with this murky liquid that is posing as coffee. "Where is everyone?"

"Faith and Lenny are running errands. Willow is at work—she works a few days a week at the bakery in town. And the boys are working on that list you made for them last night." His lip tilts up on one side.

"It's Ford's list. I simply suggested it would be more efficient if he wrote everything down and prioritized what he wanted done to keep everyone on the same page," I say. He hums in response. "Did Wyatt mention anything for me to do while he's working outside?"

"You didn't want to join them?" His lip curls similarly to his son's when he's teasing me.

"I don't know if you have enough insurance to have me help fix roofs and build fences."

"Faith left a pile of documents for you to look through. All the income reports from the last ten years or so." He nods toward the dining room table. "It didn't happen overnight. Our financial situation. It's been years in the making. Started back before I took over for my dad. Every year we get a little bit more behind."

I wonder why Wyatt is under the impression he is the reason behind all their debt.

"You did the best you could. Your family—"

"Has sacrificed a lot while I sit here and watch." He stares out the window that's filled with green pastures and a barn that looks like a dollhouse since it's so far away.

"Maybe it's time to stop watching." I finish my muffin and take my empty coffee mug back to the kitchen and rinse it out. "I need a tour," I say, holding his cane out to him.

He eyes it for a moment. "You know how to drive a Gator?"

"I'm not sure what that is but I'm a quick learner."

"Then grab your hat and put on your boots. I'll meet you outside."

Apparently a Gator is a four wheeler. I've never been on one before but it can't be too hard to figure out how to drive.

It's a rocky start as we jerk down a dirt path that leads to the flower fields.

Green stems pop out of the ground. A few with tiny buds getting ready to bloom in a variety of colors. He informs me they will harvest the flowers and sell what they can to local florists.

What happens to the flowers they can't sell? I add this to my list of questions for Wyatt.

We follow the dirt and gravel path as it curves around to the back end of the property. Mr. Rivers points out different pastures and sections of unused land. All the places they have plans to utilize in the future.

"Do you want to show the boys what you're made of?" he shouts over the wind and rumble of the engine. He points toward a large red barn. I can't quite make out who, but two of the four brothers are up on the roof.

"Hold on!" I yell before I step on the gas and we go flying over the hills. I've never done anything this crazy before. I break out in a peal of laughter and he screams wildly in excitement. I have a feeling it's been a long time since he's felt this alive.

"Circle the barn." He has a death grip on the handle above his head. I take us around the barn a few times narrowly avoiding the workstation Ford has set up.

"Someone doesn't look very happy with you," he says after our fourth trip around the barn.

"Me?" I ask. He points to Wyatt where he's standing on top of the barn with his hands on his hips.

"You better stop and talk to him."

"This was your idea, Mr. Rivers." I press my foot on the brake and put the four wheeler in park.

"Mr. Rivers is my Pa. Call me Jack. I probably should have told you I'm not supposed to be riding on these things." He slaps the dash.

"Dad. Wren," Ford says with a stern look and crossed arms. "You know the rules." Jack and I climb out of the four wheeler like chastised children.

"I asked for a tour. He tried to warn me but I insisted he come with me," I say. Jack doesn't correct me. I don't blame him as I stare down the firing squad.

"Birdie, stop lying." Wyatt climbs down the ladder that's propped up against the barn. He's shirtless and wearing a backwards hat. It's a double whammy and has me salivating. He looks like he's doused himself in oil. His skin is so slicked down with sweat.

"I'm not. I did ask for a tour." Wyatt stands in front of me. His bare chest in my face. "Can you put your shirt on, please?"

"Nah, it's too hot," he says, fanning himself. I'd have to agree with him. I'm feeling particularly warm at the moment. "Keep looking at me like that and I'm going to give you a tour of the back of the barn," he whispers in my ear. Thankfully no one else is paying attention to us. They are too busy reminding Jack about the danger of him riding on the four wheelers.

"I didn't know he wasn't allowed to ride on them."

"It's not that he can't do it. We try to keep him from doing it. He almost lost his leg in a tractor accident. If he hurts his leg again, they won't be able to save it a second time. We try to avoid any situations where that's a possibility."

"Are they that dangerous?" The four wheeler felt powerful, but not any different from a car.

"It's the land. It can be uneven and rocky. You can easily flip or roll if you aren't careful. Especially if you come in hot the way you did."

My head drops to the ground. "I should have stayed at the house," I murmur. He tilts my chin up.

"You didn't come here to stay inside all day. Come on. I'll show you around."

"Don't you need to finish?"

"They can handle the rest." He holds out his hand and I grab it. He smiles. *Stupid dimples*. "Keys, birdie."

"I wanted to drive." I pout.

"I don't think so, Evil Knievel." He ushers me back toward the vehicle. "I'm going to finish Wren's tour. Can you or Mason get Dad back home?" he asks and tosses his shirt back on. The fabric immediately sticks to his skin like glue.

"Yeah. We can do that," Ford says. He narrows his eyes on the perpetrator. Jack gives me a wink before turning his attention back to his sons.

Wyatt starts up the engine and we drive down a different dirt path that takes us deeper into the empty green pastures. We drive past hay fields for miles. He points to the barns and animals in the distance closer to the main house. His rough, warm palm lands on my thigh, startling me. Leisurely he pulls at the loose threads on the hem of my shorts. It feels even better than I imagined having his hand on my thigh while we drive around. Does he realize how much he's turning me on right now?

"Do you want to see the animals?"

"I'm not sure. Animals don't usually like me very much."

His smile disarms me. "I doubt that. I bet you'll have them eating out of the palm of your hand in no time."

"If you say so."

"I know so," he says, as if it's knowledge gained from personal experience. That sends a flutter through my belly. What is that feeling?

We pull to a stop behind another barn-like building. This barn isn't as big as the one at the back of the property that's for the horses. Wyatt informs me this is where the goats are pinned when they aren't grazing somewhere on the farm.

"We're going inside?" I ask as he opens the gate.

"They're friendly. I promise. You'll be fine."

Hesitantly, I enter the fenced area keeping my eyes out for any goats. I expected to see an empty patch of grass for the goats to run around and graze. Instead, they have a playground. There are several different apparatuses for the goats to jump and play on.

"How many goats do you have?" I spot two sitting on a swinging platform.

"Six," he says from inside the barn. He grabs a bucket from the top shelf and passes it to me.

"What am I supposed to do with this?"

"Hold it out. This is how to get them to like you," he says, then whistles. Goats begin to swarm me from every side.

"Wyatt!" I scream as they take turns digging their heads into the bucket. "Stop that." I scold a little white goat who starts chewing on my shorts. "Take your turn," I say to another goat that tries to headbutt his way to the bucket.

"Having fun yet?" Wyatt teases as he pets one of his goat friends. I am having fun. Despite the initial panic, there is something calming about being around the animals. Once the bucket is empty, Wyatt shows me how to check their water and the pens where they sleep and get shade.

"What are the goats for?" I ask, keeping one eye on the goat that is following me around. He's really cute, but I know he just wants to eat my shorts.

"Dairy. We milk them every morning."

"Do you sell the milk?"

"Sometimes. Goat milk can be a hard sell. Willow does take it up to the bakery on occasion."

He continues the tour by showing me the cows, chickens, and horses. I have a list a mile long of all the things I want to research when we get back to the house. They have everything they need to turn this place around. I'm going to prove it to them. Prove it to Wyatt. I want to show him that he doesn't have to play baseball if he doesn't want to.

After dinner I begin to sift through the paperwork Faith left out for me. Occasionally one of Wyatt's brothers would sit with me and tell me what they want to do with their portion of the farm if they had the chance. Each one of them has a vision for the future of the farm.

A future that I want to help them achieve.

When Wyatt sits beside me and drapes an arm around my chair while I research the benefits of free-range chickens, for a moment I see a future for us.

It's unrealistic considering how different our paths are, but I see it. I *feel* it. And I don't know how I'm going to let it go when it's time.

20

WYATT

The bed is empty beside me. It's not just empty, but cold. Did Wren not make it to bed last night? I left her downstairs in the dining room doing research on goat's milk of all things.

She was in her element making lists and creating spreadsheets. My mom has given her access to all our financial records and our entire operation. I overheard her asking Ford and my dad what needed to be done every day to make the farm run efficiently.

My dad has really taken a shine to her. I'll never forget the look on his face when they came flying up the bend to the barn.

I throw on some clothes and head downstairs. The house is quiet. Unusual for this time of day. Normally everyone is busy shoving food and coffee down their throats before heading out for their morning chores.

When I walk into the kitchen I see why. Half my family is gawking at Wren asleep at the table. The others are in the den staring at a wall of sticky notes like they're at an art exhibit.

"Did she make it to bed?" Ford asks me.

I shake my head. "No, looks like she's been at it all night." I glance at some of the notes she's made.

"Her ideas are good." Colt nods and taps a finger on a notepad. "We can all get what we want." I'm sure they are, but they also take money. Money we don't have.

"And how do we accomplish," I turn the paper in front of Colt, "opening a bakery right now? That's money we don't have. We can barely pay the mortgage and taxes on the land."

"Wren's working on a budget," Ford says. I shake my head laughing quietly. Ford is pragmatic. Maybe more so than Wren. The fact that he thinks a budget as flimsy as the paper it's written on will be the magic key is laughable.

"A budget still needs to be funded. Where is the money going to come from? Do we have a grove of money trees somewhere I don't know about?"

"Keep it down. You're going to wake her up," Colt says. His comment infuriates me further. As if I didn't have any concern for Wren's well-being.

"All I'm saying is she's smart. She's broken down each item into tiny steps. Hence the sticky note shrine." Ford chuckles.

"I know she's smart," I snap. It's one of the things I like about her. "I'm taking her upstairs." I slip one arm under her legs and the other around her back.

"I wasn't finished," she mumbles sleepily into my neck.

"You can work on it later. Right now you need to sleep."

Once upstairs, I lay her down on the bed and tuck her under the fluffy, down blankets. "You have my brothers thinking you can save us." I kiss her forehead then remove her glasses and put them on the table where she can find them later.

Maybe she can. She already has me believing in things I never thought I would. I guess I can try and hope for a financial miracle too.

"Today we'll work on cleaning out the barn on the south side," I overhear Ford say as I reach the bottom step. The south barn hasn't been used in years. It sits between two vacant fields we haven't had the money to put to good use yet.

"Wren's right. If we sell what we don't need, we can use that money to fix the barn and prep the fields for a summer and fall harvest," Willow says.

"We can easily clear out the whole front field by the main road for parking," Colt says.

"Parking for what?" I ask, joining my family around the table. Eyes dart around the room silently discussing what to tell me and gauging my reaction.

"Opening up the farm to the public," Mom says.

"Is that something we can do? I thought the plan was to wait until we had more money to invest," I say.

"It was the plan before because it seemed impossible to do it without funding," Ford says.

"And now?" I question.

"Now, thanks to Wren, we have a solid plan. Look at this." Colt passes me a legal pad with the Newhouse Knight logo at the top. I chuckle to myself. Only she would bring office supplies with her on spring break.

The legal pad is now a step by step guide detailing what we need to do in order to open up the farm for a summer flower picking season. She's researched everything from what flowers to grow and when to plant. How much to charge and even calculated potential revenue.

"Here is the business plan for the summer." Willow hands me another notepad. How did Wren put all of this together in one night? "It's amazing, right?"

I nod. It is. Wren is amazing. She's thought of everything.

"Willow and I will work with Wren this week getting the marketing set up while y'all clean out and fix up the old barn. We need to either sell the junk or take it to the dump," Mom says. Dad mumbles something about there not being any junk in the barn.

"Then we can start working the fields here," Mason points to one of the open fields on the blueprint, "and here for planting pumpkins in July."

"Do you think we can pull it off?" I ask. It's something we've talked about doing multiple times. We know that opening up the farm and charging an entrance fee will be a good way to get revenue, but the logistics always felt overwhelming to figure out.

Knowing how to farm and knowing how to run a business are two different things, especially when your back is up against the wall financially.

"I do. We'll start small. I think that was our problem. We wanted to do everything at once. We can begin with the front fields. Give people driving by something to look at. Then every season we can vote and determine what project is next." Ford seems confident.

"What about the debt? The foreclosure threats on the land?" I ask.

"Your dad and I are going to talk to the bank. Wren thinks if we show them the business plan they may be willing to work with us knowing money will start coming in soon. If not, we can get an investor."

Me. I'll be the investor. And while I'm playing baseball, everyone I love will be here building our legacy without me. I hate it, but it's the only way.

"We should get started on the barn. Did you want to ride out with us, Dad? Tell us what you want to sell and keep?" Colt asks.

"Can I ride in the Gator again?"

"No. You got one over on the new girl. It won't work again," Ford says.

"We'll see about that," Dad mutters.

"Mama, can you have Lenny show Wren the chickens and how to get eggs when she gets up from her nap?" I didn't take her inside the coop yesterday. The goats were enough for one day.

"Sure, honey." Mom gives me a hug. "I really like her," she whispers in my ear. I like her too, Mama. I like her a whole hell of a lot.

"How did we manage to accumulate all of this crap?" Mason asks.

We've been clearing out the barn for at least two hours and it looks like we haven't even made a dent. This old barn is one of the original buildings on the land. It's four thousand square feet of rust and garbage.

"This stuff is not junk. They're antiques. Call up one of those pickers. They'll tell you the same thing," Dad says.

"It's junk, Dad. We should be taking this stuff straight to the dump." Colt walks out with another load of scrap metal.

"I'm going to call some of the guys to come up here. You'll see. I bet we have a thousand dollars by the end of the day." Dad pulls out his phone and starts texting his friends.

"A thousand dollars?" Ford raises an eyebrow. "What do you want if you win?"

"When I win," he starts, his eyes not leaving his phone, "I get to take my woman up to our hill on the Gator."

"She'll never agree to that," Mason says.

"I know how to handle my girl. Don't you worry about that," he says and we all snicker at him. No one handles Mama. That woman rules the roost.

"Fine. And if you lose, all of this goes to the junkyard where it belongs," I say, dropping a load of spare tractor parts in a pile.

We work for another hour then decide to call it quits. We've sifted through enough to give Dad's friends an idea of what we have. There's no point in us moving it all out if they can do it for us.

As soon as I open the front door, I'm searching for a pair of blue eyes. I find her typing away on my mom's laptop. Her hair's a mess on the top of her head with two pens sticking out of the knot. She's wearing another pair of cutoff shorts and a white tank top.

I need to thank whoever told her to bring those, because they are my new favorite thing. It's a far cry from the linen pants and blazers she wears around campus, yet it suits her perfectly. I have to force myself to walk towards the fridge and not run up to her and give her a kiss.

"Hey," I say walking into the kitchen. "Did you eat yet?"

"No. Not yet," she answers, without looking up from the computer.

"You need to take a break." I get out fixings for sandwiches.

"I will after I send out this email." Wren clicks away on the keyboard.

"Who are you emailing?"

The typing stops for a moment. I glance over my shoulder. Wren is biting her lip, eyes darting around the screen. "Uh, local photographers. I thought we could invite them to come to visit for a preview day. It would be good advertising. I haven't worked out all the details yet."

We. She said we again. What does that mean? And why do I want it to mean she's going to stick around and see this project through? Would she be able to? All of this will be happening at the same time she's supposed to be getting married.

"Did Lenny take you to see the chickens?" I ask.

"She did. They weren't as friendly as the goats," she grumbles, making me laugh. "One in particular has it out for me it seems."

"They'll come around. Eat," I say, placing a plate of food on top of some papers. "Photographers are a good idea." I take a seat opposite her. "I don't know how you got all of this done in one day."

"It's not that big of a deal."

"It is though, birdie. All of your ideas. The way you get everything organized. You have everyone working together. That rarely happens. Normally Ford is yelling at Colt and Mason is off doing his own thing."

"It was everyone's ideas coming together. This is what they want. I only mapped out the most efficient way to make it happen with the resources you already have available. It isn't a foolproof plan."

"You don't give yourself enough credit. You're really good at this." I take a bite of my sandwich as I admire the blush on her cheeks.

"Thanks. This is what I want to do. I like the challenge of finding feasible solutions to help small businesses succeed." A shy smile blooms on her face.

"And this is what you'll be doing working with your dad?"

Wren nods. "Mmhmm," she says, as she chews a bite of her sandwich. "That's the plan. There are still a few details to work out."

"It's your dad's company, they would be idiots not to take you."

"We'll see." Wren's uncertainty is strange. I don't understand why she thinks she wouldn't get the job. Is this why she's getting married? To guarantee a job? That doesn't seem right. What is she not telling me?

"Did you get the barn cleaned out?" she asks, changing the subject. I'm glad. I don't like thinking about her marrying someone else.

"Good enough for now. What's next on your list?"

"I was going to start working on social media but we need a name for the farm first. Everyone seems to have their own agendas on the matter. We do have a front runner," she says, smiling again.

"I can't wait to hear this."

"Lenny Land." We both laugh.

"Of course. Why didn't I think of that one?"

"I told Lenny she can maybe build a playground. She can help design it and name it whatever she wants. What?" she asks. I realize I've been staring at her.

"Nothing. You just amaze me. I like watching your brain work. It's hot. Turns me on." I waggle my eyebrows and put the last bite of my sandwich in my mouth. "I'm going to go shower. Then I want to take you somewhere."

"Alright. I'll finish up and put all this away so the table is clean for dinner." She takes her plate to sink.

"Birdie," I say. She looks at me over her shoulder. "We need to talk about something." I'm struggling to maintain control and keep my hands to myself. Last night I folded faster than Wren can fold one of my shirts. And right now she's barefoot in my kitchen looking real pretty with the afternoon light shining through the window making her skin glow.

She turns and leans against the counter. "What's going on?"

I walk up to her and tuck a stray hair behind her ear. Her eyes cut through any defenses I still had up. "I haven't hidden the fact that I'm attracted to you. If I was a betting man I would say you're attracted to me by the way you reacted to me last night."

"It's a pretty safe bet." She crosses her arms. I smirk.

"I want you, birdie. I'm done skirting around and playing games." I run a hand up her thigh and give her a good squeeze. Her hands find my chest.

"I thought you liked playing games with me." Her head tilts to the side and she smiles at me.

"You're right I do." I can't resist her any longer. I lean in and brush my lips against hers. The kiss starts off slow like we're still testing the waters. She digs her fingers into my hair and suddenly I'm a drowning man. Lost in this woman.

I pin her against the cabinet, slipping a hand up her shorts until I reach the trim of her underwear. I toy with the edge of the fabric with my thumb. "If I were to slip my finger inside you, would you be as wet as you were last night?" I kiss down her neck and over her collarbone. Inaudible words encourage me to continue.

"I bet you are. The question is, is it for me or did making all of those spreadsheets turn you on?"

"You and your dirty shirts and backward hats."

"Do you like me dirty for you?" I kiss her after she nods. "How about tonight I make you dirty for me and then I'll lick you clean?"

The front door opens. Wren tries to pull away, but I keep her in place.

"Not in the kitchen," Ford scolds, from behind me. "Cover your eyes, Lenny."

I wink at Wren. Her cheeks are rosy. I don't know if she's embarrassed or worked up thinking about the plans I have for her tonight. "I'm going to go get that shower now. I'll be right back," I say then press my lips to hers one last time.

"The kitchen? Really? I expect that kind of behavior from my brother, but not you," I hear Ford say as I head upstairs.

"We were talking. You can't talk in the kitchen now?" she sasses him back. I'm glad she feels comfortable enough to talk back to them. You have to hold your own in this family.

"Wren, I have a daughter. I know exactly what was happening in here. But sure, we'll go with talking."

"It's not *my* fault your brother is really good with his words."

I look forward to showing her what else I'm good at later tonight.

21

WREN

Wyatt drives the four wheeler around the south side of their property. We pass the old barn they've been cleaning out most of the day. Lenny waves at us from a large pile of scrap metal she's perched on.

The wind whips my hair and I inhale the fresh spring air. The air is crisper further away from the main house and all the animals. It's lighter and invigorating. It seeps into my skin making me feel free and untethered.

"It's going to rain soon," he shouts over the wind. "We won't be able to stay long." The clouds are starting to look angry a few miles out.

We weave around dirt paths, slowly making our way up the hill through a crop of trees. The elevation is gradual. I hardly notice it until Wyatt stops at the top of one of the many rolling hills where the land flattens out and the trees disappear behind us.

Below you can see the main house and the barns in the distance. I hadn't realized we traveled that far. The land surrounding us is wide open and gives the illusion that it goes on forever.

There are no boundaries here. It explains Wyatt's abhorrence to rules—he's lived with a freedom I've never known. I'm jealous of him in that regard.

A hundred yards or so behind us is a small barn. Yet, another building that looks to be on its last legs of life. A strong breeze would likely shake a few boards loose or tear at the roof.

"I love it out here. When I was a kid I would get all my chores done and then ride my bike up to this spot. Camped out in that barn more nights than I slept in my own bed."

Wyatt settles himself on the ground and taps the space beside him. Surely he doesn't expect me to lay right in the grass. There are spiders, ants, and Lord knows what else crawling around down there.

"Nothing's gonna hurt you. Come here and watch the clouds with me while the sky's still blue."

Hesitantly I lay myself down. The grass is cooler than I expected it to be. And soft—almost fluffy like a sponge. Wyatt scoots closer until we're shoulder to shoulder. His skin is warm and comforting compared to the cooler air from the impending rain.

"It's pretty," I say.

"My favorite color blue. There is something about staring at the sky and the clouds that makes you think about your life. What are you thinking about right now?"

"Who says I'm thinking anything?" I ask.

"I can hear your mind working overtime, birdie," he jokes.

"Maybe I'm thinking about all the promises you made in the kitchen." I shift my body and turn toward him. I lean on my elbow and pick at a few blades of grass.

"I haven't stopped thinking about last night."

I run a finger through his wind blown hair. "Are we going to survive this?" I ask.

"I'm not sure what you're asking me."

I don't know if I'm sure either. "I might regret saying this, but I kind of like having you around. I don't want us to sleep together and have everything be weird afterwards."

He wraps his arm underneath my body and pulls me closer to him, grabbing my thigh and yanking it over his. "I woke up this morning with you just like this." He hugs me tighter. "I could get used to that." The heat in his eyes knocks my breath loose. "But I know I can't."

"Because you don't do relationships."

He looks away then back at me. "Right. And you don't do feelings. We're the perfect candidates for a no strings attached relationship. Purely physical." He squeezes my ass for emphasis.

"No feelings, no strings," I mumble. "Until graduation?" I question.

"Until we're done," he says. Graduation is a few months away. Considering Wyatt only sleeps with a girl once and he's done, I can see how continuing until graduation would feel like too much of a commitment.

"And then we're back to friends?"

"Always, birdie."

I hope he means that. I can't predict the future. I know we both have a lot to get through. I really want my best friend by my side for all of it.

"Good." I reach down and run a hand over his dick. He begins to harden under my touch. "Because if you haven't noticed, we aren't in your mama's house right now." Not that I was able to stick to my little rule last night.

That rule flew out the window the minute he walked out of the bathroom in his underwear.

"Fuck." He flips me on to my back. "You want me to take you right here? Fuck you into the dirt?" He rolls his hips and I feel every hard inch of him. Yes. I think I would like him to do that very much.

Out of nowhere lightning strikes in the distance and two seconds later thunder crashes.

"Damn it." He groans into my neck. "We better get out of here before it's too—" Wyatt doesn't reach the end of his sentence before gallons of water start dropping from the sky. He hops up and pulls me with him.

He is a blur in between sheets of cold rain as he runs toward the four wheeler. My glasses are fogging and I've lost my sense of direction. I'm completely disoriented. "Wyatt!" I scream out for him.

"I'm here. We're going to have to make a run for the barn. Take my hand."

The rain hits my bare arms like a thousand needles as we slip around on the slick grass. My hair is plastered to my face making it even more impossible to see.

"Almost there," he shouts. Good because my legs feel like they might give out.

He lifts the latch on the barn door and pushes me inside first. It's dark. Not quite pitch black, but it might as well be with my poor eyesight.

"Don't move. I'm going to turn on a lantern."

"You have one?" I ask, wringing the water out of my hair.

"Among other things. We'll be good here until morning."

"Morning? We can't stay here all n-night." I start to shiver. Even without the rain and wind, it's freezing in here.

"Why not? It will be an adventure," he says, as he moves around the barn. Suddenly a warm yellow light begins to glow. "It isn't much but it will do."

"I-it's b-better th-than n-nothing."

He rushes to me. "You're freezing." He pushes my wet hair off my face. "I'm going to get you a blanket."

Now that there is light, I walk around the barn in a pathetic attempt to get warm. It's nicer on the inside than I thought it would be. The ground is mainly dirt with a few patches of grass growing through the cracks between the ground and the wooden walls.

He digs inside a trunk in the corner and comes out holding a few wool blankets. They don't exactly scream cozy. I suppose now isn't the time to be picky.

He lays one down on the dirt. Then proceeds to take off his shirt.

"Wh-what are you doing?" I ask. My eyes are glued to his sculpted body.

"We'll freeze in our clothes. You need to undress and wrap up in a dry blanket." He unbuttons his jeans and begins to step out of them. With a blanket wrapped over his shoulders, Wyatt gives me his back and takes off his underwear. Interesting. Is he shy or being a gentleman again?

He's draped his clothes over one of the stall rails. I do the same with mine. Wyatt doesn't take his eyes off me as I speed walk toward him completely naked to get my blanket. If I wasn't freezing, I would have at least attempted to look sexy.

"Warmer?"

"A little." I lay down on the blanket in the fetal position and try to keep myself from shivering. It isn't working.

"Let me keep you warm, birdie." Wyatt lifts his blanket enough for me to slip underneath it. I bury myself in his chest while he works to readjust our blankets so they are layered and covering both of us. "Is this okay?"

"Fine except for your dick chaffing my thigh. Can you put it away?" I shiver and inadvertently rub myself against his erection making him growl.

"No, I can't put it away, birdie. I'm not a Mr. Potato Head. I can't remove my cock and put it back on when it's time to use it."

"That's not what I mean. Tuck it in or something."

"Sure, I'll put it away in my penis pocket." He glares at me. "You're one to talk. Your nips are drawing on my chest like a damn Etch A Sketch every time you move."

"I'm freezing. I can't help it. Isn't your dick supposed to get smaller when it's cold?"

Lightning strikes over the pasture, lighting up the barn in a quick flash. I flinch and dip my head deeper into his chest.

"Typically yes. Except you're here. And when you're around, well, this is what happens." He runs a hand down my back. It's meant to be comforting but instead it's turning me on. The light caress sends shivers down my spine.

I drag a hand down his side. His skin breaks out in tiny goosebumps under my touch. I do it again and his muscles seize. He looks at me with a fierceness that has my heart beating out of my chest.

His fingers curl around my hip. Is it a warning? Or is he encouraging me?

"You going to finish what you started outside?" he asks.

"I think I might." Snaking my arm up his chest and around his neck, I run my fingers through his hair and tug gently. Just enough to pull him closer to my mouth.

For me kissing has always been the equivalent to putting keys in a car. You do it once to start the car and get the engine going. Once I got the guy turned on, I didn't need to repeat the step again. I didn't want to.

When I kiss Wyatt, we aren't just kissing to get to the next thing. His lips roam over my body with precision as if he is drawing a map and making notes on how I respond to his touch.

He kisses my neck and scrapes his teeth over the freckle I have there making my hips buck and my body slide against his. He travels lower down my chest, his mustache grazing my sensitive skin. I've decided that I am very much pro mustache and look forward to this same feeling between my thighs.

He pushes me on my back and covers me from limb to limb. He's keeping me warmer than any blanket ever could. "I missed you last night," he says, working himself further down my body.

Cool air washes over my body as he positions himself between my legs. I'm so desperate for him after watching him walk around the house in his jeans and ripped shirts exposing all of his oblique muscles. I'll never complain about folding his old ratty T-shirts again. In fact, I may go through all his shirts and cut the sleeves off myself.

"I was looking forward to doing this all day yesterday." He drags his tongue up my left thigh. My body shivers and it isn't from the cold. "Kept thinking how good you were going to taste." He licks my right thigh and bites me at the juncture of my thigh and hip, making me whimper.

He spreads my thighs apart with his shoulders. My muscles burn from stretching further than they're used to as he licks me up my wet center and my heels dig into the blankets.

"Fucking delicious," he says, before going back for another taste. I move my ass around and pull on his hair to get him where I want him—where I need him—but he doesn't seem to care. He throws his arm over my hips, pinning me down.

"Wyatt," I plead with him. I need more.

"Is this what you want?" he asks, putting a finger inside me. "You liked this the other night." He adds a second finger stretching me. "Or maybe you want me to play with your clit.

That's what really gets you going. Doesn't it, birdie?" He licks and sucks on my clit while working his fingers inside me.

"Yes!" I moan and tighten my grip on his hair. He switches out his fingers for his tongue. His mustache tickles my skin and when he pushes against my clit, my muscles tighten and waves of pleasure roll through me. "Wyatt," I say, breathlessly as he continues to clean up the mess he's made of me.

He crawls back over my body, kissing me as he goes. He cages my head in with his arms and drags his cock between my legs. The sensation is almost too much. "Wyatt," I plead, clinging to his biceps.

"Fuck, you feel so good. Look at how desperate your greedy little cunt is for my cock." He adds a little more pressure and I almost come again. Instead he pulls back. "No way. You don't get to come again until I'm inside you," he says, then speed walks over to where we laid out our wet clothes to dry. He comes back with a condom and hands it to me. "Put it on me, birdie."

Drunk on desire he kneels between my legs like a statue. I want to study every sculpted inch of him. I run a finger along the ridge of bone at his waist. He tenses and shoots me a warning with his eyes. I rip the foil package open with my teeth and toss it aside. He releases a feral groan when I finally wrap my hand around him.

I take my time feeling the smooth velvety skin of his cock and teasing him, before my impatience gets the best of me.

He removes my glasses and puts them to the side. I start to protest. I won't be able to see him very well. I can see enough to not run into walls, but I barely caught the wink he gave me the other night. I'm guessing it was a wink. He could have just been blinking for all I know.

I don't want to miss his smile or the way his brow bends in concentration.

"Just feel me, birdie," he says, placing my hands on his face. "Feel what you do to me." He pushes the tip of his cock inside and releases a low groan. Then drags it back out slowly and pushes back in at a similar speed. He takes his time allowing me to acclimate to his size.

There is a gentleness to his touch that is unexpected. His movements are purposeful. A hand on my face. Then my breast and down my side and back again. He dips his head into my neck, kissing and nipping my sensitive skin.

"Birdie," he groans my name. "Feels fucking perfect, birdie."

My heart careens with his words, falling deeper with this man. It's too much, but I can't stop begging him for more.

"Is this the best you got?" I ask to provoke him on and remove the weight I feel on my heart. "You said you would ruin me."

He takes a slow breath, then grips me underneath my thighs and thrusts into me hard enough to knock the wind out of me. He pulls his cock out slowly, almost to the tip, then slams back into me again. "Is this what you want?" He folds himself over my body to whisper in my ear.

We're alone in the middle of nowhere. There's no need to whisper. Yet, he does. He draws me near and grips the back of my neck.

"Do you want me to fuck you so hard your cunt only craves my cock? Because I will."

"Yes. That's what I want," I say, dragging my nails across his skin clawing at his back. He grunts and growls into my neck, pumping harder, faster, striking me exactly where I need him most. The tension builds down my spine. I wrap my legs around Wyatt, pulling him closer as my pussy tightens around him and I come.

"Fuck, baby." His hair falls over his eyes and I push it out of the way. I caress his face, looking for any indication of how he's feeling. His jaw is tight and he's biting down on his lip. His cock swells then pulses inside me. "Do you feel that?" he asks, cradling my face in his hands. I nod. "Do you feel how good you milk my cock? You're fucking perfect." He leans down to kiss me.

I want to see his eyes. They tell me so much. His brown eyes turn dark when he's aroused and have a little glow when he's happy. Other than the outline of a grin and dip of his cheeks from his dimples, I'm clueless.

He collapses on top of me in a sweaty heap. I welcome the pressure. I can blame the heaviness I feel on his body weight and not the emotions I have swirling through me from having sex with my best friend.

I've always treated the act of intercourse as procedural. There were steps. The final step of getting dressed always occurs immediately after the climax, then we say goodbye and don't speak until our next hook-up.

It worked for me. It kept everything clean and easy. When the situationship ran its course, there was no love lost. We went on with our lives as if nothing happened.

There is no walking away from this—from him. My fingers comb through Wyatt's hair as we catch our breaths. His lips rest on my shoulder. One of his hands tenderly rubs circles on my side.

Once you have a man like Wyatt Rivers in your grasp, you cling to him as tight as you can and hope you are strong enough to last for the whole ride.

22

WYATT

"Well, well, well, look who the cat drug in. Did you and your little bird have a nice night?" Colt starts in on Wren and me before we've made it one step into the kitchen.

"We did," Wren answers with a gleeful smile. "Wyatt gave me five orgasms," she whisper-shouts, making Colt choke on his sandwich. I kiss the top of her head, laughing.

"I think it was more like six." We had sex one more time before we fell asleep and then I woke her up at some point in the middle of the night to do it a third time. I couldn't keep my hands off of her.

Wren uninhibited is a world wonder. Her begging for me and the feeling of being inside her was too much. I had to keep a slow pace so I wouldn't climax before I even had a chance to enjoy being inside her. That's never happened to me before.

We headed home when our stomachs started growling too much to be ignored any longer. The paths were still slick and muddy from the rain. We made it back a little dirty, but in one piece.

She starts counting her fingers. "I think you're right. It was six. Four and five kind of blend together since you did that thing with your tongue," Wren says, passing me the mayo and mustard from the fridge as if this is an ordinary conversation.

"This is too much information," Colt grumbles.

"Why so bitter? Lenny's teacher still not paying you enough attention?" I pass Wren four pieces of bread. She spreads mayo and mustard on them, then slides the plates over to me. I add the meat and cheese. Then she adds lettuce to her sandwich and tomato to mine.

We work in sync cleaning everything up and putting it away. She takes both plates to the table while I grab our drinks.

Colt stares at us dumbfounded. "How long have the two of you been together again?"

"A few months," I answer.

At the same time Wren says, "We're not together."

"What I mean is we've been friends for a few months. But Wren's right. We're not together." Why is that difficult to admit? We went over this last night and decided to be friends with benefits. And boy are there benefits.

"Right. I'm going to go join Dad and Ford in the barn. His picker friends are here. I want to see if he's going to win the bet."

"What bet?" Wren asks.

"Dad bet he could make a grand off all that scrap metal in the barn. If he wins, he gets to take his *woman* out in the Gator," I explain.

"And now you know what happens when a Rivers man takes his girl out on the Gator." Colt winks. "Are you going to do any work today or are you taking the day off?"

"I'm working. What do we need to do?"

"Ask the boss." Colt nods to Wren.

"I'm not the boss, Colt." She rolls her eyes. "Willow mentioned something yesterday about moving some of the seedlings from the greenhouse to the fields on the east side."

"That's outside," I tease Wren.

"I can handle it."

"There will be dirt and bugs. You'll probably sweat."

"I'm becoming a fan of the dirt," she says, biting her lip and eyeing my dirty T-shirt. We're both in desperate need of a shower after spending the night in the barn.

"Y'all flirt weird," Colt says, before walking out the door. He's not the first person to say that.

Wren shakes her head at Colt and goes back to eating her sandwich. "Were you flirting with me? Trying to turn me on about getting dirty?"

She ignores my questioning and eats the last bite of her sandwich. "If I was flirting with you, you wouldn't have to ask me." She takes our plates to the sink, rinsing them, and placing them in the dishwasher. "You would know."

I push away from the table and lean back in my chair. "I would, huh?"

"Yep." She crosses her arms over her chest.

"Give me an example."

"That's the thing. I'm not really a flirty person. I prefer the direct approach." She says this as if it's a bad thing.

"Give me an example."

Wren walks up to me and stands between my legs. I slide my hands up her thighs just under the hem of her shorts. I can't get enough of her wearing these damn things. She traces a finger up the veins in my arms.

"I'm going to go take a shower. I want you to join me." She starts to back away, but I pull her against me. I tuck a strand of hair behind her ear.

I want to tell her that I like her direct. I like her mean. I like her bossy. I just like her. Plain and simple. She isn't ready to hear all of this because for some reason she has it in her head that she is too much. That she's cold and unlovable.

Which is odd because I find her to be the exact opposite of everything she thinks of herself.

Instead I say, "First one naked is the first one to orgasm." I slap her ass. She yelps then takes off upstairs.

"We made good progress today." Ford takes a sip of his beer.

We're all sitting out back around the fire pit roasting marshmallows and making s'mores. Mason has his guitar out and is picking at the strings.

"I won my bet," Dad says, holding up his beer.

Wren giggles beside me. "He's never going to stop talking about that is he?"

"Probably not." I pull my marshmallow from the fire and scrape it off the stick between two graham crackers. I take a bite and hot marshmallow strings all over my mouth.

"You're a mess." Wren swipes her thumb across my lips.

She's mentioned more than once that some people find her attention to detail frustrating to deal with. They clearly haven't had her full attention on them. When I'm the one she is fixated on, I feel like a king. "It's all over your mustache too. Another reason to shave it off." She licks the sticky, white residue off her thumb.

"You weren't complaining about my mustache in the shower earlier. In fact, I'm pretty sure you said it felt good against your—" She slaps a hand over my mouth.

"You've made your point," she says, cutting me off. I grin at her.

"When are you going to hire more help?" Colt asks Ford, grabbing my attention. I know we need more hands on deck, but labor isn't free. Especially if it's something more permanent.

"I don't know. We may have to do without it this time." Ford takes a long sip of his beer. This is taking a toll on him. His brow is wrinkled with worry.

"You should check with the high school. See if there are any kids looking for volunteer hours. They can help with parking, crowd control, and the petting zoo area. The rest of you can handle ticket and product sales."

"That's a great idea, Wren," Mom says, beaming at my girl. "I'll get in touch with Donna tomorrow." Donna is the principal at the local high school.

I put my arm around Wren and kiss her on the side of her face.

Ford, Mason, and Colt discuss more logistics of the spring and summer harvest. I want to give my opinion and offer help, but it doesn't matter since I won't be here. I'll be living miles away or on the road in some hotel.

Wren squeezes my thigh as if she knows what I'm thinking. But that's impossible. There's no way this woman knows me well enough to read my mind.

But the way she is looking at me and urging me to say something to my family, proves she does know me. Maybe even better than I know myself.

"Take a walk with me?" I ask close to her ear. She nods. "We'll be back."

"Sure you will," Ford says. Giving me a knowing look. He's right. We probably won't be back.

I take Wren's hand in mine and walk her down the path that leads to the horse pasture. They are all in the barn for the night, but it's one of the safest paths to walk in the dark.

"You need to tell them." Wren rests her head on my shoulder.

"Tell them what exactly?"

She stops walking abruptly, yanking my arm back. "That you don't want to play. That you want to stay here and be a part of everything. You sat there and let them shut you out."

"It doesn't matter. I have to play. They're doing the right thing. They should be making plans without me." I kick a piece of gravel.

"You don't have to play. The debt isn't from baseball. It was a slow accumulation over the last forty years. Your daddy took over this place in debt from bad business decisions and back taxes. Add in college tuitions and hospital bills and it all stacked up. It wasn't you."

I shake my head. "It doesn't matter. It was a sacrifice either way getting me to all my practices and buying me new cleats and bats. Paying for uniforms and private coaching. You may not have found it in the paperwork but it's there. Regardless of where the debt stems from, we still need the money. I've got to pay them back."

Is it nice to know it wasn't entirely my fault that we're close to losing the place? Yes, it eases a little bit of guilt. It doesn't however change anything.

"So do it here." Wren runs her hands up my chest. "Pay them back by being here. You don't think working the fields and being a part of everything will be paying them back? You don't think they would prefer to have you with them? They want you happy, Wyatt."

"I can't risk it being enough."

"You act like you've already signed a contract in the majors. It's not guaranteed either."

I slide my hands down to her ass. "It is. I'm good, birdie. You've seen the way I play." I grin at her. Her cheeks blush. *Fucking adorable.* "I'm predicted to be drafted in the first round. San Diego needs a left-handed pitcher."

"San Diego!" Wren steps out of my reach and turns her back to me.

"It's not set but that's who keeps coming to look at me."

"It's far from home," she says quietly. It's far from me is what she means. The unsaid words squeeze my heart.

"It is but nothing a plane can't fix." I move to stand in front of her. "I'll fly to you. Every chance I get. I'll come to Atlanta and visit. You think your husband would be okay with that?" I ask. Wren flinches.

"Don't."

"Don't what? Talk about your future? It's okay to discuss mine but we can't talk about what you're going to be doing? How is that fair? Your choice will have a bigger effect on us than mine will, I promise you that."

She turns on her heel and begins walking at a fast clip down the dirt path.

"Birdie!" I yell and start chasing after her. I grab her wrist and pull her toward me. "Don't run away from me. We were talkin'."

"You're the one who's running off to California. Could you pick a place further away? At least I'll be here," she says, stomping a foot.

I grip the back of her neck. Not hard, but firm enough to get her attention. "You think that makes any of this easier?"

She'll be here in the arms of another man. I'd rather take my chances in California than have to be witness to that.

"Then stay! Believe in your family and what they're doing. Believe in me." Wren grasps at my sides hard enough to leave a mark.

"I do believe in you. I told you—"

"You told me my ideas impressed you. That I'm smart and good at what I do. But you don't believe in me. If you did, you wouldn't still be thinking about baseball. You would take the same chance with the rest of us."

"The rest of us? You say it like you're sticking around. Are you? I keep hearing you say 'we' and 'us' like you're going to be here this summer. We both know you won't." I squeeze the back of her neck. "Are we going to talk about your future now?"

"Maybe that's it," she says. "I wish I had the option to be here. I wish I could choose this." Her eyes close and a single tear drips down her cheek. I wipe it away with my thumb. "You can stay and you won't do it."

There is a lot to unpack in that statement. She wants to choose this. To choose me. Is that what she's saying? Instead I focus on me and the choice I need to make for myself.

"You really think it will work?"

"I know it will."

I pull her into my arms. "I believe in you, birdie. I'm your number one fan." I dip my head into her neck and she wraps her arms around my middle. "Will you show me everything tomorrow? Then I'll decide. But don't doubt for a second that I don't believe in you."

"I believe in you too. And your family. This place. It's something special."

Is it foolish of me to think that if I stay, maybe she will too? That maybe I can get her to believe in us one day as much as she believes in this farm and my family?

23

WYATT

"Lenny, you done with your chores already?" Ford asks when Lenny shows up where we've been planting all morning.

"Aunt Wren is getting the eggs but I finished everything else," Lenny says. I don't correct her that Wren isn't her aunt—probably because I like the sound of it too much.

"Can she do it by herself?" I ask. Last I heard, Wren still isn't on the best of terms with the chickens.

"I showed her the other day. She said she could handle it." Lenny shrugs. Ford looks at me to see what I think.

"I'm sure she'll be fine." No sooner do I get the words out there's a scream from the chicken coop. We all turn to see Wren fly out of the coop with her hair all over the place.

"I'm okay!" she shouts over to us. Then pushes her hair out of her face and walks proudly back to the house with her basket of eggs.

"Told ya she'd be fine." I grin at Ford and Lenny.

"I'm going to go check on her. She may need my help," Lenny says, then runs off to the house.

"I think Lenny likes her," I say.

"The whole family does, Wyatt. I'd say you more than like her." My brother Ford. Always so observant.

"It doesn't matter. She's not mine to like forever. Not like that." Saying it out loud doesn't make it feel any more true. She feels like she's a part of me, like someone I'm going to be missing a whole hell of a lot in a few months.

"I thought maybe the two of you were getting closer."

"We are." It's all I'm willing to say about Wren. Every day I feel myself getting more attached to her. And I think she is feeling the same way. You don't shed tears over someone leaving if you don't care.

The more I think about what she said last night. I know she's right. I can choose this. I've had it in my head for so long that baseball was the only way. But maybe she's right.

"What's got your mind turning?"

"What's next." I wipe sweat off my forehead with my shirt and adjust my hat. "I keep thinking about what's next for me."

"You're going to get drafted and play baseball." He moves to the next section of dirt with another tray of plants. The planter broke down again forcing us to do everything by hand until Colt can get it fixed.

"And if I didn't?"

"Then you work the farm with us. Unless you've got Georgia on your mind." His lip tilts in a grin.

"Is it that simple?" I ask, ignoring his Georgia comment.

"Why wouldn't it be?"

"Do you think Mom and Dad would feel the same? They won't be disappointed that I'm wasting my talent? All the time and money they spent. I'll be washing it down the drain."

"Everything they've ever done has been for us. To see us succeed. To see us happy. I sometimes think about Lenny growing up and leaving. Maybe she wants to be an astronaut."

"If anyone would try, she would."

"No shit. I'd have a hard time seeing her leave but I'd give her everything I had to make sure she was prepared to go."

"And if she decided to stay here and help run the farm?"

"I'd count my lucky stars. You'd give up the majors to muck stalls and bale hay?"

"In a heartbeat. I love the game but not more than I love being here. I don't know if I'm meant to live that life. I like nights under the stars more than I do stadium lights."

"Whatever you decide, they'll support you. They just want to see you happy."

"That's what Wren said too."

"She's a smart girl."

Wren and Lenny come strolling out of the house toward the old barn we're going to transform into a temporary store front. They both have clipboards in their hands and look like they mean business.

"I wonder what they're up to?" I ask.

Ford glances up to watch the girls walk past the barn into an empty field. "Lenny Land," he says, with a smile. "Wren asked her to draw up her plans. They are working on a presentation and proposal to show everyone. You're not the only one who's going to take a hit, if she doesn't stay. Figure out how to keep her around."

If I knew how, I would. I'm not sure I'm enough for a girl like her to stick around for. All I've got is dirt for miles and a dimpled smile. It's nothing like the life she has planned for herself back in Georgia.

Ford cleans up all the empty trays and heads back to the greenhouse for another load leaving me to my thoughts. Not really where I feel like being right now.

"What are you doing in here?" I lean against the open barn door. Wren is sitting on her knees with a piece of white poster board in front of her. She looks at me over her shoulder. I'll never get tired of having those eyes looking at me.

"I'm trying to map out the layout for the shop. Willow and Colt gave me a list of what needs to go in here but I'm not sure it will all fit."

"It'll fit. It always does. You just got to work it in." I thrust my hips back and forth.

"Do you have to make everything sexual?"

I pull her up from the ground and into my arms. "With you? Always." I give her a kiss that ends too soon for my liking. "Do you want any help?"

"Are you going to actually help me or just stare at my ass?" She raises an eyebrow.

"I can multitask. Ain't nothing going to stop me from looking at you." I push stray hairs off her face. Wren's hair has a slight wave to it now that it's being dried in fresh air and sunshine. No more slicked back ponytails. I find a feather and snag it out of her hair.

"Things got a little out of hand in the coop this morning. We have an understanding now."

"You and the chickens?" I'm trying hard to keep a straight face.

"Yes. They're going to enjoy a nice snack outside their coop in the morning while I retrieve all the eggs."

"What happened with this one?" I twirl the feather between my fingers.

"She missed the first memo. Lenny warned me that Pancake doesn't listen very well. I don't understand how she can tell them all apart."

"That's Lenny for ya. I'm glad you and the chickens are getting along now, birdie."

"Just in time to leave in a couple days." She steps out of my arms and back to her plans on the floor.

"They'll still be here when you visit." I'm planting ideas, hoping they'll grow wild in her head.

"They will probably forget our arrangement by then."

"I'll remind them while you're gone," I say.

"So, you're staying?"

"I think I am. I still need to talk to my folks. I can't imagine being anywhere but here." Except wherever Wren is. I can always see myself beside her.

"I'm proud of you for choosing what you want," she says, not taking her eyes off the drawing in front of her.

"Whatcha thinking, birdie?"

"Nothing." She's got her creepy fake smile painted on her face. "We should get started if we're going to have this done before dinner."

I tip her chin up. "I'm here when you're ready to talk about all those nothings that are bothering you." I kiss the top of her head.

Wren lets out a deep sigh that resets her back to her robotic factory setting. She directs me around the barn taking measurements and mapping out the different parts of the store. Once we're ready, Colt and Mason will build the check-out stands and flower arranging tables out of scrap wood we have lying around.

"What did Willow say she wanted over here? We were just talking about it this morning." Wren stares at the corner of the barn. "It's on the tip of my tongue. Damn it. I knew I should have written it down."

"I've got something for the tip of your tongue," I mutter to myself as I finish taping off where she wants the cutting station to go.

"What was that?" She whips around in my direction. I stand up, holding the roll of tape.

"Nothing. Don't worry about it."

She steps closer to me. "No, I want to know." Her palm meets my chest, branding me through my shirt.

A long sigh escapes me. She's not going to let me walk away from this one unscathed. Maybe if I flip my hat backwards, I can distract her. I've done it before and it's worked like a charm. Her eyes trail up my biceps as I lift my arms, removing my hat and shaking out my hair, before flipping it on backwards.

She bites on her lower lip, then raises an eyebrow. "Nice try. What." She takes a step forward and I move back one. "Did." Again, she moves closer to me until she has me pinned in the back corner of the barn. "You. Say?"

The scent of wildflowers nearly suffocates me as she push es her body against mine. Her blue eyes are a shade darker than usual. *Is my little bird turned on?*

"I said. I have something for the tip of your tongue."

Her eyes rake over my body. "Prove it." She takes a small step back and waits.

"You want me to whip out my dick?"

"If that's what you intended for my tongue? Then yes." She puts her hands on her hips. I glance at the front door of the barn. "They've seen it before, buckaroo." She smirks.

"I'm going to kill Colt for telling you about that." With a sigh, I unbutton and lower the zipper on my jeans. Then whip my dick out like I would if I were taking a piss except I'm rock hard at the moment.

Wren steps forward and drops to her knees. Her hands stroke up my thighs until she reaches the waistband of my pants and underwear. She looks up at me for consent before pulling my jeans and underwear down around my ankles.

One of her hands caresses my bare thigh and my dick grows harder in my palm. Her eyes go wide and she licks her lips. Taking my dick in her hand she strokes me gently, before licking from root to tip. "Fucking hell, birdie."

"I licked it so it's mine. That's the rule, right?"

"Yeah, it's yours, birdie. What are you going to—" *Fuckity. Fuck. Fuck. Fuck.* Wren wraps her lips around my dick and sucks me down whole. Her hands roam over my thighs and my ass while her mouth and tongue work me over.

I pull her hair out of the band and add it to the other one of hers I wear on my wrist. Collecting all of her hair, I wrap it around my hand and hold the back of her head.

"Do you know how many times I pictured those lips around my cock?" I ask. She responds with a whimper. "I jerked off more than once to the thought of your pretty eyes staring up at me like this."

Her eyes water as she bobs her head on my cock. I wipe them away when they fall on her cheeks. Hollowing her cheeks, she sucks me down faster. My grip tightens on the back of her head and she slows down, edging me back from my orgasm. I grin down at her.

"Are you going to let me cum down your throat, birdie?" I ask. She responds by running a finger down the crack of my ass and massaging my balls. Fuck. She's too good at this. "I'm close," I warn her. She nods the best she can.

My muscles tighten and I groan out her name. She slides her hands up and down my thighs as her mouth swallows every last drop from me.

When I'm done, she silently tucks me back into my briefs and buttons my jeans. I wipe the moisture from her eyes and fix her hair back up in the messy bun thing she had earlier. "Birdie." I pull her in my arms and kiss her soft and slow. She clings to me like she's desperate for me.

"Wyatt," she pleads with me.

"Do you need me to take care of you?" I kiss her down her neck and bury my face in her chest. "Did sucking my cock get you all worked up?"

She nods and scrapes her nails down my back.

"Come on. I can't do what I want to do to you in here where anyone can walk in." I take her hand in mine and start walking us out of the barn. "I can't believe you just did that."

"Are you complaining?"

"Fuck no! But the next time you do that, I want you naked and sitting on my face."

"You're pretty confident there will be a next time."

I stop in my tracks halfway to the house. "Did you not like doing it?"

"No. I enjoyed it very much."

Such a Wrenism. So polite. *I enjoyed it very much.* "Anytime you want to enjoy yourself, the pleasure is all mine. But now, the pleasure will be yours." I race us back to the house, passing my brothers on the way.

"Where's the fire?" Colt asks.

"Probably going to have another one of their talks. Is that what you're doing, Wren?"

"Yes. Very important things to discuss. Probably need to have the same conversation two or three times."

"For fucks sake," Colt curses. "This is too much information!"

"See you at dinner," she says with a wave.

God, I love this girl.

The thought should freak me out. Weeks ago it would have. But fuck, I really do love her. She's nothing like me, but fits me perfectly. She pushes me and challenges me.

I love her and it's going to hurt like hell to let her go in a few months.

24

WREN

"Are you alright? Your eyes are leaking," Lenny says. She's cuddled up with me on the couch. We've been here most of the afternoon researching ideas for her outdoor play area and drawing out plans. Now we're watching one of her favorite princess movies.

"I'm fine, Lennon. I'm happy for her," I say, referring to the princess who's flying around the sky on a magic carpet. That seems to satisfy her enough to focus on the television again.

I've watched this movie more times than I can count when I was a kid. It's always been one of my favorites. I don't ever remember crying when the prince pulls up on a flying carpet offering to show her a world of shimmering stars and wondrous places.

Being here in my own new world. Having a man open my eyes to new things.

I don't know how I'm going to leave. I...

Sucking in a ragged breath, I let another tear fall.

I know I have to go. I have things I need to deal with. A pending engagement. An engagement I don't want, but I don't know how to get out of it without knowing the ramifications of saying no.

If Fred Abbott is capable of blackmailing his own son, what could he do to my dad?

Is my happiness too big a sacrifice? Can I give up Wyatt for my family? The thought is crushing. It steals my breath and cools my blood. It didn't matter before.

Before Wyatt.

Is that how I will think about my life now? The person I was before him and who I am after him? While at my core, I am still the same person. There are parts of me that are permanently altered because of this man.

We are leaving for Newhouse tomorrow and the thought makes me sad. I'm going to miss everything about this place. I'm going to miss fighting with the chickens every morning and getting head butted by goats.

I'm going to miss late afternoon walks where the sun warms your skin and cool nights sitting around the fire with everyone.

I'm going to miss waking up to Wyatt. I'm going to miss his fingers making circles on my back or on my thigh. I'm going to miss him snuggling behind me early in the morning before he leaves for a long day out on the farm.

I'm even going to miss the dirt and all the bugs.

Jack and Faith casually offered me a job the other night after dinner. I don't need the money. Working has never been about the money to me. It's about being useful and creating something valuable. I could do that here.

I could stay. I know my mom and dad would understand. They've always encouraged me to follow my heart.

If Wyatt wanted me to and if I can solve my fiancé dilemma.

Maybe Daniel would understand. If he knew there was someone else, because there is.

I snatch my phone off the coffee table and send him a text.

ME

> I know I said we could go through with the engagement but things have changed. I'm sorry.

My phone dings almost immediately.

DANIEL

> I don't think you understand what my father is capable of. We have to see it through.

ME

> I'm sorry he is keeping your money hostage but I can't help you with that anymore. You will have to figure something else out.

DANIEL

> He knows about Wyatt and his family's situation. He's been tracking you.

ME

> Why would he do that? They have nothing to do with you and me.

DANIEL

> They will if there isn't a you and me. He's been talking to people and asking questions. I have no doubt he will try and use your attachment to Wyatt to get what he wants.

ME

> Why is being connected to my family so important to him?

DANIEL

> I don't think you understand how prominent your family is.

He's right. I don't. I know my mom came from money and my dad has paved his own way. Even though my mom is the reason this marriage was even a thought, she didn't raise me with the same beliefs and principles she grew up on.

ME

> He has to take my no as an answer.

DANIEL

> He may take it but there will be consequences.

The screen door bangs closed before I have time to really process his text.

The Rivers boys push and shove their way inside. Colt and Mason nod hello and head straight to the kitchen for sustenance.

Ford and Wyatt crave sustenance too. In the form of hugs and kisses from their girls. Ford sits on the ottoman and pulls Lenny into his arms. Wyatt is dirty and sweaty but I lean into his embrace.

"I've missed you Lenny bug. We could have used your help out there," Ford tells his daughter.

"Next time, Daddy. We had a lot of work to do before Wren leaves tomorrow," Lenny says.

"Have you been good for Wren?"

"What do you think? I even gave her extra cuddles when she started to cry. Just like you do when I'm sad."

"You were crying?" Wyatt asks. His eyes are etched with concern.

"It was a sad part in the movie. That's all," I try to reassure him.

"It wasn't really. It was the fun part when they fly around the sky." Her words are directed at her dad. Wyatt's eyes are drilling into the side of my face but I can't find the strength to look at him.

"Lenny, everyone has different experiences. It's okay that Wren got sad and it's okay that it made you happy," Ford explains.

"Are you sad?" Lenny asks.

"No," I whisper. I rub my wrist with my thumb.

"You're really going to lie to Lenny," Wyatt says into my ear. I glance at him. Tears sit in my eyes ready to fall. He sees it too. "Come with me." He stands up abruptly.

I give Lennon a quick hug and meet Ford's eyes over her head. He offers a weak smile. I don't know if he feels bad for Lennon tattling on me or if he knows Wyatt is about to interrogate me.

Taking Wyatt's hand, I let him lead me upstairs to our room.

"Strip," he says after locking the door.

"You can't boss me around like this," I say.

He doesn't even acknowledge me. Instead he goes into the bathroom and starts the shower. By the time I get in there he's already taken off his shirt and is working on his jeans and underwear.

"Birdie. I'm not asking again."

"You didn't ask me the first time," I snap. Then I rip my shirt off over my head. I step out of my shorts and underwear, and join him in the shower.

He's standing under the stream of water with his back to me. I kiss his left shoulder blade and then his right one.

Resting my head against his back, I wrap my arms around him. The pads of my fingers dig into the hard muscle of his abdomen. He sighs and the storm inside him begins to calm.

He turns to face me and maneuvers us where I'm standing under the spray. He cradles my face in his hands. His touch is tender. I want him to be demanding. That I can handle. I can fight that. Wyatt being sweet like this makes me puddy in his hands.

"I don't know why you were crying. I'm guessing it's another one of those nothings you are being surreptitious about."

"Good one," I say softly. It's been harder to play our little game out here since we're so busy, but he's managed to get a few words in here and there.

"If you need to cry, you can cry in here and no one has to know."

Wyatt kisses me with so much love I feel it in my toes. The kiss opens the floodgates. Tears stream down my face, mixing with the water from the shower.

I can't identify the feelings behind the tears. It feels like years of frustration from holding it together. For pretending to be strong when I should have let myself fall apart.

It's also sadness and grief. I feel the loss of a life I could have had with Wyatt and it's gut wrenching. In a few months there is going to be a giant hole in my heart and I don't know how to get myself out of this mess.

Wyatt is silent as he washes my hair and my body. He makes quick work of cleaning up himself while I stand numb and afraid of our future.

He wraps me up in a towel and carries me to bed. "Feel better?" he asks, tucking us in.

"A little. Thank you."

He pulls me closer into his chest and our legs tangle together.

With a sigh I say, "I don't know how I'm going to say goodbye." *To you.* I think to myself because I'm afraid to admit it out loud.

"Me too, baby," Wyatt says, squeezing me tighter. His words make me think he knows I'm talking about him and maybe he doesn't want to say goodbye to me either.

"And you said everything in that old barn was junk," Jack

gloats as we eat our ice cream sundaes on the screen porch at the back of the house.

One of the items buried in the barn was an antique ice cream maker. The kind you have to hand crank. He's spent the last couple of days cleaning it and giving it new life.

That's a personality trait he has passed on to all of his children. Each one of them sees the beauty in something when everyone else is blind to it.

"Yeah, yeah, you found maybe five things we can use," Colt says.

"That barn stored the farm's history." Jack turns to me. "My family founded the town of Rivers Bend. My great-great-granddad came here and fell in love with the place. He said the land sang to his soul. He walked this land and knew it was where his family was meant to be."

I look out to the wildflower fields and up to the hills where Wyatt plans to build a house one day. I feel the land too and the stirring in my soul. The urgency to plant roots so deep into the ground I can't be moved. I want to leave my imprint here because after a few short days it's left one on me. It only seems fair that I get to do the same.

"Are you trying to tell me those hills are alive with the sound of music?" Colt jokes, making everyone except Lennon laugh. The reference to *The Sound of Music* going over her head.

"Joke all you want kid. You know it's true. Once you're here it's hard to leave."

I squeeze Wyatt's thigh just under where my knee is resting. We're sitting on the little loveseat together. He's been keeping his hands busy running his fingers from the hem of my shorts to the top of my knee since he devoured his ice cream in three bites.

"It is true," Wyatt says. He takes hold of my hand. "Dad. Mama. I've decided I'm not going to enter the draft. I don't want to play baseball after I graduate. I want to come back home and work. I know we need the money."

"Money don't matter," his dad says, interrupting him. "Are you sure you don't want to play? Growing up that's all you wanted."

"I'm sure. Dreams change. This is what I want to be doing. It's been hard enough being away at college the past few years."

"Those years served a purpose," Faith says, looking directly at me.

"They did," Wyatt agrees. His grip on my hand tightens.

"This will make you happy?" Faith asks.

"It's a start." Wyatt's eyes burn into mine leaving so many words unsaid.

"There'll be time for that too," Faith says like the true matriarch of this family. Knowing and seeing everything we can't. She knew there was something between Wyatt and me the first time she saw us pull up in his truck.

"I'm glad you're going to be staying Wyatt. It isn't the same here without you." Willow leans over from where she's sitting and gives him a side hug.

As soon as we get back to Newhouse, I have to come up with a plan to get the upper hand with Fred Abbott. He may think he holds the match but I'm holding the fuse. I'm not going to let him get close enough to blow up my world and everyone I care about.

25

WREN

It's been two weeks since I said goodbye to Wyatt's family. Being back on campus feels wrong. I spent the first few days cleaning out my closet. None of my old clothes felt right after wearing jean shorts and sundresses.

I've taken on more tutoring jobs and buried myself in schoolwork. Anything to keep my mind occupied. If not, I'm constantly thinking about kidnapping Wyatt and driving us back to Rivers Bend.

How about that for something wild and spontaneous?

After a lot of contemplation, internal debating, and lack of communication on Daniel's end, I decided I needed to go to Georgia and handle the situation with him. I don't have the time in my schedule for this trip but it needs to be done.

I also don't have the emotional bandwidth to continue to question and guess what will happen. With graduation looming, my time with Wyatt is coming closer to an end unless I do something about it.

I told Wyatt I was going home for a few days, but I didn't tell him why. Just that I wanted to see my family. I purposefully picked a weekend he would be out of town playing so he couldn't come with me. I know he would have tried.

Honesty, I don't know what to tell him. Until I know how this is going to play out, I don't want to get his hopes up. Assuming he has hopes of us staying together and making something out of what we've started.

We aren't in a real relationship. He isn't my boyfriend. Our agreement ends at graduation or before, if one of us wants out. Even if he decides he doesn't want a relationship with me. If he decides he wants out, I can't get married.

I pull into my parents' driveway and take a deep breath. They were surprised to hear I was going to drive home for a visit. I didn't tell them I was here to speak to Daniel either. That would give my mom the wrong idea.

I find my mom in the living room reading a book. Her hair is pulled back in a tight bun, and she is lounging in a blouse and dress slacks. It looks uncomfortable and overdressed for lounging around the house after being surrounded by jeans and cotton shirts at Wyatt's house.

"Hi, Mom," I say.

"Wren, you look great." She takes in my air-dried hair and casual attire of jeans and button up shirt. Not quite what I was wearing on the farm, but more relaxed than I was dressing before. "How was your drive?" She greets me with a hug.

"Uneventful." And it was. Without Wyatt singing off tune or asking me a million questions, it was boring. I missed his enthusiasm for the alphabet game and spotting road signs.

Riding in a car will never be the same after having him drive me around for hours with his hand on my thigh.

"Sometimes that is a good thing. I'm so glad you're here. Did you have a nice spring break?" My mom takes my hands and urges me to sit on the couch with her.

"I did. I went with my friend to his family's farm for a few days."

"How was that? It doesn't sound like something you would volunteer to do," she says with a knowing smile.

"It was actually really nice. His family was very welcoming. I was mainly there to help them with resurrecting their farm and business. They were spinning their wheels trying to keep it afloat."

"Let me guess. You showed up with your brilliant mind and came up with a plan to turn things around." Her lips tilt in amusement.

"Something like that," I mumble.

"And your friend?"

"What about him?" I ask, avoiding eye contact.

"Your dad had led me to believe that the two of you were growing closer. He mentioned there might be more to your friendship than casually spending time together."

"I'm not sure how he came to that conclusion by the information I've given him. I only asked him for advice on how to handle some of the hurdles they are facing in their business," I explain.

"He knows his daughter well. So do I. There is something different about you and I have a feeling he has something to do with it. Will you tell me about him?"

I settle myself deeper into the couch cushions. "There isn't much to say about Wyatt. He's the most infuriating man I've ever met. He's messy and loud. He's impulsive. He takes one second to think about the consequences before taking action. He eats entirely too fast."

She is grinning ear to ear. "He's made quite the impression on you. You like him. Do you love him?"

"I'm not sure if that's something I'm capable of doing. But I care about him a lot. It won't matter if I can't figure out a way to get out of this situation with Daniel."

"Wren," she says with a thread of sadness. "You are capable of loving another person. I don't know why you would think you aren't. And if you do love him, which I suspect you do, there isn't a situation with Daniel to worry about."

"What about Mr. Abbott? Dad would lose a lot of business." Not that I think he will continue to work with him once I tell him what Abbott is going to do to Wyatt's family.

Mom takes my hands in hers and squeezes. "Your dad loves two things more than anything in the world. You and me. That has always been the case with him. Losing business will not faze him. If you want to be with Wyatt, then that's what you should do."

"I'm not sure how Wyatt feels about me. I'm not an easy person to love."

"What are you talking about? Why would you say that?"

"It's something I've always thought. I'm so much like dad and you said he was hard to love. I put two and two together." I shrug.

"Wren, honey, I fell in love with your father within days of meeting him. He was so smart and steady. He made me feel safe." She smiles to herself as if she just remembered a private joke between the two of them.

"I lived my life high in the sky. I was like a hot air balloon floating aimlessly until your dad came along and anchored me. If you overheard me saying he was hard to love, it was a comment to a friend in jest or annoyance. He probably abandoned another cup of coffee randomly around the house." That is something he does often. "Loving him is the easiest thing I've ever done."

"I always thought..." I shake my head. "I'm glad that is the case for you and Dad. I'm not sure it's the same for me and Wyatt."

"Have you told him how you feel about him?"

"No. I'm not sure I could."

"Sometimes it's hard to put love into words."

"It doesn't matter. My life is in Georgia."

"Yes, but your heart is in Alabama. You can't live without your heart, Wren."

"What do you suggest I do?"

"First we're going to talk to your dad about this engagement. I don't know the details of their business arrangement. What I do know is that your father will stand by his family. If this relationship needs to be severed then that's what needs to happen."

"Okay. And then?" I question.

"That's up to you. You'll need to figure out what it is that you want and how you plan on getting it. If there's one thing I know about you, it's that when you decide what you want, you don't stop until you get it."

Dad sits in a leather wingback chair behind his large oak desk. For the last hour we have been discussing my future with Daniel, or lack thereof, and his relationship with Mr. Abbott.

I let him know everything Daniel told me about his dad's intentions to get more involved in our company by marrying me off to his son, the fact he is blackmailing his own child, and potentially threatening Wyatt's family.

"He responded to my request to come over for a drink and discuss business. He should be here shortly. Remember to stay calm and don't let him get under your skin. Let him think he has the upper hand. We need to let him talk. Make him believe he is running the show."

"And if he doesn't like that we're calling everything off and severing our relationship with him?"

"Too bad. I've always known Fred was ruthless. It's part of what's made him good at what he does. I won't work with a man who thinks he can come after my family, let alone stoop low enough to target his own child to get what he wants."

"I'm sorry this isn't working out how you wanted." I look down at my hands in my lap.

"I'm not. My gut was telling me something was off with him. It has been for a while which is why I haven't been letting him in on any of my projects. Have you decided what you are going to do after graduation?"

"I'm not sure," I say. My heart is pulling me in one direction, but the idea feels as unpredictable as the wind. Wyatt hasn't asked me to stay. I feel like I'm building my future on sand during the high tide.

Dad opens his mouth to say something but decides otherwise. Instead, he clicks around on his computer pulling up the email I sent him last week. With permission from Jack and Faith, I've given my dad more details about the farm and the future plans. "Tell me more about the business."

"Like I mentioned, according to all the legal documents I've read, once the land is free and clear, the property will be divided equally between the five children."

"Will they want to sell their shares at some point?"

"No. They want to expand and build out the land with other businesses. Willow wants a bakery, and Colt has plans for a brewery."

"I see." He continues to read over the different business plans I composed with what little direction I had to go on.

Faith asked me if I could put together what I would for any other client that was looking for an investor. Then said, *"Tell your dad thank you."* I don't know if that was her way of asking for help without actually asking or if she knew I was going to ask him to help regardless of a formal request.

"Do you think we should invest in them?" he asks. It's something I've mulled over since I first learned of their situation. I always knew our firm could step in and help because we have the resources, financially and otherwise.

"No," I answer honestly. If he's surprised, he doesn't show it. "If the company helps, they will lose a large percentage of what they have worked so hard to keep. I don't want to do that to them. They need to retain all interest in their business."

"What do you want to do? While your starter plan is brilliant, it's a Band-Aid when what they need is surgery."

While the fact that Fred Abbott is digging for information about the farm behind the scenes escalates the situation, it was my heart that decided this was the right thing to do—not my head.

I readjust myself in my seat. I don't know how he will react to what I'm about to suggest. "I want to be the sole investor. My trust will cover the debt and leave enough to foot the bill for some of the smaller construction projects. It will be enough to get them off the ground and generating revenue again."

"You want to invest?" His eyebrows furrow. "I thought you didn't want to take away a percentage of the company with an investment."

"I wouldn't be. They would retain complete ownership according to the original agreement of the land when they purchased."

"Wren, I have to advise you against handing over hundreds of thousands of dollars for nothing in return." He pauses. Leaning back in his chair. "It wouldn't be, would it?" he asks, putting together what I knew after one night with Wyatt. "That money is meant for your future and your future is there with Wyatt."

Emotions begin to bubble out of nowhere. I do my best to rein them in. I don't mind crying in front of my dad, but I don't want to look like I just had an emotional breakdown before Abbott gets here.

"He hasn't asked me to stay. However, I wasn't planning on giving him much of a choice." We promised each other before we started our friends with benefits situation that we would remain friends. Even if he rejects me, I will still be there for my best friend.

"This feels like the right thing to do. It wouldn't be without any stipulations. I've thought about it." Using my trust fund and savings isn't what Jack and Faith had in mind when they asked for my help. They were entertaining a partnership. I can't do that to them. "Will you help me with the paperwork?"

"Of course," he answers. There's a loud knock on his door. "We'll talk more about the details later. Remember, give nothing away." I nod. "Come in," he calls out.

I steel my spine and wait for Fred to enter the room. My dad stands to greet him. The energy in the room shifts immediately. For someone who is so eager to be associated with my family, you would think he could hide his disdain a little better.

"Wren, how nice to see you," he says, greeting me.

"Hello." I don't bother getting up.

Fred takes the seat beside me while my dad fetches them both drinks. It's tempting to have one myself but I prefer to have all my wits about me for this conversation.

"If we are discussing wedding plans, shouldn't Daniel be here as well for this conversation?" Fred asks.

"That won't be necessary. Wren and I have been talking. There isn't going to be a wedding," Dad says. He's relaxed in his chair with his scotch while Fred looks ready to erupt.

"It is happening. We decided years ago."

"Years ago when they were teenagers, it was idle chatter. It had no weight to it. You were the one who presented the idea again a few years ago. Why?" Dad's tone is casual. He is doing his best to be amicable. Friendly fire still has a twenty percent death rate. The question is, who's going to shoot first?

Fred's eyes narrow slightly. "They would be a power couple. Together they would run both companies. They make sense together." His hand grips tighter on his scotch. "Daniel cares about Wren. He will be devastated."

I scoff. Dad's eyes dart to me with a warning to stay calm.

"I agree both of our children will make great assets to each of our firms, but they are on different paths. I've gone over the logistics and it's no longer beneficial for us to partner up, personally or professionally."

Fred's face flushes and his eyes narrow on my dad. "What are you saying exactly?"

"I'm saying that we will no longer be doing business with you. I am severing this connection." My dad leans forward onto his desk.

"You may want to rethink that," Fred warns.

"Are you threatening me? Remember, I have just as many connections in this city as you do. You do not want to mess with me or my family."

Fred stares at my dad silently for a moment. Then he turns his attention to me. "Did you have a nice spring break, Wren?"

"It was fine." I refuse to elaborate or offer him a modicum of ammunition to use on me later. He doesn't know I'm already aware of everything he is about to say to me thanks to Daniel's warning.

"I never thought you would be one to go on vacation in Rivers Bend. There isn't much to that town anymore." He pauses for me to respond. I stare at him waiting for him to continue until it gets awkward. It is an interview tactic I've picked up from watching murder documentaries with Wyatt. Fred will have to fold or reveal his cards. I'm not saying anything.

"Except for your friend. The farmer." His stare is cold and calculating. "It is quite the predicament they have themselves in. I would hate to see them lose everything."

Dad stands and leans on his desk. "Is that a threat?"

"Take it for what you will. I've done my research. That land they are sitting on will make a pretty penny parceled off and developed."

It takes all my strength to keep my mouth closed and to stay seated in my chair. I know that what I want to say will only infuriate him further and push him even more over the edge. I can't do anything that will make him take action against Wyatt's family.

There is only one thing I can say that will stop him but I'm not willing to do that either. We will have to call his bluff another way. I will have to beat him to the punch.

Fred stands and pulls something out of his pocket. He places a small box on the edge of dad's desk. "I'll leave this here. I trust you to make the right choice. If not for you, then for your friend. I'll be watching," he says, before heading toward the door.

"Oh, and Wren, you may want to end your little fling sooner than later. It will be easier. If not, I'll send Daniel up one weekend to take care of it for you. I'll see myself out."

Once he clears the room, I feel like I can breathe again.

"Bastard." My dad curses which is something he never does. It makes me laugh. I'm sure I look psychotic. My dad joins me. It feels good to laugh. It's as cathartic as crying.

It might even be better. Laughing feels like winning. Crying feels like defeat. I won't let that man win this battle. It isn't about me anymore.

Wyatt and I are partners. Maybe not in an official capacity. And it may only ever be friends. I can accept that. What I can't accept is delivering the enemy to his door. He has fought too hard to lose everything because of me.

"I'm not going to let him ruin Wyatt's family," I say, once I get my emotions under control. I stare at the ring box. "If this is what it takes, then I'll do it. I just need to hold him off long enough to get the property free and clear and in their names. Can you start the paperwork with getting the money out of my trust and paying off the debt?"

"It could take a while."

"I know. This is the only way. Otherwise Abbott will call in favors and try to get to them before we do."

"I think it might be best if I handle the correspondence with the Rivers family. I don't want there to be a connection to you until it's necessary. If he's been watching you at school, who knows where else he has eyes. We have to be careful. I can cover all our interactions under a different project name."

"Okay. That sounds smart."

"Can you give me the list of stipulations you have? I will get the papers drawn up for the family to sign when it's time."

"I can do that."

"And Wren. I think you should limit your interaction with Wyatt as much as possible. You don't want to give Fred any reason to make him act before we're ready."

I agree. It would be smart to keep a safe distance. Make it appear that we aren't seeing each other. Considering all I want to do right now is crawl into Wyatt's arms and seek the comfort I know only he can give me, limiting our interactions won't be happening.

When did the guy who only offered a good time start feeling like forever?

WYATT & WREN

WYATT

Have you seen my shirt?

The Morgan Wallen one.

Check behind the couch cushion.

That's where you ripped it off me.

We should do that again.

WREN

Not there. Maybe you left it at your parents' house.

WYATT

Or maaaaayyyyybe...

You took it.

WYATT

325

Are you coming over?

I just got home.

WREN

I'm about to leave. Do you want me to get dinner?

WYATT

Already ordered.

Get over here woman.

WREN

Koa just showed up at Sydney's. He's knocking and yelling through the door.

WYATT

What else is happening?

WREN

I can't see much through the peephole.

WYATT

Go outside and redo your bulletin board or something.

WREN

I'm not going to do that.

WYATT

I don't want to play today.

WREN

I'm going to tell Ford to stop texting you.

WYATT

It's not that.

I just don't care.

WREN

Do you care about Hart? Koa? The rest of your team?

WYATT

Yes.

WREN

Those guys are still fighting for their jobs.

You don't quit on people. Finish what you started.

Win and make them look good.

WYATT

That was a lot of texting birdie.

Get here early so I can kiss you before the game.

26

WYATT

"Saw Wren in the stands," Koa says as he slips on his shoes.

"Yeah." I smile thinking about the make out session we had in my truck before the game started. "She's coming over tonight." I pull a clean shirt over my head.

"Never thought I'd ever see you with a girlfriend."

I wince. "She's not my girlfriend. We're friends." I throw a few things into my duffle and add, "With benefits." I'm crossing my fingers and toes that she's enjoying said benefits enough to stick around this summer.

"Wren was cool with that?" Koa asks.

"Wren doesn't do relationships either. Never found the need for them. She wouldn't have said yes if I asked her to be my girlfriend or anything serious. We agreed to no strings attached over spring break."

"How's that working out for you?" Hart asks. There are only a few of us left in the locker room. Usually he is one of the first guys showered after the game and rushing out the door to see Lauren.

How is that working for me? Not good. I laugh. "There are so many strings I could do fucking macrame over here."

"What the fuck is macrame?" Hart's eyebrows scrunch together.

"It's when you take cord or yarn or whatever and knot it together to create art, a plant holder, jewelry, all kinds of things," Koa informs Hart.

"How do you know that?" Hart asks him.

"Syd got into making them for a little while. She has a giant wall hanging and a few holders for her plants." He shrugs.

"That's great. Now, back to me," I say. "Should I tell Wren I want more?" Asking her to be my girlfriend feels wrong. Not because I don't want to be exclusive with her. Fuck, I am exclusive with her. I've bent and broken every rule I've ever had for this girl.

I'm not ready to book a church and call the preacher, but the word girlfriend doesn't feel like a big enough title for what she means to me.

I know something happened when she went home to visit her parents a few weeks ago. I expected our relationship to change when we got back to school. I knew our lives would take over once we left the little bubble we created on the farm.

I'm busy with practice and traveling for games. She has her tutoring gig that is monopolizing more of her time than I would like.

There's something off beyond our busier schedules. Call it gut instinct or intuition or my newfound ability to hear Wren speak in her silence.

Anytime I ask what's bothering her, she shuts me out and says everything is fine. I know my girl. She is keeping something from me. Just like the day she was crying over that movie she was watching with Lenny. There was something else going on then too.

Wren doesn't break down, but to have her cry in front of me stirred up a whole new set of feelings. It about broke my heart to see her upset like that.

"Can you do long distance? She lives in Georgia," Koa says, giving me information I'm well aware of.

"She can always move." I throw my bag over my shoulder. "She knows where I'll be. She was the one who encouraged me to stay home in the first place. Wren wouldn't have done that unless she was okay with living there too."

"Or if she had no intention of the two of you being more than something to pass the time. She has dreams of her own just like you do," Hart says.

"Way to kill the vibe," I grumble. Wren is ambitious. It's one of the things I love about her. We head out of the locker room to find the girls waiting for us outside near the parking lot.

"If you want her, tell her." Hart gives one final piece of advice before he goes to Lauren.

He's right. I need to say something. But bringing it up will change everything. I'm not ready for her to call it quits and walk away if it's not what she wants.

It's a worry for another day. Right now Wren looks edible in a black tank top and jean shorts. I'm happy to see they have made it into her campus wardrobe.

I greet Wren with a kiss. Her arms wrap around my neck. I let my bag drop to the ground. Pulling her closer, I revel in the way she melts against my chest.

"Hi, ," I mumble into her neck as I inhale her sweet perfume.

"Hi. You looked good out there."

My hand roams up her side, until I reach her boobs. I really like playing with these. I run my thumb under the cup of her bra and her body responds to me immediately.

"I wanted to look good for my girl."

"I bet she was impressed." Wren fingers comb through my hair.

"I have a few more things I can impress you with." I bite her ear. "Let's go home." I pick up my bag and take her hand.

"How did your coach take the news about not entering the draft?"

I squeeze her hand. It was a conversation I wasn't looking forward to having but I'm glad it's out of the way. "I don't think he was surprised. He scouted me. He knows my story. Family has always been a priority."

"How do you feel now that everyone knows?"

I place my hand on her thigh once we're situated in my truck. I don't know how to drive without my hand resting here. "Relieved. The pressure I've felt building the past year is gone. As soon as I committed to my family, I could breathe, birdie. I have been drowning for years. I was finally able to break through the surface and take a breath."

"Do you think you'll miss playing? I'm going to miss seeing you out there," Wren says, unabashedly.

"I won't miss the sore shoulder after every game. I can always play in the beer league in town if I ever feel like throwing the ball around." Sometimes I think it would be nice to build a field on the farm for kids to come play or host charity games.

"For the record," Wren says while she waits for me to unlock the front door. I open the door for her and she walks in under my arm. "You look even hotter when you're hauling hay." She tosses the words over her shoulder.

I drop my bag by the door and chase after her. Before she can reach the stairs I throw her over my shoulder like I would a bale of hay. "Tell me more." I smack her ass making her squeal.

"I will but first you need to get naked." She pushes her hand down the back of my shorts and smacks my ass back.

"Jesus. Fuck, birdie." I jump when her finger hits my asshole, making me trip. Her giggle is her only saving grace. Otherwise I would punish her for making me almost fall down the stairs while I'm carrying her.

"Can you put me down please? All the blood in my body is rushing to my head."

"I can relate," I say, sliding her down my body. "I need you naked and on my bed." I tear my shirt off over my head and throw it onto the floor along with my shorts and underwear. Wren looks at the pile of clothes strewn all over the room. "We'll get it later, birdie. Arms up."

She raises her arms and I strip her of her tank top and bra. She slips out of her shoes while I work on her shorts and underwear.

I jump onto the bed and lay down, making myself comfortable. "Come sit on my face, I'm hungry." Wren walks to me with confidence. I've always loved this about her. Not a shy bone in her body, but she saves it all for me.

She straddles my thighs and takes my cock in her hand. With a firm grip she begins to stroke me. Damn I love it when her hands are on me. She knows exactly where to put more pressure. "Shouldn't I be the one rewarding you? You had the win today."

"This is rewarding me." I take her hand in mine and help her get into position. "Now, hold on to the headboard and tell me what else I do around the farm that makes you wet."

"We could be here a while," she sasses.

"I've got all night, baby."

Fuck, this view is everything. Blue eyes peer down at me over the curve of her breasts. I slide my hands up her torso and cup them in my palm. Her head drops back elongating her neck.

Wrapping my hand gently around the base of her throat I say, "Start talking." I run my thumb over the length of her neck as she swallows. The simple movement makes my cock thicken even more.

I grasp her hips and position her over my face. She hovers for a moment before fully seating herself. *Fucking heaven.*

I run my tongue through her center. Her moan sends a direct message to my dick. I bite her thigh when she stays silent. She inhales a sharp breath. As much as I love all the little noises she likes to make, I need her words right now.

"Talk or I'll bite you again."

"Your shirts," she says. I flick my tongue against her clit. "The ones that are ripped down the side. I like that I can see all your muscles through the big hole." She grinds down against my face hoping I'll stay on her clit. I know exactly where my girl needs me but I'm not going to give it to her too soon. She's going to have to work for this one.

"Hats," she moans. "Baseball caps or the cowboy hat. I don't care. When you take your shirt off and tuck it into the back pocket of your jeans." She gasps when I dip my tongue into her tight hole.

I lap at her skin, trying to get every last drop. She chases after her orgasm, completely forgetting about our deal. When I start to lift her up she fights against me. "What are you doing? I was close."

"I know. I'll take care of ya, but you have to be a good girl and keep talking."

Her frustrated growl is so fucking cute and turns me on even more.

"Hammering fence posts, mending the roof, playing with the goats." She gasps. "Wyatt," she draws out my name on a moan. Pressing down on my face, she stretches into my tongue, putting even more pressure onto her clit. "Oh, God," she moans.

Without giving her a moment to recover, I flip her on to her back. I have a condom on before she can blink and I'm sliding inside of her. Nothing feels as good as being inside Wren and having her come on my cock.

Her fingers run through my hair guiding me as I kiss and nibble on her skin. "You know what gets me hot?" I ask, slowing my pace.

"What?" Her hips flex, urging me to speed up, but I won't give her what she wants. I'm in charge right now.

"Your shorts. Your legs fucking drive me nuts." I squeeze the outside of her thigh. "The way your hair blows in the wind. The way your ass looks in a pair of jeans. Do you want me to keep going?"

"Yes." Her eyes burn into mine.

"The way you think. You're so smart. Fuck, it's hot the way your brain works. When you sing while you do laundry. I can barely hear you but it gets me hard every time." I work my hips faster. If she keeps clenching around me like she is, I'm not going to last much longer.

"The way you smell." I dip my face into her neck. "The way you pretend that I annoy you."

"I'm not pretending," she rasps. The slight tilt to her lips tells me otherwise.

"Birdie, I know you're lying." I lean back to switch up the angle. "And even if I do annoy you." Thrusting into her harder, I say, "You love it. Are you going to give me another one?" I ask, stroking my thumb over her sensitive clit.

She nods and locks her legs around my waist. Driving into her deeper with this position, my spine starts to tingle and my balls tighten. "Fuck, Wren." I pump into her a few more times as she tightens and spasms around me.

I hold her for a minute then give her one more kiss before pulling out and going to the bathroom to clean up. A few moments later, Wren pops the door open joining me.

"What are you wearing?" I stop in my tracks. She has on that damn Newhouse baseball jersey. "You need to take that off." I'm seconds from losing it. I know she is not wearing that motherfucker's jersey after I was just inside her.

"Are you sure?" She bites her bottom lip. She's lucky she's so fucking cute.

"Yes, birdie. Take it off."

"Fine." She sighs, turning around to change.

I don't know why she turns around. She's never hid her body from me, but then I see it. My last name is on her back.

"Stop." I take a deep breath. "Leave it. Please," I beg.

She freezes with her arms half raised over her head. She smirks at me over her shoulder. "I can't believe they were right. You realize this is crazy?"

"Don't give a fuck. You look so fucking hot right now." I wrap my arms around her and pull her tight against me. "Come on, I need you again."

"Seriously?"

"Yes, I'm running out of days where I'll be able to do this." I don't want to think about how true that statement is. Graduation hangs over my head like an anvil waiting to drop.

Is that when we say goodbye? How do I get her to fight for something with me? Because I'm willing to tear apart anyone who tries to steal her away.

27

WYATT

The worst part about a string of road games used to be bad hookups and hangovers. Now, it's being away from Wren for several days in a row. It's been sleepless nights because she isn't in my arms.

I miss her like crazy. Even with text messages and video calls, it isn't the same as holding her or kissing her goodnight.

I barely made it off the bus before I was texting to let her know I was coming over. She should be home studying if she's sticking to her usual schedule.

I climb the stairs to her dorm room two at a time. I'm impatient. I'm dying to see her. After a few quick knocks, Charlie opens the door and lets me in.

"Hey, Charlie."

"Wyatt. Congrats on your wins," she says, locking the door.

"Thanks. Is she in her room?"

"Yeah. She's had a rough couple of days. She'll be glad to see you."

Wren never mentioned anything on any of our calls. She did seem more tired than usual, but I assumed she stayed up too late waiting for me to get back to my hotel or studying.

I open her door slowly. The lock clicks getting her attention. Wren throws the book she's reading on the bed and catapults herself into my arms.

"Hey, baby." I bury my face in her neck. It's like coming home every time. She might as well get a tattoo of my lips in the spot on her collarbone since I kiss her here so often.

"I missed you." She presses her lips against mine. Her hands rake over my face and into my hair, and her thighs clamp down around my waist. It's a spiritual experience having her in my arms. She makes a believer out of me.

"I missed you too." I cup her face with one hand and her ass in the other.

"Only seven more games left in the season."

It's a bittersweet reminder of what's coming. It's not something I like to think about. I want to play this game with her for keeps and I'm worried she's still playing pretend.

Having her welcome me like this leads me to believe she sees a future for us in some capacity. I know I need to man the fuck up and ask her about it, but I'm a greedy motherfucker. There's a chance I could bring it up and send her running in the other direction.

I walk us over to the bed and put Wren down. She backs up to lean against the headboard and opens her arms and legs to me. That's an invitation I can't refuse.

I kick off my shoes and crawl onto the bed to rest my head on her stomach. She runs her fingers through my hair. She's going to put me to sleep if she's not careful.

"How's your shoulder?" she asks as she moves her hands down my neck and over my back.

"It's been worse." It hurts like a bitch. I'm glad I'm not starting the next few games. If we weren't trying to win another championship, I would ask Coach to bench me.

Wren's legs jostle underneath me. "Switch places with me and take your shirt off."

"What are you doing?" I ask when she straddles my legs and sits on my thighs. I wish she was a little higher, but this is a good start. She's still within reach.

"Give me your hand." She squirts lotion into her palm.

"Can't wait to see where this is going. Looks kinky." I place my left hand in hers. She lifts an eyebrow and grins.

"When you pretended to need a tutor all those months ago, you put your hand on top of mine." She runs her palm over the top of my hand spreading the lotion around. "I couldn't believe how cracked and abused your hands were. I thought it was all from baseball. I didn't know."

Wren uses both of her hands to work the lotion into my knuckles and fingers. They do look like shit after years of baseball and farming. She adds pressure, massaging the overworked joints. After several days of pitching, this feels amazing.

She's really fucking good at this.

"I didn't know how hard you worked and everything you carried on your shoulders. I judged you. I'm sorry. I thought you were...a joke." She bites down on her lip. "I didn't think you knew how to take anything seriously, including the importance of a good moisturizer."

She adds more lotion to her hands and works her way up my forearm and to my shoulders. She finds a knot in my pitching arm and massages it with her fingers and knuckles.

"Now I know the truth. You're the hardest working person I know. You love your family. You carry the world on your shoulders." She squeezes said shoulders, then slides her hands up my neck and into my hair. "I'm sorry I was so mean to you."

"I told ya, I like you mean." I kiss her sweet lips.

Her fingers dig in my scalp and she massages my temples.

"Fuck, birdie. You're going to have to do this for me every night." I grip her ass and yank her forward. "So you can reach me better." I grin as she settles on my dick.

"Yes, this is much better." She rolls her hips.

"You weren't exactly my favorite person either," I say to let her off the hook for forming a bad opinion about me in the beginning.

"And now?"

"And now I'm not sure how I'm going to be able to walk away," I answer honestly.

It's the painful truth of it all. The more time I spend with her, the more I want to keep her with me in Alabama. I want her to make the farm her home.

I tuck a piece of hair behind her ear. "I told you months ago, you're a strange bird, baby," I say softly.

"That's not exactly a compliment, Wyatt." Her glasses slip and I push them up on her nose for her.

"Do you know what strange means?"

"Of course I do. It means weird."

I shrug my shoulder. "It also means unusual, extraordinary, remarkable. You've always been those things to me. Intriguing and unexpected. I've fallen in love with you, birdie. Stay with me in Alabama. Start a life with me." The words tumble out of my mouth. I didn't mean to say all of that at once but she's always made me forget how to use my filter.

Wren doesn't move. Her hands freeze on my arms. Her eyes glaze over. If it wasn't for her chest rising and falling, I would think she stopped breathing too.

"You can't love me. That's not what this was supposed to be." She attempts to move off my lap but I hold her in place.

"Maybe not, but it's what it is. That's what happened. I've fallen in love with you. I want to start a life with you. I want to build a house on the hill with you. I want a tire swing in the tree so I can push you and watch your hair blow in the breeze. And I want you."

Wren stares at my chest. She's refusing to look me in the eye.

"Say something." I duck my head to get in her line of sight. "Tell me you don't feel the same. Tell me you don't want those things too. We both know you'd be lying. I like fighting with you. If you want to go that route, we can. I was never much of a brawler until you gave me something worth fighting for."

"For the past few days I've felt like part of me was missing," she whispers. "I'd do all the things I usually do. I made my lists. I stuck to my routines. I did everything I could to find some kind of normal but nothing helped. When you aren't around, everything feels wrong. I'm miserable without you. I hate you for that." She smirks.

"I'm not sorry about that, baby."

"Didn't think you would be. I've always told myself that falling in love wasn't for me. I never wanted to do it. That's why this arrangement was perfect for me." She takes a deep breath and wipes at her cheek. I don't like where she is going with this. I grip her tighter than I should. If this is over, I need her to say it.

"I think my way of doing relationships worked because there was never a worthy opponent. No one ever challenged me or pushed me. There was never anything at stake. Not until you. You're right. I do love you. I tried not to. I really did. But it was a wasted effort because I fell in love with you anyway." Her words are so sweet my heart starts pumping honey into my veins.

"Say it again."

"I love you." I capture her lips with mine. My hands dig into her hair refusing to let go.

"Tell me you'll stay, birdie. Tell me you want to start something real with me."

"We've already started something real."

I squeeze her tighter. "You're right. We have."

"But, I can't go home with you. Not yet."

"Why?"

"I have some things I need to take care of first."

"Fiancé things? You can tell him to fuck right on off over the phone." When she looks down at her lap. "You can't be serious."

"I never lied to you about my situation. You knew going into this what I was dealing with," she fires back at me.

"I know but things change. I never thought that—" I start to say.

"That you could love me?" She tries to finish my thought but she's a terrible mind reader.

I shake my head. "No, birdie. I knew I could do that. That was the easy part."

"Oh," she whispers. "Then what?"

"I never thought you would fight so hard against loving me."

"I'm not fighting it. I...I'm having to figure it out as I go. That is not something I do. I plan everything." She gestures wildly with her hands. "But I didn't plan on you. This is all your fault."

"My fault?" I rear my head back.

"Yes. Your fault." She climbs off my lap and starts pacing the room. "You're the one who wanted my help hooking up with Charlie. I never would have come up with something so silly on my own. Then you had to be sweet and thoughtful. No one's ever treated me the way that you do. You and your stupidly handsome face with dimples. And that mustache!" She throws her hands up in the air.

I roll my lips to keep from laughing at her little fit.

"Stop. This isn't funny."

"I'm not laughing."

She takes a calming breath and turns to face the wall. Her body hiccups and she sniffles. I roll off the bed and walk over to her. I wrap my arms around her chest and bury my face in the crook of her neck. "Talk to me, baby. Tell me what's going on."

"I'm...I'm trying my best here, Wyatt. There are things going on that I have no control over." She breaks free from my hold and walks over to her dresser. After digging around in the top drawer she places a small box on top of the dresser.

"What is that?" I demand. "It looks a lot like a fucking ring box."

"It is. When I went to see my parents."

I spin her around to face me. "The least you can do is look at me when you tell me why you're picking him."

"I'm not picking him. Daniel's dad is not a nice man. He's threatening my family. I have to go home after graduation and settle things with the Abbotts once and for all. Believe me. I don't like the situation any more than you do."

"I don't fucking like it all."

"I hadn't noticed," she snarks. "I don't know how long it will take. If you still want me, I'll come to Alabama. Everything you said, I want that too. I want a life with you."

"Baby, I will always want you. There isn't any part of me that doesn't beg to be in your presence. I want to help. We can both go to Georgia. I can help you pack and stop shaking your head."

"You can't be there. Then he'll know I'm not going to marry his son. My parents will be there. They'll help me."

"But I'm your man. I should be there for you."

"Is that what you are, my man? I like the sound of that."

"Damn straight. It's going to kill me to not be there with you. I just got you and now you're going to leave."

"It won't be forever. Just long enough for me to make him hurt for ever thinking he could mess with the people I love."

I feel sorry for the man who thinks he can battle against my girl. She won't back down until she gets what she wants. I've been in her line of fire before. Wren is a straight shooter with good fucking aim.

I realize she is going to war for her family and this techni-cally has nothing to do with me. It doesn't make it any easier to sit idly by and wait for her to come back to me.

A FEW WEEKS LATER

"Where are you off to?" Nash asks when I pass him in the den. He's lucky he doesn't have to move and do all this packing bullshit. He's staying here through the summer along with his friends that are moving in for their senior year.

Now that we've graduated and the season is over there's nothing left to do here. I'm not sad about heading home. It's the fact that I'm leaving without my road trip partner. *My everything partner.*

"Wren's place. I'm going to bring her all her stuff." I can't look at it anymore. For every two things of mine I packed up, there was one of hers.

How our lives melded together so quickly, I'll never understand. This box is a punch in the gut every time I look at it. It's a reminder that she isn't coming with me to Alabama and that she is still shutting me out of parts of her life. I don't know how she can tell me she loves me in one breath and keep secrets in the next.

I should be going to Georgia with her. I should be by her side until we can come home together. But she doesn't want me there. She's too independent for her own good.

"Are you breaking up with her?" he asks.

I reel my head back. "No. Why would you think that?"

"She's going to think you're removing her from your life if you bring all of that over to her."

That's impossible. There is no removing Wren from my life. She sang her way into my heart before either one of us knew it was happening.

28

WREN

"Do you want any of the mugs?" Charlie yells from the kitchen. We're finally getting around to packing up what remains in the kitchen.

I can't believe I'm saying goodbye to Newhouse, Charlie, the girls, and Wyatt.

Driving to Georgia tomorrow is going to be the hardest thing I've ever done. It feels like my heart is going in one direction and I'm headed in another.

The time we'll be separated has no end date and that's the hardest part. Like walking through the desert with no destination in sight. If there was a timeline. If I knew it would be two weeks and we could count down together, it would make the distance easier.

"You can have them." I join her in the kitchen. "Except this one." I reach into the cabinet and grab the hedgehog mug Wyatt bought me.

My heart speeds in a panic. It's been weeks, maybe months, since I've felt a rush of paralyzing anxiety. Charlie watches me with concern. "I'm fine." I take the mug and bring it to my room.

Sitting on my bed, I take a few deep breaths.

It's temporary.

Weeks, maybe days.

He loves me. Being apart changes nothing.

You are stronger than this.

I inhale one last deep breath and wipe the tears from my eyes.

"Feel better?" Charlie asks when I enter the living room.

"Not really but I have to be," I say, bringing her an empty box. "I'm going to miss you too."

She wraps her arms around me. "I know, but those tears aren't for me. We already cried and laughed those out." Any free night we had, Charlie and I have spent together watching movies, drinking wine, laughing about all of her bad dates over the years.

Charlie is more than a friend. She's family. She is someone that I will never forget. I will miss her fearlessness. She isn't afraid to try new things. If it doesn't work out, she dusts herself off and tries something else. Her resiliency is inspiring.

"I'm still sad we won't be roommates anymore."

"I'm going to miss you keeping my life together. I might end up joining the circus without you keeping me in line," she jokes.

"Have you decided what you're going to do when you get home?"

"Okay, don't laugh at me." She wraps a bowl in newspaper and places it in the box. "I think I'm going to get a job on a yacht. I saw an advertisement for a company hiring stewardesses for the summer. They'll be sailing through the Mediterranean."

"There will be a lot of potential husbands in the Mediterranean."

"I know!" She squeals.

"I was joking, Charlie."

"I'm not. That's my goal this summer. Get engaged. Look at us. You're looking to ditch a fiancé and I'm trying to lock one down," she says, grinning. I can't seem to muster up the same amount of amusement.

Not with my whole situation being unpredictable. My feelings for Wyatt are the only thing that feels steady and true. Knowing he will be waiting for me when this is all over pushes me to keep fighting until the end.

"It will all work out, you know. If anyone can make a man regret crossing them, it's you. You're smart and you were born with a sharp tongue. You know where to cut him to make it hurt the most."

"I'm glad you are confident in me. I just want it to be over with," I admit. Charlie passes me a box to tape. I secure it shut and walk the box over to her stack of growing cargo.

"I think I'm going to hire some guys from the hunky moving company to help me with all of that." She nods toward her growing pile of things.

There's a quiet knock on our door. "What would your Mediterranean fiancé think of you flirting with other men?" I joke, before opening the door.

"Hi," I greet Wyatt who's currently holding a large moving box of his own. He looks devastatingly handsome in a backwards hat, jeans, and T-shirt.

"Hi." He brushes his lips against mine for a quick kiss. "Hey, Charlie."

"Hi, Wyatt. Good to see you. I'm going to check on Syd. See if she needs any help packing up all her books." Charlie walks out of the room. Once the door closes, I direct my attention back to Wyatt.

"What's in the box?"

He sighs. Then walks the box to my room. "Looks like you're almost done packing," he says, glancing around the room.

"What's in the box, Wyatt?" I ask again, ignoring his stalling tactics.

"All your stuff I found while I was packing up my room. I thought you might need it in Georgia," he says, void of any emotion.

I lift the lid and glance inside. It appears to be a bunch of random pieces of clothes, underwear, a hairbrush, a few books. Nothing I can't live without.

"You could take it with you and keep it for me."

"How long is that going to be? Weeks? Months? I don't know if I can stare at a box of your stuff for that long." His face hardens except for the slight feathering of the muscle in his jaw.

"I don't know. Let's say it will be months. I think I'll manage living without old notebooks and highlighters." I push the box out of the way.

"There's more than that in there. Your stuff was every-where cluttering my room."

I almost laugh at that. "If you think you are getting anything back from me, you're shit out of luck."

"I don't want all my clothes you stole." He leans in closer. "I know you've been taking all my T-shirts. But that's fine, you can keep them. Wear 'em at night and think of me."

"I always think of you. Every choice I've made has been with you in mind, Wyatt." My hands ball into fists so tight my nails are going to cut through my skin. "If it wasn't for you, I wouldn't give a fuck. This is all happening because of you. You've made me feel something. This is the fallout you've caused."

"Right, this is all my fault. How quickly I forgot. I'm sorry I love you so fucking much that the thought of being away from you is driving me insane."

"We've been driving each other insane for months. This should be like wearing an old hat. You're already good at doing that," I tease, nodding toward the hat on his head.

"My dad bought me this hat my senior year in high school. It was a reminder of my dream of playing baseball and be-coming a knight. I've worn it almost every day since." He takes the hat off and throws it against the wall with a curse. "I hate this," he whispers before sitting on the bed and burying his face in his hands.

"I hate it too. I would rather be at the farm with all the bugs than dealing with this snake of a man. My dad seems to think it won't take longer than two months." I step in between his legs and wrap my arms around his neck.

"A lot can happen in two months." His hands slide over my hips and down my backside. "I fell in love with you in less time." His eyes fill with raw emotion. "Why aren't you telling me everything? I feel like I'm the one who's laying it all out there and you're keeping secrets."

"I'm telling you everything I can," I say softly. "I don't know what else you want from me."

"I want you to trust me."

"I do trust you."

"Doesn't look like it from where I'm sitting."

I let out a shaky breath. "I'm doing this for you. For us."

"It doesn't feel that way," he mumbles. "It feels like you're leaving me."

Tears spring to my eyes. "You're breaking my heart."

"I don't think that's possible."

"It is possible. I feel it." I rub a palm over my chest to ease the ache that's pressing on me.

"I can't break your heart, if you never really gave it to me."

"What are you talking about? I have given you all of me. If I'm not enough. If you need something else, then maybe you need someone else." I turn my back to him.

Wyatt spins me around and wraps his strong arms around me. "You are all I need. But I need you with me. You say you've given me your heart but I don't believe you. If you did, you wouldn't be hurting. That pain you feel. That's on you. You're the one clamping down so hard you're bleeding out. Let me have it, birdie. Give me your heart and I promise I'll take care of it."

"Maybe, I want to take care of you." I wipe a tear off his cheek. "Maybe you need to trust me," I beg. "Trust me to handle this. I'm not going to ask you to believe in me again but I need you to believe in us."

"Baby, I do. I would feel better if I knew the whole story. I can't help you if I don't know how."

"If I tell you, you will jump into action and try to fix it yourself. That's what you do. You help everyone. It's one of the things I love about you. It's my turn to help you." I've already said too much. His eyebrows furrow trying to figure out what I mean. I press my lips against his. He can't find out I'm doing this for him and his family. *Please let me do this.*"

"Fine," he sighs.

"Good. Now that we've settled that." I reach for the hem of his shirt. "I want to enjoy our last night together."

Wyatt stands and silently strips me of all my clothes. I work his jeans off him. Getting on my knees, I help him step out of his pants, underwear, and socks. My hands glide up his muscular thighs.

"Birdie." I can't tell if he's warning me or asking me.

"One taste," I say before swirling my tongue around his dick and taking him in my mouth. He begins to groan when I suck him all the way to the back of my throat.

His fingers dig into my head and he gently pulls me off him. "I need to be inside you." He helps me stand and escorts me to the bed. "Spread your legs for me."

I'm dripping for him. His eyes darken as he stares me down from the end of the bed. "You're gonna have to change your sheets when I'm done with you, birdie." He kneels at the end of the bed. Rough palms wrap around my calves and with one swift motion he yanks me to the edge of the mattress, making me yelp in surprise.

With my legs propped up on his shoulders, he dips his fingers into my core while his tongue works over my clit. I know I hated on his mustache when we first met but it does wonders rubbing against my inner thighs.

My spine tingles and tightens as he pulls every bit of pleasure he can from me. "Wyatt," I moan his name, and my hands dig into the sheets. "Don't stop." I can feel him smile against my thigh as he moves away from clit. I need to stop warning him that I'm close. He does this every time. "I said don't stop." I try to redirect his face, but he slaps my hand away.

He flattens his tongue and leisurely roams at my core. "You know, for someone who eats every meal with Flash like speed, you sure do take your time with me," I say annoyed and desperate.

"That's because you're the best thing I've ever tasted. Don't worry, baby. I'm going to let you come. But first, I'm going to enjoy my favorite meal of the day." He squeezes my thigh.

This time he immediately does the thing I like with his mouth where he alternates licking and sucking on my clit. My heels dig into his flesh and my back bows as I climax.

"We're going to have to do that a few more times before tomorrow morning," he says, kissing me and lifting me off the bed. I'm so relaxed I'm basically dead wait. Once we've settled back on the mattress, I flex my hips, rubbing myself against his erection. "Is this okay?" he asks, the tip of his cock waiting to enter my pussy.

"Yes. I'm clean. I'm also on birth control."

"I'm clean too. I've never had sex without a condom before. Fucking hell," he groans, sliding inside. Wyatt rocks his hips back and forth making me feel so full. "Your pussy is so greedy for me, birdie. Look at the way you pull my cock in. Just like that."

"I need more." I'm already so close. My nails dig into his back. He will have scratch marks in the morning, but I can't help it. This orgasm is strong and intense—my toes curl and I see stars.

He pulls my legs up over his shoulders and thrusts into me in quick succession until he is groaning my name and cumming inside me. Wyatt covers me with his body. His elbows rest on either side of my face.

I graze my fingers up and down the sides of his body while he pushes my hair out of my face. "I'm going to miss you. Not sure I can make it two months without you."

"You were prepared to move to California a few weeks ago."

"I wasn't thinking straight. Ain't no way I would have been able to do that. That was never a viable choice after I met you.

It died the minute you started throwing insults my way. I was fooling myself for even considering it still."

Wyatt slips out of me and rolls me onto my side. He kisses me on my shoulder and pulls me tight against his chest. "It'll be alright, birdie," he says when my first tear falls.

"I'm a mess. I'm falling apart. You've reduced me to pieces," I whisper, wiping tears off my cheeks.

"Baby, you can always fall apart with me. I'll pick up every single piece and carry it for you. You're not alone anymore."

Sometime in the middle of the night, Wyatt woke me up and made love to me. He moved carefully in and out of me as if he was afraid one of us would break irrevocably.

With every kiss he said I love you.

With every touch he said I'll miss you.

With every thrust he said don't forget about me.

"Fly back to me, birdie," he whispers into the hollow of my neck while I cling to him for dear life.

It's an easy promise to make and one I don't intend on breaking.

WILLOW & WREN

I don't know what's going on with you and Wyatt. It isn't my business but that's never stopped me. I thought you should see these. Hurry back to him. He's a mess.

She's impossible.

You should hear the music she listens to.

It's terrible.

She finally wore something other than beige.

Blue is her color.

Her eyes are really pretty.

I can't stop staring at them.

I made her laugh today.

I picked the wrong girl.

How do I tell her I want her instead?

You should have seen her dancing tonight.

She's downstairs in my bed.

All I want to do is go down there and hold her.

She's supposed to marry another man.

But she feels like mine.

Don't scare her away this week.

FWD TEXT FROM WYATT

I love her.

FWD TEXT FROM WYATT

But I don't know if I can keep her.

FWD TEXT FROM WYATT

How do I keep her?

FWD TEXT FROM WYATT

She's going to Georgia after graduation.

FWD TEXT FROM WYATT

I won't survive if she doesn't come back to me.

FWD TEXT FROM WYATT

I miss my best friend

FWD TEXT FROM WYATT

I need her here.

FWD TEXT FROM WYATT

I'm not going to make it much longer without her.

29

WREN

I've been home for two weeks. The first few days were hard. Then Willow sent me a string of texts Wyatt had messaged her over the last few months and the last eleven days became even harder.

During the day I've been in the office meeting with lawyers, finishing up the paperwork for Wyatt and his siblings to sign, getting all the payoff amounts from the bank.

I miss Wyatt desperately. Regular text messages and video calls do very little to fill the empty hole in my heart. I'm not sure how many more days I will be able to handle being away from him.

Yesterday I googled if it was possible to become addicted to a person.

It is.

And I am.

I have all the symptoms.

There is nothing more that I can do on my end for this deal. Checks have been signed. Paperwork has been turned in. I'm waiting on the bank to get everything approved, signed and delivered.

With no end date in sight, I've decided I'm not going to let the Abbotts hold me hostage in my own home. If I want to go to Wyatt, I'm damn well going to.

I'm far enough along in the process that there is nothing Abbott can do to change the tides. Ownership of the property is all semantics at this point.

The original plan for tonight was for Daniel and I to go out to dinner with his dad and put on a show. Pretend to be the perfect fiancé. I don't have it in me. I've never been a good actress. Wyatt will be the first one to tell you I'm also a terrible liar.

I sent Daniel a text letting him know my change of plans. He replied saying his only regret is not being able to see his dad's face in person when I call his bluff and tell him it is over.

After my meeting this afternoon, I'm doing something I never thought I would do.

Flying in a plane.

In three hours, I'm going home. The thought of seeing Wyatt's face and being able to touch him motivates me to do what I have to do next.

"Do you have everything you need?" Mom asks as I pack the last of my things in my bag.

"I think so." I take one last look around my bedroom.

"I'll donate all the clothes for you. We'll store all your other things until you're ready for them," she says, with a tremor in her voice. "I'm proud of you, Wren. You are the strongest person I know. You've always fought and loved fiercely. You care for people effortlessly. I think that's why you sometimes feel you're not good at it. Loving people is just what you do."

"Maybe. I never thought about it that way. I'm going to miss you." I wrap my arms around her.

"I'm going to miss you too. We'll be there for the grand opening. That's only a few months away. I'm going to ask Faith for the name of a good real estate agent. Maybe it's time for all of us to have a change of scenery. How do you think I'd look in a pair of those jeans?" She points at my legs.

"Incredible," Dad says from behind me. "We need to get going if you're going to make your flight." He kisses Mom on the forehead before grabbing my bag.

Mom and I hug goodbye one last time. I inhale a deep breath of perfume and commit it to memory. I did the same thing when she dropped me off at Newhouse for the first time. "You can do this," she whispers in my ear, before letting me go.

"Are you ready?" Dad asks, parking the car in front of Fred Abbott's office building.

"Ready as I'll ever be." I may not be wearing a power suit today but I have on my power cowboy boots. Each step I take into the building is a reminder of my purpose and strengthens my resolve.

"How can I help you?" the receptionist asks.

"We're here to see Mr. Abbott," I say.

"Is he expecting you?"

"No, but he'll want to see us. Tell him Ivan and Wren Ellington are here to speak with him about an urgent matter," Dad tells her.

A few moments pass before we are allowed entry into his office.

I keep checking my watch. Getting on the plane is giving me enough anxiety. I don't need to add being late on top of it.

"Wren, Ivan, what a pleasant surprise. I didn't expect to see you until later this evening. Please, take a seat. What can I do for you?" Fred asks.

"I think I'll stand thank you," I say. "I only came by to drop this off." I place the ring box he gave me on the edge of his desk. "I've made my choice. I won't be marrying Daniel. I appreciate the offer but I'll have to pass."

Fred stands from his chair. "You should reconsider. You will lose everything if you walk away."

"I'll lose everything if I don't," I say, standing my ground. Everything I want is on a farm in Alabama. If I don't walk away, I get nothing. "Now if you excuse me I have a plane to catch."

"All it takes is one phone call to the bank and I will own every inch of their land," he threatens.

"You will have to take that up with the new owners. The bank no longer has a say. I suggest you stop threatening my family. You aren't the only person in the room who knows how to throw threats around. Mark my words, if you continue down this road with me, it will be painful," I say tersely.

"You have a lot of nerve, little girl."

"You're right. I do." I smile back at him.

"Ivan, are you going to let her speak to me like this?"

"I see nothing wrong with what she's saying. Wren has always spoken her mind."

"I can ruin you."

"You could." Dad shrugs. "You won't." He types something out on his phone. "There are documents in your email listing all the clients you have stolen from over the years. Threaten my family again and I will send it to the press."

"Where did you get this?" he demands.

"My newest employee. You're going to need a new business analyst by the way. I just took your best one since mine just bought a farm."

Fred picks up his phone and places a call. If I had to guess, it's to his son. When Daniel's lawyers came through with access for his trust, a new blackmail plan began. Before he packed up his office, he managed to get everything we needed to put Fred on a leash.

"Have a great day, Fred." I walk out of his office with my shoulders back and head held high.

"You did great in there," Dad says as he buckles himself in the car.

My nerves are frazzled as we pull off on the highway toward the airport. I don't know if it's adrenaline from confronting Abbott or anxiety for my impending flight.

"Thanks, Dad. Do you think he'll try anything?" I chew on my lower lip.

"He won't risk losing his business. He's nothing without it."

That offers a small bit of comfort. I won't feel completely secure until the paperwork has been signed by all members of the Rivers family.

"He's lucky to have you," Dad says, staring down the highway in front of him. "I've had you for twenty-two years. I know better than anyone."

"I'm the lucky one. I've been loved by two of the best men I've ever met."

"You're going to make your old man cry. Promise me you'll take care of each other," he says, pulling into the drop off lane.

"We will. I love you, Dad."

"Love you too. We'll be there soon. I can't wait to see what you've done with the place." He leans in to give me a hug.

"Don't expect too much. We are still working with a small budget."

"You don't give yourself enough credit. You've always been very resourceful. Text us when you land."

I grab my bags out of the trunk and wave him off. I take a few deep breaths before entering the airport. I can do this. It's a short flight. And Wyatt is on the other side.

My seat is by the window. I don't know if that's better or worse. It likely doesn't matter since I don't plan on opening my eyes the entire time we're in the air.

As the plane takes off, I take one peek out the window to wave a final goodbye to Georgia.

I step out of the cab and my body sags with relief.

I'm home.

I drop my bags off on the porch and set off to find Wyatt. There's still a few good hours of daylight left. He has to be out here working somewhere.

He isn't with the goats or chickens. The barn is also empty. I'm about to give up and go back to the house when I hear the rumble of a four wheeler in the distance.

As soon as the four wheeler is visible, I take off running. I pump my arms and legs as fast as they can go. My boots slip over the gravel, but I don't care. He's right there.

Wyatt hops out of the passenger seat before Colt even gets it parked. He sprints in my direction, losing his hat on the path. His long legs quickly eat the distance between us.

We crash into each other. I don't feel anything but Wyatt's arms wrapping around me and lifting me off the ground. He cups my face in one hand as if he's checking to see if I'm real.

"Hi," I say, breathlessly. The sound of my voice must break the dream like trance he is in. Next thing I know his lips are on mine. He kisses me slowly, nipping at my lips, savoring the taste. His tongue licks against my lips parting them open.

I claw my way closer to him. I've never missed another person this much before. Not even my first year at college. I was excited to be on my own. I couldn't wait for my parents to leave so I could explore the university.

I was missing Wyatt the second he got in his truck and drove away.

"What are you doing here?" His eyes glance behind me. "How did you get here?"

"Last I checked birdies knew how to fly." I grin.

"You flew here? On an airplane. You hate flying."

"I know. I couldn't wait any longer. I had to get to you." I hug him tightly around the top of his shoulders.

He kisses me up and down my neck and the top of my shoulder. "Fuck, I missed you. I can't believe you flew in a plane for me."

"I would do anything for you," I say earnestly. My legs drop to the ground. Before I can walk away, he grabs my face and kisses me again.

"Tell me you're here to stay." He leans his forehead against mine.

"I'm here to stay," I whisper.

"My girl is home! Birdie's home!" he shouts, spinning me around until I'm giggling. My feet land on solid ground and we run back to the house.

He grabs my bags off the porch and takes them in the house. "Everyone is out working, but I'll send them a text. I'm afraid I'm going to have to add you to the family chat now that you're home for good." He looks at me. "I'll never get tired of saying that."

I unzip my suitcase and start unpacking. "Add me if you have to, but I'm putting it on mute. If it's an emergency, they will need to text me separately. I'm not going to read through a hundred messages to find out someone got hurt or something."

"God, I missed you. Everyone's too nice around here. I've missed this mouth." He leans down and kisses me quickly. "Let me help you unpack so we can take advantage of the house being empty." He thrusts his hips a few times in the air. God, he's ridiculous but he's mine.

"Baby, why is my shirt on your pillow?" He holds up my lifeline while I was in Georgia.

"Actually, that's my shirt. And that isn't a pillow. It's Wyatt Wallen. I slept with him every night. He smells like you." I give the pillow stuffed inside Wyatt's, I mean my, Wallen T-shirt a hug and then throw it in the middle of the bed.

"It's definitely my shirt. You were with me when I bought it," he says. I wave him off. "I'll let you keep it, but you have to take it off the pillow. That's just weird."

"Wyatt Wallen was the only way I was able to sleep." I frown.

"Now you've got the real thing. You don't need it any-more. I can't promise I'm going to let you sleep much tonight though." He wraps himself around me from behind, pressing his erection into my ass.

"I should fucking hope not," I say, making him chuckle.

"Enough unpacking for now." He flips me around and throws me over his shoulder. "If I don't have you naked in the next ten seconds, I'm going to lose it."

It feels good to be home, I think, as I strip my man naked and spend the next few hours familiarizing myself with his body again.

30

WYATT

I've barely let Wren out of my sight since she got here a week ago—I've stuck to her like glue. The only time we've been apart is when Willow kidnapped her and took her into town. Otherwise, she's always within reach.

I still can't believe she's here some days. I wake up in the morning and think I'm still dreaming. But she's there in the flesh, sleeping away in my arms.

"Do you know what this is about?" Mason asks from his seat across from me at the kitchen table.

"No idea. Dad and Mama said they needed to talk to us about something and called a house meeting." I absentmindedly pull at the strings on Wren's shorts. There's something calming about it. To me at least, Wren is squirming in her seat, rubbing her thighs together. I snicker at her and she sends a glare back my way.

"We haven't had one of these since Colt accidentally drove Ford's truck into the barn. That was over ten years ago," Willow says.

"No. I remember having a house meeting when Willow was sixteen and was dating that little twerp Eric," Ford says, shaking his head. "He was terrible. I don't know what you saw in him."

"We all can't get it right the first time like Wyatt. You should know that better than anyone, Ford," she says, rolling her eyes. "And that meeting doesn't count because it was just the four of you. It was an ambush of the brotherly kind."

"Did Mama mention anything to you on one of your walks?" I ask Wren. The two of them have been very buddy buddy walking all over the property.

"No. She hasn't mentioned anything new."

I eye her suspiciously. She doesn't appear to be lying, but I'm not convinced she's telling me the whole truth. Wren knows something.

"Is everyone here?" Dad asks, walking into the kitchen. He hobbles around the table with his cane, giving everyone a kiss on the head. I'm waiting for him to shout '*goose*' and make a run for it.

"We're all here. You going to tell us what this is all about?" Colt asks before taking a bite of the sandwich in front of him.

Dad and Mama exchange glances. "We sold the farm," Mama says, clutching hard to the stack of papers in her arms.

"What?" Ford bellows. "Can you repeat that? I thought I heard you say you sold the farm, but that can't be without talking to us first. Dad, I'm supposed to be in charge here."

"Slow down, son." Dad holds up his hand stopping Ford from saying anything else. "Your mama and I owned the farm. It was in our names. We could sell if we wanted to."

"You said *owned*. How much did you give away in this deal?" Mason asks, leaning forward on the table. His hands clenched in front of him.

"We know you have questions, but let us explain." Everyone nods in agreement at Mama's request. "Good. It was a deal we couldn't refuse. An investor offered to take care of all of our debt and leave enough money to start a small reserve fund."

I clench my hand around Wren's thigh. An investor came in and paid for everything? Her dad wouldn't have done that, would he? Is this what she was taking care of? I glance in her direction. Her face is a mask. She's staring emotionlessly at her glass of sweet tea.

"The new owners will own one hundred percent of the farm. All the land, buildings, existing businesses, everything," Dad explains.

"You've got to be fucking kidding me?" Ford fumes.

"I'm not joking. The investor set a few stipulations. As long as the new owners agree, the property will transfer to them." Mama passes out the packets of papers she's been holding onto. She places one in front of everyone but Wren.

"Look over everything. If you agree, sign the documents. Mama and I will take care of filing the rest of the paperwork." Dad squeezes Mama's hand. She's about two seconds from crying.

"We're the owners?" Mason questions, his eyes scanning over the first page.

"If all five of you sign, then you will each own an equal share." Mama walks into the kitchen to fix her and Dad a cup of coffee.

"What about the investor? How much do they get?" Ford peers up from his paper.

Dad glances in my direction. "They didn't want any interest in the business. It's all in there. Keep reading."

I realize Dad wasn't looking at me. He was looking at Wren. "What did you do?" I ask her.

"Nothing you wouldn't have done," she says, without looking at me.

"God damnit, Wren." I stand from the table and walk outside. I can't believe she paid off everything.

"Birdie," she shouts from the front porch while I pace the gravel drive.

"What?"

She stomps down the stairs. "My name is birdie. I like it when you call me birdie."

"Oh now you like it do ya? I can't call you that when I'm mad at you. I didn't quit baseball for you to come in and pay off our debt."

"No you didn't. You stopped playing because this is where your soul feels alive. You quit because this is where you belong. I didn't do it to come in and play hero. I did it because I belong here too. I did it because that evil man was threatening to buy the farm. I wasn't going to let him hurt my family." She pounds a fist into her chest.

"Before you said he was coming after your family. That was why you wanted to take care of this on your own."

"You're right. I did say that. And he was threatening my family. Your family is my family too. I'm a fucking Rivers woman. I have been for quite some time now if you haven't noticed." She moves closer to me. "We don't stand by and let the men do all the work. We like to get our hands dirty too."

"You sure do." I sigh, dropping my head. "I don't like that you used your money to bail us out. I'm supposed to be taking care of you." I take her hands in mine and lace our fingers together.

"I'm glad you feel that way because I'm broke. I need a job, a place to live, and food to eat. If you would go read the fine print of the contract it's all there."

I chuckle at her. "I guess we should go back inside then."

"Probably. If I had to guess, everyone else has already signed."

All eyes are on us as we reenter the house and sit back down on the bench seat.

"You're the investor," Ford states. It isn't a question. He's staring Wren down under the brim of his baseball cap.

"Yes. I believe in each of you. I had the funds. It is a smart investment." She takes a quick sip of her tea.

"You didn't ask for anything in return," Colt says.

"No. I asked for all of those things. If you don't do them, then you have to pay back every penny. I've set it up where I'm guaranteed to get everything I want one way or the other," she tells my brother.

"Why don't you read 'em out loud?" Dad suggests.

"Alright, the investor is allocated an unlimited budget for sticky notes and office supplies." Ford grins.

"Of course that would be your first request," I grumble.

"I felt it was important," she replies.

"Can I continue?" Ford asks. We both nod. "The Rivers Family Farm must be renamed to...Songland Farms. All current businesses and any new endeavors will be considered an entity of Songland Farms." Ford coughs, clearing his throat.

"After hearing Jack talk about the land and how it sang to the soul, I thought it was appropriate," Wren says.

"Songland Farms," Willow whispers as her eyes fill with tears. "It's perfect." She glances at Wren.

"I thought so too." Mama squeezes Wren's shoulder.

"Each owner is allocated a parcel of land of their choosing to build a first or secondary residence. If the owner chooses not to live in said dwelling full time, they are required to come home to Songland Farms for all major holidays and birthday celebrations," Colt reads.

"That is a very specific requirement," Mason says to Wren.

Wren blushes as she wipes at the condensation on her glass of tea. "I've never been a part of a big family. It's only been me, my mom, and Dad. Having everyone home together for Christmas sounds kind of nice."

"You say that until you have to fight someone for the last dinner roll," Colt jokes.

"Each owner," Willow starts, "if they choose, is allocated at minimum ten acres of land to construct and open a business of their wildest dreams." Willow looks up at Wren. "Will you help me with it?"

"That's one of the stipulations. I need a job. I would like to help all of you with your business plans and take over the paperwork side of managing the farm."

"Thank God. It's all yours," Ford says.

"I thought you would say that. It will give you more time to work on the farm and be with Lennon. At some point we may want to hire a financial adviser and a marketing manager. I can handle those things for now."

"You thought of everything," I say, kissing her cheek.

"She sure did. Keep reading Wyatt." Mason rolls his lips to keep from smiling.

I scan the document. Wren's listed everything from Lenny Land being the first business to be constructed to requiring Mama to plant new wildflowers every year.

"Wyatt Rivers is not allowed to alter his facial hair without the consent of the investor." I laugh.

"I told you it was growing on me."

"I know exactly why you like my mustache," I say.

"Because it makes you look more handsome."

"Sure, we can go with that." I level her with a look. "Wyatt Rivers also agrees..." I close my eyes and inhale a breath. "To take Wren Marie Ellington as his partner in all of his business plans and in life. He agrees to love her always, even when she's mean. He agrees to talk to her every day and hold her close at night." I can barely get the words out as the love I have for this woman bubbles to the surface.

"Mama, is there anything else you need from me or birdie?" I ask, scribbling my signature on the document. It's the easiest contract I've ever signed. I would lay down my life for this woman. She didn't barter for enough if you ask me. I would have given her a hell of a lot more.

"No. I think we're good here," she says, smirking at us.

"Great. Come on, birdie. We're going to have a little talk." I hold out my hand and pull her up from the bench. "We'll be back for dinner."

We walk to the front door and stop to put our boots on.

"Wish I had a girl who enjoyed talking as much as Wren," I hear Colt say.

Wren shrugs a shoulder not embarrassed at all that my whole family knows I'm about to remind my girl how much she likes my mustache between her thighs and how much I love her.

I drive the four wheeler out to my spot, our spot now. I have to force myself to keep my eyes on the road ahead and not on Wren. Her hair whips freely in the wind. Her face is pointed toward the sky, letting the sun soak into her skin.

I'm a lucky bastard. I don't know what I did to become God's favorite but I'm fucking grateful to him for bringing Wren into my life.

Wren and I walk hand in hand around the land that we'll build our home on one day.

I've always been someone who knew what they wanted. I come across as the jokester of the group, but I'm well rooted.

It would take a lot to blow me away, but Wren manages to do it every time.

I lead her into the old rickety barn. I'm not sure if it is worth salvaging, but I would like to. We've been making a lot of good memories in here.

Wren stretches out on the bed of blankets we made the first night she came home. I lay down beside her and tangle my legs with hers.

"The first time I heard you sing, it was from behind the closed door of your dorm. You were singing about finding whatever makes a person happy. My first thought was that those things weren't going to be found at Newhouse. I thought I needed to be here to be happy. But I was miserable while you were gone." I position myself over her body. Her hands immediately go under my shirt.

"I always felt stuck at school. I couldn't wait to get out of there and chase after the things I thought were going to make me happy. Turns out my happiness was behind that door the whole time. I heard you singing, but Charlie opened the door. I thought it was her."

She lets out a full belly laugh. "You didn't ask Charlie to sing for you, did you?"

"No. She told me the truth on our little date."

"Why didn't you ever say anything?" she asks, her fingers tickle up the side of my chest.

"It didn't matter. I already knew it was you. Whether you were the one singing or not, it was always going to be you and me. I don't know how I'm ever going to be able to thank you for everything you've done for my family." I glide my hand up and down her side. I need to feel her. Have my hands on her.

"*Our* family and you don't need to say thank you. I did it for me. I'm pretty selfish that way. Now you're all mine. You've got to put up with my smart mouth for the rest of your life." Her eyes sparkle with mirth.

"I love your smart mouth." I lean down and kiss her lips. "We've been throwing strikes at each other for months. Every barb, every insult, you hit the mark every time. We learned each other's weaknesses and exploited them with efficiency. You know what it takes to bring me to my knees. Baby, you do it by breathing.

"I want you selfish." I kiss down her neck to her chest. "I like you greedy." I move down her body and unbutton her shorts. "I fucking love you mean." I strip her of her clothes. "And I love that you're mine."

31

WYATT

In an hour, Songland Farms will officially be open for business.

The last month has been all hands on deck getting everything ready for the grand opening of our first summer season. Wren has worked herself to the bone lining up influencers and photographers to come out and document everything.

Mason and Colt, along with their foreman, Lenny, built Lenny Land, to her exact specifications. Complete with a giant silo slide. It turned out to be the biggest selling point for families. We sold out of all our tickets for both days in a few hours.

It isn't opening day jitters that has me jumping from boot to boot unable to stay still. Wren's mom and dad should be here any minute. They got into town late last night and are staying at a bed and breakfast a town over from here.

I know I'm not the country club guy they thought their daughter would end up with. Even with her using all her money to get my family out of debt, our financial differences have never been an issue. It doesn't stop me from worrying about them liking me.

I quickly finish setting up the pre-cut flowers in the shop. It's the last thing I have to do on my list. I want to find Wren and see if she needs help with anything else.

She's been running around like a chicken with its head cut off making sure everything is set up correctly and all of our volunteers know what they are supposed to be doing.

There's been a learning curve as we transition to a large scale operation. Lucky for us, my girl knows how to manage people. Her direct approach may come across as abrasive to some but it gets the job done. Most people have embraced her no-nonsense attitude. They know she is the person to go to with any compliments, complaints, and concerns. If something isn't working efficiently, you best believe Wren will take care of it.

Walking out of the barn, I see Mason over by the play area. "Have you seen Wren around?" I ask. He's checking to make sure everything is bolted down and ready for hundreds of kids to go wild.

Last weekend Lenny invited a bunch of her friends—excuse me, her test group—over. Wren helped her type up a questionnaire and everything. It reminded me of her student profile she wanted me to fill out.

"I think she's up front by the road. You should call her on the walkie."

"I'm not calling her on the damn walkie."

"You lost yours didn't you?" He smirks at me.

"It's not lost. It's around here somewhere," I grumble.

"One of the guys drove her down to the parking lot. If you hurry, you can be the one to bring her back home," he shouts. I'm already stomping through the gravel halfway to my four-wheeler. I don't know which one of these high school numbskulls thought it was a smart idea to take my girl for a ride.

When I pull up behind the other vehicles, Wren is directing her army of parking attendants. These guys will handle crowd control with the cars, making sure everyone is safe and using the parking lot efficiently.

A few of the guys are paying more attention to Wren's legs than her instructions. I stand beside her and cross my arms over my chest. She does a double take and rolls her eyes when she sees me glaring down her admirers.

"You're ridiculous," she murmurs to me.

"I think you underestimate the power of frayed denim and tanned legs," I say, while keeping my eyes straight ahead.

"Does anyone have any questions?" Wren asks, ignoring me. A few kids ask questions which Wren answers expertly.

"Great. We open at ten. You can start allowing cars in fifteen minutes early. We need to keep the road clear if possible," I tell the crew. They nod and go off to do whatever Wren asked them to do while they wait.

Wren glances at the main road. "Cars are already starting to line up."

"You did a great job, birdie. You've turned this whole place around." I throw an arm over her shoulder and walk her back to the four wheeler.

"We all did this. It was a family effort."

"You're right. It was." I kiss the top of her head. "Get in. I'll take you back to the house. What time are your parents getting here?"

"Any minute. They wanted to be here early in case we needed help. I expect my mom to be full on Dolly with pink cowboy boots and big hair."

"Think she'll want to borrow my silver chaps?" I joke.

"Don't tempt her with a good time," Wren deadpans. "Can you drive us to the barn? I've got something for you."

"We don't have time for that, birdie."

"That is not what I'm talking about," she says, slapping my arm.

Once I park, she hops out of the four wheeler and I follow her inside the barn. She digs around in one of the boxes we have full of branded T-shirts. I'm not sure why, I already have mine.

With one hand behind her back, she stalks toward me. She reaches up and removes my old Newhouse hat from my head. "We've got new dreams now," she says, before placing a Songland Farms hat on my head.

"How did I get so lucky?" I ask, swallowing down the emotions I feel with starting this new dream with her.

"I don't know. I ask myself the same thing every day." She tilts her head and gives me a kiss under the bill of my hat.

"Thank you, birdie," I say, wrapping my arms around her and pulling her close.

"Knock, knock. Sorry to interrupt," a female voice calls out from the front of the barn.

Wren breaks our kiss and looks over my shoulder. "Mom. Dad!" She rushes to greet them.

Great. Of course they would show up when I'm making out with their daughter. Not the first impression I was hoping for.

"This is Wyatt," Wren says, pulling me closer to them.

"Hello. It's nice to meet you both," I say. Wren's mom—who is wearing pink cowboy boots—pulls me into a hug.

"It's nice to finally meet you too," she says, when she lets me go. "He's so handsome, Wren." She winks at her daughter and fans her face with her hand. I have to bite down on my lip to keep from laughing.

"Alright, Mom, that's the one compliment you're allotted for today. I already told him he looked good this morning. Any more and we'll give him a complex."

"That is not what you said this morning," I say. "Do you need me to remind you?"

"No," she says through gritted teeth. "I remember just fine."

"I'd like to know," her dad says, with a playful smile.

"Oh darn, look at the time. We should head back to the house and introduce y'all to the rest of the family. I know Faith and Jack are dying to meet you both," Wren says and starts walking out of the barn.

"I'll tell you later," I say to Ivan and Abby.

"Wyatt," Wren warns, making her parents laugh.

"He's perfect for you Wren," her mom says, laughing. Wren sighs then beams a smile in my direction.

"I know. But seriously no more compliments. You don't understand the damage you are doing to his ego right now. I won't hear the end of it."

I run up to Wren and throw an arm around her. "Stop being so mean. You're turning me on," I whisper in her ear. Then give her a quick kiss.

There are people everywhere.

They are in the sunflower fields. The playground. They are with the chickens and the goats. You can't walk anywhere without running into someone.

It's unbelievable. This is better than we could have hoped for.

Leaning against the fence, I watch as Wren helps a group of kids feed the goats. She's become a seasoned pro when it comes to the animals. She's taken over all the milking and feeding for the goats, cows, and chickens.

It's hard to believe a few months ago she was wearing slacks and blouses. Now the only suit she wears is her birthday one. Ain't no complaints about that.

Wren's dad walks around the side of the barn. I should probably stop thinking about Wren naked with him so close by.

Ivan spots me and joins me in admiring his daughter. He watches her with a smile on his face. "She looks happy," he says.

"She is. I didn't know if she would like it here. If she would fit in my world. The first time she met the goats she was so scared. Look at her now. She's a natural."

"She fits you, that's why it works. When you find the person that you're meant to be with, everything else falls into place. I never thought I would end up with a beauty pageant queen. I was working as a valet at the country club the first time I saw her." Ivan gets a dreamy far off look in his eye.

"Abby came to the club every Sunday with her family. During the summer, she would come to swim and play tennis with her friends. She was the most beautiful woman I had ever seen, but we were completely different people—she was flighty and just wanted to have fun, while I worked two jobs and had goals and dreams. I was going to community college and working at my startup. We were heading in different directions."

"What happened?"

"I changed course. I wasn't going to let her go. Together we built the life we wanted. Her parents didn't like it at first. I was the help after all. They thought we were too young to know what love is. I told them they're old and they still don't know what love is." He smirks.

"I know I love your daughter. She's the most important person in my life. She's my best friend. There's nothing I wouldn't do for her."

He looks at me. His eyes brimming with emotion. "I know what an honor it is to hold that position. I was her best friend for many years."

His words hit home. It is an honor to be her best friend. To know her inside and out. To be the one she turns to when she's tired and weary. To be the only one who can make her feel better.

"I promise I'll take care of her."

"I don't have any doubt about that." He slings an arm around my shoulder and gives me a quick hug.

"I don't think I've ever been this tired." Wren stretches her legs over my lap.

We're out back, sitting on the porch. Everyone else has gone to bed. It's been a good day, but a long one.

"Did you have fun?" I start massaging her calve muscles.

"I did. It was a lot of work, but it was fun."

"I'm glad you thought so because we get to do it all over again tomorrow and the next day. And the day after that," I tease.

"And the day after that?" she asks, and her tone is more serious.

"Everyday until we're done." I reach across the couch and pick Wren up and drop her on my lap.

"What if I'm never done with you?" She drags her fingers up my face and into my hair.

"That's why we're so good together because I'm never going to be done with you either."

1 YEAR LATER

WREN

"If someone does not get this man away from me, y'all might as well call the police and put me in cuffs now," Willow exclaims, pointing a finger at Jasper—one of the new farm hands we hired a few months back.

"Now, Willow, that is no way to treat your future husband," Jasper jokes with her. He's been chasing after her since the first day he started working here. She hasn't quite warmed up to him yet.

"Over my dead body," she seethes.

"I think what you meant to say is 'til death do us part." Jasper risks his life and takes a step closer to my sister. Technically we aren't sisters yet, but after working and living together for a year, I can't imagine calling her anything else.

"Turn around Jasper. What do you see?" Willow asks.

"Grass," he says.

"Close. That," she points toward the vacant fields, "is acres and acres of land. I can hide your body where no one will find you." Willow glares at Jasper. Most men would buckle, but he smiles gleefully.

"So, that's a yes to getting married then?" he asks her. Willow throws her hands up and screams. Then storms off toward the main house. "I think I'm wearing her down," Jasper says, before chasing after her like a little puppy.

Wyatt's deep chuckle has me spinning around. "You're done early," I say, wrapping my arms around him. He spent the day laying the foundation for Willow's bakery, while I spent most of my time working in the general store.

We were able to open the store last spring. After a good summer and fall season, it left us with enough funds to build a decent size store near the main road.

It's become quite the attraction. People from all over stop by to buy homemade pies, cakes, jams, and jellies—all made fresh here on the farm. Charlie's even visited a few times with her boyfriend.

"I couldn't stay away any longer. You ready to go home?" His hands slip into the back pockets of my shorts.

"I am. Let me tell Mama I'm leaving. I only came outside because I saw Willow and Jasper cutting across the field. I thought the porch needed a good sweeping."

Wyatt chuckles. "You're catching on. What did you figure out?"

"If I had to guess, Willow's pissed she's attracted to Jasper. Instead of giving in she keeps making death threats. He of course calls it progress."

"Willow could do worse. Jasper's a good guy. I like him."

"You like that he gives Willow hell. It's payback for all the teasing she's given you over the years."

"She gives it back. That's what you Rivers women do. I'm pretty sure '*Give 'em Hell*' is your motto," he jokes, as he opens the door to the general store.

"We should get T-shirts made," I suggest.

"T-shirts for what?" Mama asks from behind the counter.

"Wyatt just came up with a new slogan for the farm," I tell her. It isn't a bad idea. I'm always looking for new ways to advertise. A fun slogan on a shirt is a great way to do that.

"We can talk about it at the next meeting. I'm taking her home. We'll see you tomorrow. Is Dad coming to get you?" Wyatt asks.

"Yes, he'll be here soon. I'll get everything closed up and wait for him on the porch. Y'all get out of here."

Dad has been allowed to drive the four wheeler from the main house to the store to pick up *his woman*. Sometimes they drive straight home but most nights you can find them taking a long drive around the property with Mama behind the wheel.

They claim they like the serenity that comes right before dusk. It's just them, the crickets, and the summer breeze. I think they like admiring everything their children are accomplishing—everything they've accomplished.

Wyatt parks the truck beside our little trailer. We saved up enough money from the summer and fall harvest last year to buy ourselves a one bedroom trailer. Someday we'll have our dream house built here. Until then, this is perfect for the two of us.

We've talked about getting married and having kids a few times. There's no rush. I don't need a ring on my finger to know this man is my forever. He completes me and fills me in places I didn't know were empty.

Good thing that was an inside thought. Wyatt would *definitely* make a joke about it.

"What are you smiling about?"

I shake my head. "Nothing. I have a surprise for you. Follow me." I grab his arm and drag him past the trailer into the open field. "Stand here and close your eyes."

Once his eyes are closed, I turn him where he's facing our future front yard. "What's going on, birdie?"

"I got you something. I know we're a long way off from getting our house built, but I wanted to give you this. Open your eyes."

His eyes bounce from me to the giant oak tree in the front yard. It's the only reason we chose to have our house face this direction. It's the best tree to hang a tire swing on.

"When did you do this?" Holding hands, we walk to the swing.

"This morning after you went to work. Ford and Lenny helped me."

"This was the important business meeting he had this morning?" Wyatt holds the swing and steps inside.

"I guess. I didn't tell him to make up stories. Want me to push you?"

"Hop on." He pats the other side of the swing.

"I don't know if it will hold both of us." I look skeptically at the ropes tied around the branch.

"Look how much fun it is." Wyatt walks backward as far as he can before lifting his feet and flying into the air. "You know what else we could do on here?" He waggles his eyebrows.

"Absolutely not," I say, laughing. "It's not a sex swing, Wyatt."

"Not with that attitude it isn't." He stops swinging and climbs out. "Get on. Let me push you, baby."

He holds the swing still while I attempt to climb on. "Stop laughing at me." I know I look ridiculous as I try to balance on one foot and climb over the edge of the tire. "I've never done this before."

"Are you sure this can't be a sex swing because you look hot as fuck right now." He bites down on his lip as he circles around me. His forearms flex as he pulls me back towards his body. "Keep your legs up for me," he whispers into my ear.

Damn him. He said the same thing to me last night and now it's all I can think about as I fly back and forth through the air.

The swing begins to slow down and Wyatt helps me get down.

"Thank you for this. It's exactly what I wanted."

"We'll get the house one day too."

"Two out of three ain't bad." His hand grips the back of my head and he pulls me in for a kiss. My stomach does a little flip. Just like it did the first time I kissed him. "I've got the most important thing right here in my arms."

I couldn't agree with him more.

Thank You

I had the best time writing Wyatt and Wren's story. Their playfulness and the way they banter with each other is one of a kind. They are so different but fit each other perfectly. I have to thank the two of them for taking over their story halfway through and making it into what it became.

This book would not have been written without the help of several people.

My Family. I love you so much. You have to live with me on a daily basis. You witness every high and every low. You listen about all of my plot ideas – good and bad. Your support is why we're here right now. I love dream chasing with all of you.

Kelsey. Again, I couldn't do this without you and I wouldn't want you. Having you to bounce ideas off of 24/7 is the best. I appreciate you so much.

Author Friends. I have met so many amazing authors over the past six months. Thank you for supporting me through all the highs and lows of this job. You keep me laughing and somewhat sane.

Beta Team. Thank you so much for taking the time to read the book and give feedback. I hope you read Strike Zone for a second time and see how impactful you're feedback was. You truly made this book better.

Julie & Team at Books & Moods. Thank you so much for all of your help with this cover. It is absolutely perfect. You nailed every detail.

Kristen at Kristen's Red Pen. You made me a better writer. All of your advice and insight was priceless. I am so grateful to be working with you and having your knowledge and expertise at my fingertips. Thank you so much!

Lemmy and the team at Luna Literary Management. You are a creative and marketing genius. I am continuously blown away by your talent. Thank you for your support and encouragement throughout this process and for putting together the best ARC team a girl could ask for.

Newhouse Nation! You make it worth it. I am filled with joy and gratitude when I think of the community we are building. Your love and support means so much to me. I feel like I won the lottery with all of you.

To anyone who picks up this books. Thank you. I don't care if you love it or hate. I appreciate you taking a chance on Wyatt & Wren.

About the Author

Ginger Walls is most known for her Newhouse University series. She writes steamy contemporary romance with a mix of humor and heartbreaks. Her characters go through real-life struggles with strength and a side of vulnerability. You will laugh, cry, and swoon your way through every page.

When Ginger isn't writing she enjoys reading books about motorcycle clubs and seven-foot-tall aliens. She also enjoys listening to music and spending time with her family.

Follow her on social media (@gingerwallsauthor) to stay up to date on her upcoming book releases or the latest antics from her family.

Other Books

WHAT'S NEXT

Grab your boots and cowboy hat. We are going to Rivers Bend, Alabama and visiting Songland Farms while the Rivers' family rebuilds their legacy.

JOIN NEWHOUSE NATION

Made in the USA
Columbia, SC
02 October 2024

42931217R00248